FUGITIVE PIECES

ANNE MICHAELS

B L O O M S B U R Y

LONDON • OXFORD • NEW YORK • NEW DELHI • SYDNEY

Bloomsbury Paperbacks
An imprint of Bloomsbury Publishing Plc

50 Bedford Square
London
WC1B 3DP
UK

1385 Broadway
New York
NY 10018
USA

www.bloomsbury.com

BLOOMSBURY and the Diana logo are trademarks of Bloomsbury Publishing Plc

First published in 1996 in Canada by McClelland & Stewart, Toronto
First published in Great Britain 1997
This paperback edition first published in 2017

British Library Cataloguing-in-Publication Data
A catalogue record for this book is available from the British Library.

ISBN: PB: 978-1-4088-9135-3
          ePub: 978-1-4088-0568-8

2 4 6 8 10 9 7 5 3 1

Printed and bound in Great Britain by CPI Group (UK) Ltd, Croydon CR0 4YY

MIX
Paper from
responsible sources
FSC
www.fsc.org   FSC® C020471

To find out more about our authors and books visit www.bloomsbury.com.
Here you will find extracts, author interviews, details of forthcoming events and
the option to sign up for our newsletters.

During the Second World War, countless manuscripts – diaries, memoirs, eyewitness accounts – were lost or destroyed. Some of these narratives were deliberately hidden – buried in back gardens, tucked into walls and under floors – by those who did not live to retrieve them.

Other stories are concealed in memory, neither written nor spoken. Still others are recovered, by circumstance alone.

Poet Jakob Beer, who was also a translator of posthumous writing from the war, was struck and killed by a car in Athens in the spring of 1993, at age sixty. His wife had been standing with him on the sidewalk; she survived her husband by two days. They had no children.

Shortly before his death, Beer had begun to write his memoirs. "A man's experience of war," he once wrote, "never ends with the war. A man's work, like his life, is never completed."

I

THE DROWNED CITY

Time is a blind guide.

Bog-boy, I surfaced into the miry streets of the drowned city. For over a thousand years, only fish wandered Biskupin's wooden sidewalks. Houses, built to face the sun, were flooded by the silty gloom of the Gasawka River. Gardens grew luxurious in subaqueous silence; lilies, rushes, stinkweed.

No one is born just once. If you're lucky, you'll emerge again in someone's arms; or unlucky, wake when the long tail of terror brushes the inside of your skull.

I squirmed from the marshy ground like Tollund Man, Grauballe Man, like the boy they uprooted in the middle of Franz Josef Street while they were repairing the road, six hundred cockleshell beads around his neck, a helmet of mud. Dripping with the prune-coloured juices of the peat-sweating bog. Afterbirth of earth.

I saw a man kneeling in the acid-steeped ground. He was digging. My sudden appearance unnerved him. For a moment he thought I was one of Biskupin's lost souls, or perhaps the boy in the story, who digs a hole so deep he emerges on the other side of the world.

Biskupin had been carefully excavated for almost a decade. Archaeologists gently continued to remove Stone and Iron Age relics from soft brown pockets of peat. The pure oak causeway that once connected Biskupin to the mainland had been reconstructed, as well as the ingenious nail-less wooden houses, ramparts, and the high-towered city gates. Wooden streets, crowded twenty-five centuries before with traders and craftsmen, were being raised from the swampy lake bottom. When the soldiers arrived they examined the perfectly preserved clay bowls; they held the glass beads, the bronze and amber bracelets, before smashing them on the floor. With delighted strides, they roamed the magnificent timber city, once home to a hundred families. Then the soldiers buried Biskupin in sand.

~

My sister had long outgrown the hiding place. Bella was fifteen and even I admitted she was beautiful, with heavy brows and magnificent hair like black syrup, thick and luxurious, a muscle down her back. "A work of art," our mother said, brushing it for her while Bella sat in a chair. I was still small enough to vanish behind the wallpaper in the cupboard, cramming my head sideways between choking plaster and beams, eyelashes scraping.

Since those minutes inside the wall, I've imagined that the dead lose every sense except hearing.

The burst door. Wood ripped from hinges, cracking like ice under the shouts. Noises never heard before, torn from my father's mouth. Then silence. My mother had been sewing a button on my shirt. She kept her buttons in a chipped saucer. I heard the rim of the saucer in circles on the floor. I heard the spray of buttons, little white teeth.

Blackness filled me, spread from the back of my head into my eyes as if my brain had been punctured. Spread from stomach to legs. I gulped and gulped, swallowing it whole. The wall filled with smoke. I struggled out and stared while the air caught fire.

I wanted to go to my parents, to touch them. But I couldn't, unless I stepped on their blood.

The soul leaves the body instantly, as if it can hardly wait to be free: my mother's face was not her own. My father was twisted with falling. Two shapes in the flesh-heap, his hands.

I ran and fell, ran and fell. Then the river: so cold it felt sharp.

The river was the same blackness that was inside me; only the thin membrane of my skin kept me floating.

From the other bank, I watched darkness turn to purple-orange light above the town; the colour of flesh transforming to spirit. They flew up. The dead passed above me, weird haloes and arcs smothering the stars. The trees bent under their weight. I'd never been alone in the night forest, the wild bare branches were frozen snakes. The ground tilted and I didn't hold on. I strained to join them, to rise with them, to peel from the ground like paper ungluing at its edges. I know why we bury our dead and mark the place with stone, with the heaviest, most permanent thing we can think of: because the dead are everywhere but the ground. I stayed where I was. Clammy with cold, stuck to the ground. I begged: If I can't rise, then let me sink, sink into the forest floor like a seal into wax.

Then – as if she'd pushed the hair from my forehead, as if I'd heard her voice – I knew suddenly my mother was inside me. Moving along sinews, under my skin the way she used to move through the house at night, putting things away, putting things in order. She was stopping to say goodbye and was caught, in such pain, wanting to rise, wanting to stay. It was my responsibility to release her, a sin to keep her from ascending. I tore at my clothes, my hair. She was gone. My own fast breath around my head.

I ran from the sound of the river into the woods, dark as the inside of a box. I ran until the first light wrung the last greyness out of the stars, dripping dirty light between the trees. I knew what to do. I took a stick and dug. I planted myself like a turnip and hid my face with leaves.

My head between the branches, bristling points like my father's beard. I was safely buried, my wet clothes cold as armour. Panting like a dog. My arms tight against my chest, my neck stretched back, tears crawling like insects into my ears. I had no choice but to look straight up. The dawn sky was milky with new spirits. Soon I couldn't avoid the absurdity of daylight even by closing my eyes. It poked down, pinned me like the broken branches, like my father's beard.

Then I felt the worst shame of my life: I was pierced with hunger. And suddenly I realized, my throat aching without sound – Bella.

~

I had my duties. Walk at night. In the morning dig my bed. Eat anything.

My days in the ground were a delirium of sleep and attention. I dreamed someone found my missing button and came looking for me. In a glade of burst pods leaking their white stuffing, I dreamed of bread; when I woke, my jaw was sore from chewing the air. I woke terrified of animals, more terrified of men.

In this day-sleep, I remembered my sister weeping at the end of novels she loved; my father's only indulgence – Romain Rolland or Jack London. She wore the characters in her face as she read, one finger rubbing the edge of the page. Before I learned to read, angry to be left out, I strangled her with my arms, leaning over with my cheek against hers, as if somehow to see in the tiny black letters the world Bella saw. She shrugged me off or, big-hearted, she stopped, turned the book over in her lap, and explained the plot . . . the drunken father lurching home . . . the betrayed lover waiting vainly under the stairs . . . the terror of wolves howling in the Arctic dark, making my own skeleton rattle in my clothes. Sometimes at night, I sat on the edge of Bella's bed and she tested my spelling, writing on my back with her finger and, when I'd learned the word, gently erasing it with a stroke of her smooth hand.

I couldn't keep out the sounds: the door breaking open, the spit of buttons. My mother, my father. But worse than those sounds was that I couldn't remember hearing Bella at all. Filled with her silence, I had no choice but to imagine her face.

~

The night forest is incomprehensible: repulsive and endless, jutting bones and sticky hair, slime and jellied smells, shallow roots like ropy veins.

Draping slugs splash like tar across the ferns; black icicles of flesh.

During the day I have time to notice lichen like gold dust over the rocks.

A rabbit, sensing me, stops close to my head and tries to hide behind a blade of grass.

The sun is jagged through the trees, so bright the spangles turn dark and float, burnt paper, in my eyes.

The white nibs of grass get caught in my teeth like pliable little fishbones. I chew fronds into a bitter, stringy mash that turns my spit green.

Once, I risk digging my bed close to pasture, for the breeze, for relief from the dense damp of the forest. Buried, I feel the shuddering dark shapes of cattle thudding across the field. In the distance, their thrusting heads make them look as if they're swimming. They gallop to a stop a few feet from the fence then drift towards me, their heads swinging like slow church bells with every glory step of their heavy flanks. The slender calves quiver behind, fear twitching their ears. I'm also afraid – that the herd will bring everyone from miles away to where I'm hiding – as they gather to rest their massive heads on the fence and stare down at me with rolling eyes.

I fill my pockets and my hands with stones and walk into the river until only my mouth and nose, pink lilies, skim the air. Muck dissolves from my skin and hair, and it's satisfying to see floating like foam on the surface the fat scum of lice from my clothes. I stand on the bottom, my boots sucked down by the mud, the current flowing around me, a cloak in a liquid wind. I don't stay under long. Not only because of the cold, but because with my ears under the surface, I can't hear. This is more frightening to me than darkness, and when I can't stand the silence any longer, I slip out of my wet skin, into sound.

Someone is watching from behind a tree. I stare from my hiding place without moving, until my eyeballs harden, until I'm no longer sure he's seen me. What's he waiting for? In the last possible moment before I have to run, light coming fast, I discover I've been held prisoner half the night by a tree, its dead, dense bole carved by moonlight.

Even in daylight, in the cold drizzle, the tree's faint expression is familiar. The face above a uniform.

The forest floor is speckled bronze, sugar caramelized in the leaves. The branches look painted onto the onion-white sky. One morning I watch a finger of light move its way deliberately towards me across the ground.

I know, suddenly, my sister is dead. At this precise moment, Bella becomes flooded ground. A body of water pulling under the moon.

~

A grey fall day. At the end of strength, at the place where faith is most like despair, I leaped from the streets of Biskupin; from underground into air.

I limped towards him, stiff as a golem, clay tight behind my knees. I stopped a few yards from where he was digging – later he told me it was as if I'd hit a glass door, an inarguable surface of pure air – "and your mud mask cracked with tears and I knew you were human, just a child. Crying with the abandonment of your age."

He said he spoke to me. But I was wild with deafness. My peat-clogged ears.

So hungry. I screamed into the silence the only phrase I knew in more than one language, I screamed it in Polish and German and Yiddish, thumping my fists on my own chest: dirty Jew, dirty Jew, dirty Jew.

~

The man excavating in the mud at Biskupin, the man I came to know as Athos, wore me under his clothes. My limbs bone-shadows on his strong legs and arms, my head buried in his neck, both of us beneath a heavy coat. I was suffocating but I couldn't get warm. Inside Athos's coat, cold air streaming in from the edge of the car door. The drone of engine and wheels, once in a while the sound of a passing lorry. In our strange coupling, Athos's voice burrowed into my brain. I didn't understand so I made it up myself: It's right, it's necessary to run. . . .

For miles through darkness in the back seat of the car, I had no idea where we were or where we were going. Another man drove and when we were signalled to stop, Athos pulled a blanket over us. In Greek-stained but competent German, Athos complained that he was ill. He didn't just complain. He whimpered, he moaned. He insisted on describing his symptoms and treatments in detail. Until, disgusted and annoyed, they waved us on. Each time we stopped, I was numb against his solid body, a blister tight with fear.

My head ached with fever, I smelled my hair burning. Through days and nights I sped from my father and my mother. From long afternoons with my best friend, Mones, by the river. They were yanked right through my scalp.

But Bella clung. We were Russian dolls. I inside Athos, Bella inside me.

I don't know how long we travelled this way. Once, I woke and saw signs in a fluid script that from a distance looked like Hebrew. Then Athos said we were home, in Greece. When we got closer I saw the words were strange; I'd never seen Greek letters before. It was night, but the square houses were white even in the darkness and the air was soft. I was dim with hunger and from lying so long in the car.

Athos said: "I will be your koumbaros, your godfather, the marriage sponsor for you and your sons. . . ."

Athos said: "We must carry each other. If we don't have this, what are we. . . ."

On the island of Zakynthos, Athos – scientist, scholar, middling master of languages – performed his most astounding feat. From out of his trousers he plucked the seven-year-old refugee Jakob Beer.

THE STONE-CARRIERS

The shadow past is shaped by everything that never happened. Invisible, it melts the present like rain through karst. A biography of longing. It steers us like magnetism, a spirit torque. This is how one becomes undone by a smell, a word, a place, the photo of a mountain of shoes. By love that closes its mouth before calling a name.

I did not witness the most important events of my life. My deepest story must be told by a blind man, a prisoner of sound. From behind a wall, from underground. From the corner of a small house on a small island that juts like a bone from the skin of sea.

On Zakynthos we lived close to the sky. Far below, the restless waves surrounded us. According to myth, the Ionian Sea is haunted by an error of love.

There were two rooms upstairs and two views. The small bedroom window opened emptily to sea. The other room, Athos's study, looked down our stony hill to the distant town and the harbour. Winter nights, when the wind was relentless and wet, it seemed we were on the bridge of a ship, shutters creaking like masts and rigging; the town of Zakynthos shimmered, luminescent, as if under the waves. During the darkest part of summer nights, I climbed through the bedroom window to lie on the roof. In the days, I stayed in the small bedroom, willing my skin to take on the woodgrain of the floor, to take on the pattern of the rug or the bedcover, so I could disappear simply by stillness.

The first Easter in hiding, at the midnight climax of the Anastasimi Mass, I watched from the window in Athos's study. The procession candles were carried, a faint snaking line flickering through the streets, retracing the route of the epitafios then dispersing into the bare hills. At the edge of town, as each worshipper walked home, the line broke into sparks. With my forehead against the glass, I watched and was in my own village, winter evenings, my teacher lighting the wicks of our lanterns and releasing us into the street like toy boats bobbing down a flooded gutter. Wire handles clinked against the hot globes. The rising smells of our damp coats. Mones swinging his arms, his lamp skimming the ground, his white breath glowing from below. I watched the Easter procession and placed this parallel image, like other ghostly double exposures, carefully into orbit. On an inner shelf too high to reach. Even now, half a century later, writing this on a different Greek island, I look down to the remote lights of town and feel the heat of a lamp spreading up my sleeve.

I watched Athos reading at his desk in the evenings,

and saw my mother sewing at the table, my father looking through the daily papers, Bella studying her music. Any given moment – no matter how casual, how ordinary – is poised, full of gaping life. I can no longer remember their faces, but I imagine expressions trying to use up a lifetime of love in the last second. No matter the age of the face, at the moment of death a lifetime of emotion still unused turns a face young again.

I was like the men in Athos's stories, who set their courses before the invention of longitude and never quite knew where they were. They looked at the stars and knew they were missing information, terra nullius raising the hair on their necks.

On Zakynthos we lived on solid rock, in a high and windy place full of light. I learned to tolerate images rising in me like bruises. But in my continuous expectation of the burst door, the taste of blood that filled my mouth suddenly, many times a day, I couldn't conceive of any feeling stronger than fear. What is stronger than fear; Athos, who is stronger than fear?

On Zakynthos I tended a garden of lemon balm and basil in a square of light on the floor. I imagined the thoughts of the sea. I spent the day writing my letter to the dead and was answered at night in my sleep.

~

Athos – Athanasios Roussos – was a geologist dedicated to a private trinity of peat, limestone, and archaeological wood. But like most Greeks, he rose from the sea. His father had been the last Roussos mariner, carrying to conclusion the family shipping business dating from the 1700s, when Russian vessels sailed the Turkish Straits from the Black Sea to the Aegean. Athos knew that no ship is an object, that a spirit animates the ropes and wood, that a sunken ship becomes its ghost. He knew that chewing raw fish quenches thirst. He knew that there are forty-four elements in sea water. He described the ancient Greek cedar galleys, caulked with bitumen and outfitted with sails of silk or bright linen. He told me about Peruvian balsa rafts and Polynesian straw boats. He explained how the huge Siberian rafts made of spruce from the taiga were built on frozen rivers and set free when the ice melted in the spring. Sometimes two rafts were bound together, creating a vessel so large it could carry a house with a stone fireplace. From his father, Athos inherited sea charts that had been passed down from captains and hydrographers, augmented by generations. He drew his great-grandfather's trading routes for me in chalk on a black slate learner's globe. Even as a child, even as my blood-past was drained from me, I understood that if I were strong enough to accept it, I was being offered a second history.

To share a hiding place, physical or psychological, is as intimate as love. I followed Athos from one room to the other. I was afraid, as one who has only one person to trust must be afraid, an anxiety I could only solve by devotion. I sat near him while he wrote at his desk, contemplating forces that turn seas to stone, stone to liquid. He gave up trying to send me to bed. Often I lay at his feet like a cat, surrounded by books piled ever higher on the floor beside his chair. Late at night, while he worked – a solid concentration that put me to sleep – his arm dangled like a plumb line. I was soothed by the smells of bindings and pipe tobacco and the weight of his safe, heavy hand on my head. His left arm reaching down to earth, his right arm reaching up, palm to heaven.

During the long months, I listened to Athos recount not only the history of navigation – heightened dramatically by ancestral anecdote, pictures from books and maps – but the history of the earth itself. He heaped before my imagination the great heaving terra mobilis: "Imagine solid rock bubbling like stew; a whole mountain bursting into flame or slowly being eaten by rain, like bites out of an apple. . . ." He moved from geology to paleontology to poetry: "Think of the first phototropic plant, the first breath inhaled by any animal, the first cells that joined and did not divide to reproduce, the first human birth. . . ." He quoted Lucretius: "'The earliest weapons were hands, nails, and teeth. Next came stones and branches wrenched from trees, and fire, and flame. . . .'"

Gradually Athos and I learned each other's languages. A little of my Yiddish, with smatterings of mutual Polish. His Greek and English. We took new words into our mouths like foreign foods; suspicious, acquired tastes.

Athos didn't want me to forget. He made me review my Hebrew alphabet. He said the same thing every day: "It is your future you are remembering." He taught me the ornate Greek script, like a twisting twin of Hebrew. Both Hebrew and Greek, Athos liked to say, contain the ancient loneliness of ruins, "like a flute heard distantly down a hillside of olives, or a voice calling to a boat from a shore."

Slowly my tongue learned its sad new powers. I longed to cleanse my mouth of memory. I longed for my mouth to feel my own when speaking his beautiful and awkward Greek, its thick consonants, its many syllables difficult and graceful as water rushing around rock. I ate Greek food, drank from Zakynthos's wells until I too could distinguish the different springs on the island.

We entered a territory of greater and greater tenderness, two lost souls alone on deck on a black and limitless ocean, the wind howling off corners of the house, no lights to guide us and none to give our position away.

By early morning Athos was often close to tears of admiration for his brave lineage, or for the future: "I will be your koumbaros, your godfather, the marriage sponsor for you and your sons. . . . We must carry each other. If we don't have this, what are we? The spirit in the body is like wine in a glass; when it spills, it seeps into air and earth and light. . . . It's a mistake to think it's the small things we control and not the large, it's the other way around! We can't stop the small accident, the tiny detail that conspires into fate: the extra moment you run back for something forgotten, a moment that saves you from an accident – or causes one. But we can assert the largest order, the large human values daily, the only order large enough to see."

Athos was fifty when we found each other at Biskupin. He was bluntly handsome, heavyset but not heavy, and his hair was halfway grey, the shade of a good silver ore. I watched him comb his hair, wet against his scalp, into deep furrows. I continued to scrutinize, as if watching a science demonstration, his hair turning thick as foam as it dried, his head slowly expanding.

His study was crammed with rock samples, fossils, loose photos of what seemed to me to be undistinguished landscapes. I'd browse, picking up an ordinary-looking lump or chip. "Ah, Jakob, what you hold in your hand is a piece of bone from a mastodon's jaw . . . that's bark from a thirty-five-million-year-old tree. . . ."

Immediately I put down whatever I held; scalded by time. Athos laughed at me. "Don't worry, a rock that's survived so much won't be hurt by a boy's curiosity."

He always had a cup of coffee on his desk – schetos – black and strong. During the war when his supply ran out, he reused the same grounds until he said there was not an atom of flavour left. Then futilely he tried to disguise a bland blend of chicory, dandelion, and lotus seeds by continuing to prepare it in his brass briki one cup at a time, a chemist experimenting with proportions.

Bella would have said Athos was just like Beethoven, who counted out exactly sixty beans for each cup. Bella knew everything about her maestro. Sometimes she piled her hair on top of her head, put on my father's coat (on Bella, a clown's coat with sleeves hanging past her fingertips), and borrowed his unlit pipe. My mother obliged with the composer's favourite meal: noodles and cheese (though not Parmesan) or potatoes and fish (though not from the Danube). Bella drank spring water, which Ludwig apparently imbibed by the gallon – a predilection that pleased my father, who, in these costume dramas, drew the line at Beethoven's beer drinking.

After dinner, Bella pushed her chair from the table and loped towards the piano. When she took off my father's loose coat, she shed all comedy. She sat, collecting herself, pressed like a cameo in the amber of the piano lamp. During dinner she'd made her secret choice of music, usually slow, romantic, yearning with sorrow; sometimes, if she felt well-disposed towards me, "The Moonlight." Then my sister played, drunk and precise, trying to keep on the straight line while swaggering with passion, and my mother would wring the dish towel in her hands with pride and emotion, and my parents and I would sit, stunned again by our silly Bella's transformation.

~

They waited until I was asleep, then roused themselves, exhausted as swimmers, grey between the empty trees. Their hair in tufts, open sores where ears used to be, grubs twisting from their chests. The grotesque remains of incomplete lives, the embodied complexity of desires eternally denied. They floated until they grew heavier, and began to walk, heaving into humanness; until they grew more human than phantom and through their effort began to sweat. Their strain poured from my skin, until I woke dripping with their deaths. Daydreams of sickening repetition – a trivial gesture remembered endlessly. My mother, after the decrees, turned away by a storekeeper, then dropping her scarf in the doorway, bending down to pick it up. In my mind, her whole life telescoped into that single moment, stooping again and again in her heavy blue coat. My father standing at the door, waiting for me to tie my laces, looking at his watch. Skipping stones on the river with Mones, wiping the mud off our shoes with the long grass. Bella turning the pages of a book.

I tried to remember ordinary details, the sheet music beside Bella's bed, her dresses. What my father's workshop looked like. But in nightmares the real picture wouldn't hold still long enough for me to look, everything melting. Or I remembered the name of a classmate but not his face. A piece of clothing but not its colour.

When I woke, my anguish was specific: the possibility that it was as painful for them to be remembered as it was for me to remember them; that I was haunting my parents and Bella with my calling, startling them awake in their black beds.

∾

I listened to Athos's stories in English, in Greek, again in English. At first I heard them from a distance, an incomprehensible murmur as I lay face down on the rug, anxious or despondent in the long afternoons. But soon I recognized the same words and began to recognize the same emotion in Athos's voice when he talked about his brother. I rolled onto my stomach so I could see his face, and eventually I sat up to learn.

Athos told me about his father, a man who'd scorned tradition most of his life, who'd raised his sons more European than Greek. His father's maternal relatives had been prominent in the large Greek community in Odessa, and his uncles had moved in the social circles of Vienna and Marseilles. Odessa: not far from the village where my father was born; Odessa, where, as Athos told these stories, thirty thousand Jews were being doused with gasoline and burned alive. His family had shipped the valuable red dyes for shoes and cloth from Mount Ossa to Austria and made their fortune. From his father, Athos learned that every river is a tongue of commerce, finding first geological then economic weakness and persuading itself into continents. The Mediterranean itself, he reminded me, had seduced its way out of rock – the "inland sea," the womb of Europe. Athos's older brother, Nikolaos, died at eighteen in a traffic accident in Le Havre. Shortly after, his mother fell ill and died. Athos's father was convinced the family was being punished for his own sin of neglecting the Roussos origins. So he returned to the village of his birth, the place where his father had also been born. There, he paved the town square and built a public fountain in Nikos's name. And this is where Athos took me: the island of Zakynthos, scarred by earthquakes. Its barren west and fertile east. Its groves of olives, figs, oranges, and lemons. Acanthus, amaranth, cyclamen. These were the things I did not see. From my two small rooms, the island was as inaccessible as another dimension.

Zakynthos: mentioned with affection by Homer, Strabo, Pliny. Twenty-five miles long and twelve miles wide, its highest hills fifteen hundred feet above the sea. A port on the maritime trade route between Venice and Constantinople. Zakynthos was the island birthplace of no less than three beloved poets – Foscolo, Kalvos, and

Solomos, who wrote the words to the national anthem there when he was twenty-five. A statue of Solomos presides over the square. Nikos bore a slight resemblance to the poet, and when Athos was a child he thought the statue had been erected to honour his brother's memory. Perhaps this was the beginning of Athos's love for stone.

When Athos and his father returned to Zakynthos after the deaths of Nikos and his mother, they went on a night journey to Cape Gerakas to watch sea turtles lay their eggs on the beach. "We visited the salt pans at Alykes, the currant vineyards in the shadow of the Vrachionas Mountains. I was alone with my father. We were inconsolable. We stood silent at the blue grotto and in the pine groves." For two years, until Athos could no longer avoid school, they were inseparable.

"My father took me along while he did his business with the shipbuilders at Keri Bay. I watched them caulking seams from the springs of pitch that bubble up from the black beach. We saw a man at the docks who knew my father. The muscles of his arms bulged like massive figure-eights, his licorice hair melted with sweat, he was stained with pitch. But he spoke katharevousa, the high Greek, like a king. After, my father scolded me for my rudeness; I'd been staring at him. But it was as if his voice came from a ventriloquist! When I said that, my father was truly angry. It was a lesson I never forgot. Once, in Salonika, my father left me in the charge of a hamal, a stevedore, while he attended to business with the harbour master. I sat on a bollard and listened to the hamal's fantastic tales. He told me about a ship that had sunk completely and then risen again. He'd seen it with his own eyes. Its cargo was salt and when it dissolved in the hold the ship bobbed up. That was my first encounter with the magic of salt. When my father retrieved me, he offered the hamal some money for looking after me. The man refused. My father said, 'That man is a Hebrew and he carries the pride of his people.' Later I learned that most of the men who worked at the docks in Salonika were Jews and that the yehudi mahallari, the Hebrew quarter, was built along the harbour.

"Do you know what else the hamal told me, Jakob? 'The great mystery of wood is not that it burns, but that it floats.'"

～

Athos's stories gradually veered me from my past. Night after night, his vivid hallucinogen dripped into my imagination, diluting memory. Yiddish too, a melody gradually eaten away by silence.

Athos pulled books off the shelves and read to me. I dove into the lavish illustrations. His was an old library, a mature library, where seriousness has given way to youthful whim. There were books on animal navigation and animal camouflage, on the history of glass, on gibbons, on Japanese scroll painting. There were books on icons, on insects, on Greek independence. Botany, paleontology, waterlogged wood. Poetry, with hypnotizing endpapers. Solomos, Seferis, Palamas, Keats. John Masefield's *Salt Water Ballads*, a gift to Athos from his father.

He read to me from a biography of the sixteenth-century Flemish botanist Clusius, who went on plant-hunting expedititions in Spain and Portugal where he broke his leg, then fell off a cliff on his horse, breaking his arm, landing in a prickly shrub he named Erinacea, hedgehog broom. In similar fashion he stumbled upon two hundred new species. And from the biography of the eighteenth-century botanist John Sibthorpe, who went to Greece to hunt all six hundred plants described by Dioscorides. On his first journey, he met with plague, war, and rebellion. On his second, he travelled with an Italian colleague, Francesco Boroni (immortalized by the boronia bush.) They came down with fever in Constantinople, botanized their way to the summit of Mount Olympus, and escaped capture by Barbary pirates. Then, in Athens, Boroni fell asleep by an open window and fell out, breaking his neck. Sibthorpe continued their work alone until he became ill at the ruins of Nicopolis. He staggered home to die at Oxford. His work was published posthumously, except his letters, which were accidentally burned as rubbish.

For four years I was confined to small rooms. But Athos gave me another realm to inhabit, big as the globe and expansive as time.

Because of Athos, I spent hours in other worlds then surfaced dripping, as from the sea. Because of Athos, our little house became a crow's nest, a Vinland peathouse. Inside the cave of my skull oceans swayed with monstrous ice-floes, navigated by skin-boats. Mariners hung from mizzen-masts and ropes made from walrus hide. Vikings rowed down the mighty rivers of Russia. Glaciers dredged their awful trails across hundreds of miles. I visited Marco

Polo's "celestial city" with its twelve thousand bridges, and sailed with him past the Cape of Perfumes. In Timbuktu we traded gold for salt. I learned about bacteria three billion years old, and how sphagnum moss was pulled from swamps and used as surgical dressing for wounded soldiers because it contained no bacteria. I learned how Theophrastus thought fossil fish swam to mountaintops by way of subterranean rivers. I learned that fossil elephants were found in the Arctic, fossil ferns in Antarctica, fossil reindeer in France, fossil musk ox in New York. I listened to Athos's story of the origins of islands, how the mainland can stretch until it breaks at the weakest points, and those weaknesses are called faults. Each island represented a victory and a defeat: it had either pulled itself free or pulled too hard and found itself alone. Later, as these islands grew older, they turned their misfortune into virtue, learned to accept their cragginess, their misshapen coasts, ragged where they'd been torn. They acquired grace – some grass, a beach smoothed by tides.

I was transfixed by the way time buckled, met itself in pleats and folds; I stared at a picture in a book of a safety pin from the Bronze Age – a simple design that hadn't changed in thousands of years. I stared at fossil plants called crinoids that looked like the night sky etched on rock. Athos said: "Sometimes I can't look you in the eye; you're like a building that's burned out inside, with the outer walls still standing." I stared at pictures of prehistoric bowls, spoons, combs. To go back a year or two was impossible, absurd. To go back millennia – ah! that was . . . nothing.

Athos didn't understand, as I hesitated in the doorway, that I was letting Bella enter ahead of me, making sure she was not left behind. I paused when I ate, singing a silent incantation: A bite for me, a bite for you, an extra bite for Bella. "Jakob, you're such a slow eater; you have the manners of an aristocrat." Awake at night, I'd hear her breathing or singing next to me in the dark, half comforted, half terrified that my ear was pressed against the thin wall between the living and the dead, that the vibrating membrane between them was so fragile. I felt her presence everywhere, in daylight, in rooms I knew weren't empty. I felt her touch on my back, my shoulders, my hair. I turned around to see if she was there, to see if she was looking, to see if she was standing guard, though if anything were to happen to me, she wouldn't be able to prevent it. Watching with curiosity and sympathy from her side of the gossamer wall.

Athos's house was isolated, a steep climb. Although we could see anyone approaching from afar, we also could be seen. It was a two-hour walk to town. Athos made the trip several times a month. While he was away, I barely moved, frozen with listening. If anyone climbed the hill, I hid in a sea chest, a box with a high curved lid; and each time less of me emerged.

We relied on one merchant, Old Martin, for supplies and news. He had known Athos's father, and Athos since he was a child. Old Martin's son, Ioannis, had a Jewish wife. One night, he and Allegra and their little son appeared at our door, their arms full of their belongings.

We hid Avramakis – Match, for short – in a drawer. While German soldiers stretched out their legs under the tables of the Zakynthos Hotel.

~

Because Athos's love was paleobotany, because his heroes were rock and wood as well as human, I learned not only the history of men but the history of earth. I learned the power we give to stones to hold human time. The stone tablets of the Commandments. Cairns, the ruins of temples. Gravestones, standing stones, the Rosetta, Stonehenge, the Parthenon. (The blocks cut and carried by inmates in the limestone quarries at Golleschau. The tombstones smashed in Hebrew cemeteries and plundered for Polish sidewalks; today bored citizens, staring at their feet while waiting for a bus, can still read the inscriptions.)

As a young man, Athos marvelled at the invention of the Geiger counter, and I remember him explaining to me, shortly after the end of the war, cosmic rays and Libby's new method of carbon dating. "It's the moment of death we measure from."

Athos had a special affection for limestone – that crushed reef of memory, that living stone, organic history squeezed into massive mountain tombs. As a student, he wrote a paper on the karst fields of Yugoslavia. Limestone that develops slowly under pressure into marble – Athos describing the process made it sound like a spiritual journey. He was rhapsodic about the French Causses and the Pennines in Britain; about "Strata" Smith and Abraham

Werner, who, he said, like surgeons "folded back the skin of time" while surveying canals and mines.

When Athos was seven, his father brought him home fossils from Lyme Regis. When he was twenty-five, he was entranced by Europe's new sweetheart, a limestone fertility goddess that had risen from the earth fully formed, the "Willendorf Venus."

But it was Athos's fascination with Antarctica, which began when he was a student at Cambridge, that was to become our azimuth. It was to direct the course of our lives.

Athos admired the scientist Edward Wilson, who was with Captain Scott at the South Pole. Among other things, Wilson, like Athos, was a watercolourist. His pigments – the deep-purple ice, the lime-green midnight sky, white stratus over black lava – were not only beautiful but scientifically accurate. His paintings of atmospheric phenomena – parhelions, paraselenae, lunar haloes – depicted the exact degrees of the sun. Athos relished that Wilson made watercolour sketches in the most perilous circumstances, then at night read the adventures of Sherlock Holmes and poetry in the tent. I was intrigued to know Wilson tried his own hand at writing the occasional poem – an activity, Wilson noted modestly, "that is perhaps an early symptom of polar anaemia."

Always hungry ourselves, we commiserated with the starving explorers. In their howling tent, the exhausted men ate hallucinatory meals. They smelled roast beef in the frozen darkness and savoured each bite in their imaginations as they swallowed their dried rations. At night, rigid in their sleeping bags, they discussed chocolate. Silas

Wright, the only Canadian on the expedition, dreamed of apples. Athos read me Cherry-Garrard's account of their food nightmares: shouting at deaf waiters; sitting at laden tables with their arms tied; the plate that falls to the floor the moment it's served. Finally, just as they taste their first mouthful, they fall into a crevasse.

At their base at Cape Evans during the long winter night, each member of the expedition gave a lecture on his particular specialty: polar sea-life, coronas, parasites. . . . This was serious passion for knowledge; a biologist once traded a heavy pair of socks for extra geology lessons.

Geologizing quickly became a mania, even among the non-scientists. Strongman Birdie Bowers turned into a rockhound, and every time he brought in a sample for identification he made the same announcement: "Here's a gabbroid nodule impaled in basalt with feldspar and olivine rampant."

Like the lectures at Cape Evans, these tales were told by Athos in the evenings, with the lantern on the floor between us. The light animated lithographs of Carboniferous ponds and polar wastes, and glinted off the glassed-in shelves of minerals and wood samples, the jars of chemicals. Details gradually came clear, as I learned the words. By late evening the floor would be littered with volumes open to pictures and diagrams. In that lamplight, we might have belonged to any century.

"Imagine," said Athos, his pale voice an emanation in the dark room, "reaching the pole only to discover Amundsen had reached it first. The entire globe hung beneath their feet. They no longer knew what they looked like, not the distant white flesh under their clothes, nor their leather faces. The sight of their own naked bodies was as far from them as England. They'd walked for months. Ceaselessly hungry. The snow turned their eyes to tinder and their faces glowed blue with frostbite. Across endless terrain split by invisible seams ready to swallow them without warning and without a sound. It was forty degrees below. They stood beside the only human evidence for a thousand miles – a mere square of cloth, Amundsen's flag – and knew they faced every step of the homeward journey. Yet, there's a photo of Wilson at their camp at the bottom of the world, and the camera has caught him with his head leaned back. Laughing."

At the head of the Beardmore Glacier, in the rare exposed surface, Wilson collected fossils from the fringe of an inland sea three million years old. These rocks later helped prove that Antarctica had been tectonically torn from an immense continent, from which Australia, India, Africa, Madagascar, and South America fractured, crumbled, strayed. India smashed into Asia, the crumpled point of collision becoming the Himalayas. All of which the earth achieved with staggering patience – a few centimetres a year.

The men, barely able to drag themselves, continued to haul back thirty-five pounds of fossils from the Beardmore. Wearied beyond recovery, Wilson kept on recording his observations: ice that resembled, to his homesick eyes, gorse or sea-urchins. The rest of the expedition waited for the five who'd made the final march to the pole. When winter set in, they knew their companions would never return. In the spring, a search party discovered the tent. When the bodies were dug out of the snow, Scott's arm was around Wilson, and the bag of fossils was lying next to them. They'd carried it with them to the end. This thrilled Athos, but for me, another detail proved Wilson's nobility. Wilson had borrowed a book of Tennyson's poetry for the final march to the pole and, even when every ounce tore at his thighs and shoulders, he persisted in carrying it back, in order to return it to its lender. I could easily imagine carrying a favoured item to the ends of the earth, if only to help me believe I'd see its beloved owner again.

After the First World War, Athos had returned to Cambridge to visit the new Scott Polar Research Institute. Of England he recounted nothing of castles or knights. Instead he described flowstone, dripstone, and other marvellous cave formations; spasms in time. Marble curtains bulging with petrified breezes, gypsum blossoms, clusters of stone grapes. He'd brought back a small postcard of the Scott Institute, which he showed me. And hanging above his desk was an especially prized possession: a reproduction of Wilson's "Paraselena at McMurdo Sound," which gave me a shock when I first saw it. It was as if Wilson had painted my memory of the spirit world. In the forefront was a circle of skis like a sparse and ghostly forest and, above, the breathtakingly divine haloes of the paraselena itself, swirling, suspended like smoke.

For many months all I saw were stars. My only prolonged experience of the outside world was late at night; Athos let me climb through the bedroom window to lie on the roof. Flat on my back, I dug a hole in the night sky. I inhaled the sea until I was light-headed, and floated above the island.

Alone, in space, I imagined the Antarctic auroras, billowing designs of celestial calligraphy, our small portion of the sky like the corner of an illuminated manuscript. Stretched out on a cotton mat, I thought of Wilson, lying on an ice-floe in the darkness of a polar winter, singing to Emperor penguins. Looking up at the stars, I saw massive islands of ice swaying on the sea, opening and closing a passage, the wind moving floes from hundreds of miles away; one of Athos's lessons in "remote causes." I saw ice-fields pale gold with lunar light. I thought of Scott and his frozen men starving in the tent, knowing that an abundance of food waited, inaccessible, only eleven miles away. I imagined their last hours in that cramped space.

~

The Germans looted the harvests of the fruit groves. Olive oil was as rare as if we lived on the ice cap. Even on lush Zakynthos we craved citrus. Athos carefully sliced a lemon in half and we sucked out the sourness down to the skin, ate the skin, then smelled our hands. Since I was still young, the rationing and restrictions affected me more than Athos. Eventually my gums began to bleed. My teeth came loose. Athos watched me falling apart and wrung his hands with worry. He softened my bread in milk or water until it was a spongy porridge. As time went on, no one had anything left to sell. We grew what we could, and Athos foraged the sea and the hedges, but it was never enough.

We survived on the overlooked sea peas and vetches, on hyacinth beans and nasturtium pods. Athos described his plant-hunting to me as he prepared our meals. He tugged out capers growing from cracks in the limestone and pickled them; we were inspired by the sturdy contrariness of the plant, which sprang from the rocks and had a marked preference for volcanic soil. Athos looked up recipes in Theophrastus and Dioscorides; he used Pliny's *Natural History* as a cookbook. He unearthed yellow asphodels and we ate "roasted tubers à la Pliny." He boiled asphodel stems, seeds, and roots to remove the bitterness and mixed the smashed concoction with a potato to make bread. We could even have made a liqueur from the flower, and then after dinner resoled our shoes or bound a book with glue made from the roots. Athos pored over Parkinson's *Theatre of Plants*, a useful book that tells you not only what to cook for supper but how to dress your wounds if you have an accident in the kitchen. And, if the meal is a complete disaster, Parkinson even tells you the best recipe for mummification. Athos liked Parkinson's book because it was originally published in 1640, which, as he explained, was "the year the first café opened in Vienna." Athos took pleasure in rhyming off long Latin names while dishing out a sinister-looking green soup. Just as I lifted the spoon to my lips, he commented slyly that "the soup contains capers, not to be confused with 'caper spurge,' which is highly poisonous." Then he waited for the effect. The spoon hovered outside my mouth while he casually speculated, "Unfortunate errors have, no doubt, occurred. . . ."

~

The Italian soldiers who patrolled Zakynthos had no quarrel with the Jews of the zudeccha – the ghetto. They saw no reason to disturb the three-hundred-year-old community, a peaceful mix of Jews from Constantinople, Izmir, Crete, Corfu, and Italy. On Zakynthos at least, the macaronades seemed mystified by the German agenda; they lounged in the afternoon heat and sang to the sunset crinkling over the waves. But when the Italians surrendered, life on the island changed drastically.

The night of June 5, 1944. Through the rustling darkness of the fields, late-night voices: a wife turns to her husband who's already asleep telling him there will be another child by Christmas; a mother calls for her son across the sea; drunken promises and threats of German soldiers in the kafenio in Zakynthos town.

In the zudeccha, the Spanish silver siddur with hinges in the spine, the tallith and candlesticks are being buried in the earth under the kitchen floor. Letters to absent children, photos, are buried. While the men and women who place these valuables in the ground have never done so before, they go through the motions with centuries of practice guiding their hands, a ritual as familiar as the Sabbath. Even the child who runs to bring his favourite toy, the dog with the little wooden wheels, in order to place it in the hold in the kitchen floor, seems to act with knowledge. All across Europe there's such buried treasure. A scrap of lace, a bowl. Ghetto diaries that have never been found.

After burying the books and dishes, the silverware and photos, the Jews of the Zakynthos ghetto vanish.

They slip into the hills, where they wait like coral; half flesh, half stone. They wait in caves, in the sheds and animal stalls of the farms of Christian friends. In their cramped hiding places, parents tell their children what they can, a hurriedly packed suitcase of family stories, the names of relatives. Fathers give their five-year-old sons advice for married life. Mothers pass down recipes not only for the haroseth on the Seder plate but for mezedhes, for cholent as well as ahladhi sto fourno – baked quince, for poppyseed cake and ladhera.

All night and day and night, on the floor next to the sea chest, I wait for the sign from Athos. I wait to close myself up inside. In the hot silence I can't read or think past listening. I listen until I sleep, until I wake again, listening.

It was the night the families of the zudeccha went into hiding that Old Martin's son, Ioannis, and his family came to us. The following night, Ioannis took them to a better hiding place, on the other side of the island. At the end of the week he came again, with news. He was stricken. His narrow face looked even narrower, as if it had been squeezed through a pipe. We sat in Athos's study. Athos poured Ioannis the last inch of ouzo then filled the glass with water.

"The Gestapo ordered Mayor Karrer to write down the name and profession of every Jew. Karrer took the list to Archbishop Chrysostomos. The archbishop said: Burn the list. That's when they sent the warning to the zudeccha. Almost everyone managed to escape the night we came to you. The next day, the streets were empty. I passed through the ghetto on the way to my father's. In the daylight it seemed impossible that hundreds of people could have disappeared so quickly. All you could hear were the trees rustling."

Ioannis drained the glass with one tilt of his head.

"Athos, did you know my wife's family is from Corfu? They lived on Velissariou Street, Velissariou Street, near Solomou. . . ."

Athos and I waited. The shutters were half closed against the sun. The room was very hot.

"The boat was overflowing. I saw it with my own eyes. The boat was so full of Jews from Corfu that when it reached Zakynthos harbour the soldiers couldn't cram on a single soul. The poor few they rounded up were waiting in the noon sun. Mrs. Serenos, old Constantine Caro! In Platia Solomou, right under the Virgin's nose, with their hands above their heads, at gunpoint. But then the boat didn't stop. My father and I waited at the edge of the square, to see what the Germans would do. Mr. Caro started to weep. He thought he was saved, you see, we all thought that, we weren't thinking properly, and we weren't thinking too that if our Jews were saved, it was because the Corfu Jews had been taken in their place."

Ioannis stood, he sat down. He stood up again.

"The boat sailed right past the harbour. Archbishop Chrysostomos said a prayer. Mrs. Serenos started to shout, she began to walk away shouting that she'd die in her own home, not in the platia with all her friends looking on. And they shot her. Right there. Right in front of us all. In front of Argyros's where she used to shop . . . sometimes she brought a little toy for Avramakis . . . she lived across the street. . . ."

Athos put his hands over his ears.

"The others were pushed onto a truck that stayed in the blazing platia the rest of the afternoon, with ss all around, drinking limonadha. We were trying to think what to do, to do something. Then suddenly the truck took off, in the direction of Keri."

"What happened to them?"

"No one knows."

"And the people on the boat? Where were they taking them?"

"My father guesses to the train station at Larissa."

"And Karrer?"

"No one knows where he is, my father heard he escaped by kaiki the same night we came to you. The archbishop stayed with the Jews, he wanted to get in the truck with them but the soldiers wouldn't let him. He stood all day next to the truck, talking to the poor people inside. . . ."

He paused.

"Maybe Jakob shouldn't hear any more."

Athos looked uncertain.

"Ioannis, he's already heard so much."

I thought Ioannis was going to weep.

"If you're looking for the ghetto of Hania, Crete's two-thousand-year-old ghetto, look for it a hundred miles off Polegandros, at the bottom of the sea. . . ."

As he spoke, the room filled with shouts. The water rose around us, bullets tearing the surface for those who took too long to drown. Then the peaceful blue sheen of the Aegean slipped shut again.

After a while Ioannis left. I watched as Athos walked with him partway down the hill. When he returned, Athos went to his desk and wrote down what Ioannis had told us.

∼

Athos would no longer let me go out on the roof at night.

He had been so careful to maintain order. Regular meals, daily lessons. But now our days were without shape. He still told stories, to try and cheer us, but now they were aimless. How he and Nikos learned about Chinese kites and flew a handmade dragon above Cape Spinari while the children from the village perched on the coast, waiting their turn to feel the tug of the string. How they lost the kite in the waves. . . . All his stories went wrong halfway through, and reminded us of the sea.

The only thing that calmed Athos was to draw. The greater his despair, the more obsessively he drew. He took down a battered copy of Blossfeldt's *Elementary Forms* and, in pen and ink, copied the photographs of magnified plants that transformed stems into burnished pewter, blossoms into fleshy fish mouths, pods into hairy accordion pleats. Athos collected poppies, lavatera, basil, broom and spread them on his desk. Then, in watercolours, he made precise renderings. He quoted Wilson: " 'Nature's harmonies cannot be guessed at.' " He explained as he painted: "Broom grows in the Bible. Hagar left Ishmael in a clump of broom, Elijah lay in broom when he asked to die. Perhaps it was the burning bush; even when the fire goes out, its inner branches continue to burn." When he was finished, he gathered what was edible and we used it for supper. Important lessons: look carefully; record what you see. Find a way to make beauty necessary; find a way to make necessity beautiful.

By the end of summer Athos rallied enough to insist that our lessons resume. But the dead surrounded us, an aurora over the blue water.

At night I choked against Bella's round face, a doll's face, immobile, inanimate, her hair floating behind her. These nightmares, in which my parents and my sister drowned with the Jews of Crete, continued for years, continued long after we'd moved to Toronto.

Often on Zakynthos and later in Canada, for moments I was lost. Standing next to the fridge in our Toronto kitchen, afternoon light falling in a diagonal across the floor. About something I can't remember Athos answered me. Perhaps even then the answer had nothing to do with the question. "If you hurt yourself, Jakob, I will have to hurt myself. You will have proven to me my love for you is useless."

Athos said: "I can't save a boy from a burning building. Instead he must save me from the attempt; he must jump to earth."

~

While I hid in the radiant light of Athos's island, thousands suffocated in darkness. While I hid in the luxury of a room, thousands were stuffed into baking stoves, sewers, garbage bins. In the crawlspaces of double ceilings, in stables, pigsties, chicken coops. A boy my age hid in a crate; after ten months he was blind and mute, his limbs atrophied. A woman stood in a closet for a year and a half, never sitting down, blood bursting her veins. While I was living with Athos on Zakynthos, learning Greek and English, learning geology, geography, and poetry, Jews were filling the corners and cracks of Europe, every available space. They buried themselves in strange graves, any space that would fit their bodies, absorbing more room than was allotted them in the world. I didn't know that while I was on Zakynthos, a Jew could be purchased for a quart of brandy, perhaps four pounds of sugar, cigarettes. I didn't know that in Athens, they were being rounded up in "Freedom Square." That the sisters of the Vilna convent were dressing men as nuns in order to provide ammunition to the underground. In Warsaw, a nurse hid children under her skirt,

· 45 ·

passing through the ghetto gates, until one evening – a gentle twilight descending on those typhus-infected, lice-infested streets – the nurse was caught, the child thrown into the air and shot like a tin can, the nurse given the "Nazi pill": one bullet in the throat. While Athos taught me about anabatic and katabatic winds, Arctic smoke, and the Spectre of the Bröcken, I didn't know that Jews were being hanged from their thumbs in public squares. I didn't know that when there were too many for the ovens, corpses were burned in open pits, flames ladled with human fat. I didn't know that while I listened to the stories of explorers in the clean places of the world (snow-covered, salt-stung) and slept in a clean place, men were untangling limbs, the flesh of friends and neighbours, wives and daughters, coming off in their hands.

~

In September 1944, the Germans left Zakynthos. Across the hills, music from town spun through the air frail as a distant radio. A man rode across the island, his high-pitched yelps and the Greek flag snapping above his head. I didn't go outside that day, though I went downstairs and looked into the garden. The next morning Athos asked me to sit with him by the front door. He carried two chairs outside. Sunlight blared from every direction. My eyeballs jangled in my skull. I sat with my back against the house and looked down at myself. My legs did not belong to me; thin as lengths of rope knotted at the knees, skin dripping where muscle used to be, tender in the strong light. The heat pressed down. After a while Athos led me, dazed, inside.

I grew stronger, each day climbing further down and up the hill. Finally I walked with Athos to Zakynthos town, which gleamed as if an egg had been cracked on the sharp Venetian details and dripped shiny over the pale yellow and white plaster. Athos had described it so often: the hedges of quince and pomegranate, the path of cypresses. The narrow streets with laundry drying from the grillwork balconies, the view of Mount Skopos, with the convent Panayia Skopotissa. The statue of Solomos in the square, Nikos's fountain.

Athos presented me to Old Martin. There was now so little to sell that his tiny shop was mostly empty. I remember standing next to a shelf where a few cherries were scattered like rubies on ivory paper. During the occupations, Old Martin tried to satisfy the cravings of his patrons. This was his private resistance. He bartered secretly with ship captains for a delicacy he knew a customer pined for. Thus, cunningly, he bolstered spirits. He kept track of the larders of the community, efficient as a caterer at a fine hotel. Martin knew who was buying food for Jews in hiding after the ghetto was abandoned, and he tried to save extra fruit and oil for families with young children. The Patron Saint of Groceries. Old Martin's short hair stood up in several directions. If Athos's hair was silver ore, Martin's was jagged and white as quartz. His knobbly arthritic hands trembled as he reached deliberately for a fig or a lemon, holding one at a time. In those days of

scarcity his shaking care seemed appropriate, an acknowledgement of the value of a single plum.

Athos and I walked through the town. We rested in the
platia where the last Jews of the zudeccha had waited to
die. A woman was washing the steps of the Zakynthos
Hotel. In the harbour, ropes tapped against the masts.

For four years I'd imagined Athos and I sharing secret
languages. Now I heard Greek everywhere. In the street,
reading signs for the farmakio or the kafenio, I felt pro-
fanely exposed. I ached to return to our little house.

In India there are butterflies whose folded wings look
just like dry leaves. In South Africa there is a plant that's
indistinguishable from the stones among which it grows:
the stone-copying plant. There are caterpillars that look
like branches, moths that look like bark. To remain invisible, the plaice changes colour as it moves through sunlit
water. What is the colour of a ghost?

To survive was to escape fate. But if you escape your
fate, whose life do you then step into?

≈

The Zohar says: "All visible things will be born again
invisible."

The present, like a landscape, is only a small part of a
mysterious narrative. A narrative of catastrophe and slow
accumulation. Each life saved: genetic features to rise
again in another generation. "Remote causes."

Athos confirmed that there was an invisible world, just as real as what's evident. Full-grown forests still and silent, whole cities, under a sky of mud. The realm of the peat men, preserved as statuary. The place where all those who have uttered the bony password and entered the earth wait to emerge. From underground and underwater, from iron boxes and behind brick walls, from trunks and packing crates. . . .

When Athos sat at his desk, soaking wood samples in polyethylene glycol, replacing missing fibres with a waxy filler, I could see – watching his face while he worked – that he was actually traipsing through vanished, impossibly tall Carboniferous forests, with tree bark like intricate brocades: designs more beautiful than any fabric. The forest swayed one hundred feet above his head in a prehistoric autumn.

Athos was an expert in buried and abandoned places. His cosmology became mine. I grew into it naturally. In this way, our tasks became the same.

Athos and I would come to share our secrets of the earth. He described the bog bodies. They had steeped for centuries, their skin tanning to dark leather, umber juices deep in the lines of palms and soles. In autumn, with the smell of snow in the dark clouds, men had been led out into the moor as sacrificial offerings. There, they were anchored with birch and stones to drown in the acidic ground. Time stopped. And that is why, Athos explained, the bog men are so serene. Asleep for centuries, they are uncovered perfectly intact; thus they outlast their killers – whose bodies have long dissolved to dust.

In turn I told him of the Polish synagogues whose sanctuaries were below ground, like caves. The state prohibited synagogues to be built as high as churches, but the Jews refused to have their reverence diminished by building codes. The vaulted ceilings were still built; the congregation simply prayed deeper underground.

I told him of the great wooden horses that once decorated a synagogue near my parents' house and were now desecrated and buried. Someday perhaps they would rise in a herd, as if nothing had occurred, to graze in a Polish field.

I fantasized the power of reversal. Later, in Canada, looking at photographs of the mountains of personal possessions stored at Kanada in the camps, I imagined that if each owner of each pair of shoes could be named, then they would be brought back to life. A cloning from intimate belongings, a mystical pangram.

Athos told me about Biskupin and its discovery by a local teacher out for an evening stroll. The Gasawka River was low and the huge wooden pylons perforated the surface of the lake like massive rushes. More than two thousand years before, Biskupin had been a rich community, supremely organized. They harvested grain and bred livestock. Wealth was shared. Their comfortable houses were arranged in neat rows; the island fortification resembling a modern subdivision. Each gabled home had ample light as well as privacy; a porch, a hearth, a bedroom loft. Biskupin craftsmen traded with Egypt and the Black Sea coast. But then there was a change in climate. Farmland turned to heath, then to bog.

The water table rose inexorably until it was obvious that Biskupin would have to be abandoned. The city remained underwater until 1933, when the level of the Gasawka River dropped. Athos joined the excavation in 1937. His job was to solve the preservation problems of the waterlogged structures. Soon after Athos made the decision to take me home with him, Biskupin was overrun by soldiers. We learned this after the war. They burned records and relics. They demolished the ancient fortifications and houses that had withstood millennia. Then they shot five of Athos's colleagues in the surrounding forest. The others were sent to Dachau.

And that is one of the reasons Athos believed we saved each other.

~

The invisible paths in Athos's stories: rivers following the inconsistencies of land like tears following the imperfections on skin. Wind and currents that stir up underwater creatures, bioluminescent gardens that guide birds to shore. The Arctic tern, riding Westerlies and Trades each year from Arctic to Antarctica and back again. On their brains, the rotating constellations, the imprint of longing and distance. The fixed route of bison over prairie, so worn that the railway laid its tracks along it.

Geography cut by rail. The black seam of that wailing migration from life to death, the lines of steel drawn across the ground, penetrating straight through cities and towns now famous for murder: from Berlin through Breslau; from

Rome through Florence, Padua, and Vienna; from Vilna through Grodno and Łódź; from Athens through Salonika and Zagreb. Though they were taken blind, though their senses were confused by stench and prayer and screams, by terror and memories, these passengers found their way home. Through the rivers, through the air.

When the prisoners were forced to dig up the mass graves, the dead entered them through their pores and were carried through their bloodstreams to their brains and hearts. And through their blood into another generation. Their arms were into death up to the elbows, but not only into death – into music, into a memory of the way a husband or son leaned over his dinner, a wife's expression as she watched her child in the bath; into beliefs, mathematical formulas, dreams. As they felt another man's and another's blood-soaked hair through their fingers, the diggers begged forgiveness. And those lost lives made molecular passage into their hands.

How can one man take on the memories of even one other man, let alone five or ten or a thousand or ten thousand; how can they be sanctified each? He stops thinking. He concentrates on the whip, he feels a face in his hand, he grasps hair as if in a passion grasp, its matted thickness between his fingers, pulling, his hands full of names. His holy hands move, autonomous.

In the Golleschau quarry, stone-carriers were forced to haul huge blocks of limestone endlessly, from one mound to another and back again. During the torture, they carried their lives in their hands. The insane task was not futile only in the sense that faith is not futile.

A camp inmate looked up at the stars and suddenly remembered that they'd once seemed beautiful to him. This memory of beauty was accompanied by a bizarre stab of gratitude. When I first read this I couldn't imagine it. But later I felt I understood. Sometimes the body experiences a revelation because it has abandoned every other possibility.

~

It's no metaphor to feel the influence of the dead in the world, just as it's no metaphor to hear the radiocarbon chronometer, the Geiger counter amplifying the faint breathing of rock, fifty thousand years old. (Like the faint thump from behind the womb wall.) It is no metaphor to witness the astonishing fidelity of minerals magnetized, even after hundreds of millions of years, pointing to the magnetic pole, minerals that have never forgotten magma whose cooling off has left them forever desirous. We long for place; but place itself longs. Human memory is encoded in air currents and river sediment. Eskers of ash wait to be scooped up, lives reconstituted.

How many centuries before the spirit forgets the body? How long will we feel our phantom skin buckling over rockface, our pulse in magnetic lines of force? How many years pass before the difference between murder and death erodes?

Grief requires time. If a chip of stone radiates its self, its breath, so long, how stubborn might be the soul. If sound waves carry on to infinity, where are their screams now? I imagine them somewhere in the galaxy, moving forever towards the psalms.

~

Alone on the roof those nights, it's not surprising that, of all the characters in Athos's tales of geologists and explorers, cartographers and navigators, I felt compassion for the stars themselves. Aching towards us for millennia though we are blind to their signals until it's too late, starlight only the white breath of an old cry. Sending their white messages millions of years, only to be crumpled up by the waves.

VERTICAL TIME

"I met Athos at the university," said Kostas Mitsialis. "He shared my office. Whenever I came in, no matter how early or how late, he was already there, reading by the window. The books and articles piled on the sill! English poetry. How to preserve leaf skeletons. The meaning of pole carvings. He had a beautiful watch from his father. It had an inlay of a sea monster on its case and on its face, with a tail that curled around eleven o'clock. Athos, do you still have it?"

Athos smiled, opened his jacket, and dangled the watch from its chain.

"I told Daphne about him, the shy fellow who took away my privacy in my own office! She wanted to see for herself. One afternoon she came to pick me up, greeting me with a tug on my ears the way she still likes to do. Daphne was only twenty then and always in a good mood. Come to dinner, she said to Athos. Athos asked, Do you like music?

"Those days between the wars, the tavernas were filled with tango, but we had no use for Spaniard music because we had our own: the slow hasapiko and the songs sung with bouzouki that come from the sailors on the docks and the hamals and the plum-juice vendors."

"And the drug dens," winked Athos.

"He took us to a small place off Adrianou Street. There we heard Vito for the first time. His voice was a river. It was glikos, black and sweet. Athos, do you remember? Vito was also the cook. After preparing the food, he came from the kitchen rubbing the rosemary and oil from his fingers onto his apron, and then he stood among the tables and sang a rembetiko that he made up on the spot. A rembetiko, Jakob, always tells a story full of heartache and eros."

"And poverty and hashish," said Athos.

"After Vito sang, he played santouri music that somehow told the story again. One night he did not sing first, but played something so mysterious . . . a story I seemed to know, to remember. It gave me an ancient, suspenseful feeling, like an orchard when the sun moves in and out of the clouds . . . and later that night Daphne and I decided to marry."

"And if you hadn't heard the song?" I asked.

They laughed.

"Then it would have been moonlight, or the cinema, or a poem," said Kostas.

Athos rubbed my hair. "Jakob writes poems," he said.

"Then you have the power to make people marry," said Daphne.

"Like a rabbi or a priest?" I asked.

They laughed again.

"No," said Athos. "Like a cook in a café."

In Athens, we stayed with Daphne and Kostas – Professor Mitsialis and his wife – old friends of Athos's who lived on the slopes of Lykavettos in a small house with rubble where the front steps had been. Daphne had set a pot of flowers in the pile. A vegetable and herb garden in the back. Past Kolonaki Square, between Kiphissia and Tatoi, past the foreign embassies, palms and cypresses, past parks, past tall white apartments. Past the statue of revolutionary Mavrocordatos, where an Athenian kneeled in 1942 and sang Solomos's national anthem and was shot.

It had taken Athos and I close to two weeks to travel the wounded landscape from Zakynthos to Athens. Roads were blocked, bridges out, villages in ruins. Farmland and orchards had been devastated. Those without a scrap of land to work or money for the black market were starving. This would be the case for years. And, of course, peace did not come to Greece at the end of the war. About six months after the fighting ended in Athens between communists and British, with an interim government still in place, Athos and I closed up the house on Zakynthos and crossed the channel to Kyllini on the mainland.

In Athens, Athos would begin to search for news of Bella and the only other member of my family I knew of, an aunt I'd never met, my mother's sister Ida, who'd lived in Warsaw. We both understood that Athos must search so that I could give up. I found his faith unbearable.

On the boat, Athos brought out bread and a spoonful of honey for our breakfast, but I couldn't eat. Looking out at the waves of Porthmos Zakinthou, I thought nothing would ever be familiar again.

We took lifts whenever we could, in carts and on the

backs of bone-rattling lorries that stirred up the dust climbing hairpin turns and spiralling down again. We travelled long distances me ta podhia – on foot. There are two rules for walking in Greece that Athos taught me as we climbed a hill and left Kyllini behind. Never follow a goat, you'll end up at the edge of a cliff. Always follow a mule, you'll arrive at a village by nightfall. We paused often to rest, in those days more for my benefit than Athos's. When we were both worn out, we waited with our satchels by the side of the road, hoping someone might come by to take us to the next village. I looked at Athos in his frayed tweed jacket and his dusty fedora and saw how much he'd aged in the few years I'd known him. As for me, the child who'd entered Athos's house was gone, I was thirteen years old. Often while we were walking, Athos put his arm across my shoulders. His touch felt natural to me, though all else was like a dream. And it was his touch that kept me from falling into myself too far. It was on that journey from Zakynthos to Athens, on those crumbling roads and in those dry hills, that I realized what I felt: not that I owed Athos everything but that I loved him.

The landscape of the Peloponnesus had been injured and healed so many times, sorrow darkened the sunlit ground. All sorrow feels ancient. Wars, occupations, earthquakes; fire and drought. I stood in the valleys and imagined the grief of the hills. I felt my own grief expressed there. It would be almost fifty years and in another country before I would again experience this intense empathy with a landscape.

At Kyllini, we saw that the great medieval castle

had been dynamited by the Germans. We passed outdoor schools, children in rags using slabs of rock as desks. A shame hung over the countryside, the misery of women who could not even bury their dead, whose bodies had been burned or drowned, or simply thrown away.

We descended the valley to Kalavrita, at the foot of Mount Velia. Since disembarking at Kyllini, everyone we'd spoken to had told us of the massacre. At Kalavrita, in December 1943, the Germans murdered every man in the village over the age of fifteen – fourteen hundred men – then set fire to the town. The Germans claimed the townspeople had been harbouring andartes – Greek resistance fighters. In the valley, charred ruins, blackened stone, a terrible silence. A place so empty it was not even haunted.

At Korinthos, we climbed aboard a lorry that was filled to overflowing with other travellers. Finally, on a hot afternoon in late July, we arrived in Athens.

Dusty and tired, we sat in Daphne and Kostas's living room, with Daphne's paintings of the city on the wall – all light and edges, a radiant cubism that in Greece is close to realism. A small glass table. Silk cushions. I was afraid that when I stood up my dirty clothes would leave an imprint on the pale sofa. A little dish of wrapped candies on the table distracted me, gave me a painful glimmer, as when part of you falls asleep and then blood returns to the place. I didn't understand I could help myself. My elbows rubbed against my sleeves, my legs against my shorts. In a large silver-framed mirror, I saw my head looming above the thin stem of my neck.

Kostas led me into his room and he and Athos picked out some clothes for me. They took me to a barber for my first real haircut. Daphne drew me to her, her hands on my shoulders. She was not much taller than me and almost as thin. She was, as I look back, like a very elderly girl. She wore a dress with a pattern of birds. Her hair was fastened in a knot on top of her head, a little grey cloud. She served me a stifhado of beans and garlic. I ate karpouzi outside with Kostas, who showed me how to spit the melon seeds all the way to the bottom of the garden.

Their kindnesses were mysterious and welcome to me as the city itself – with its strange trees, its blinding white walls.

The morning after we arrived, Daphne, Kostas, and Athos began to talk. Starved, they fell into conversation, cleaning their plate as if they'd find a truth painted on the bottom. They talked as if everything must be told in a single day. They talked as if they were at shivah, at a wake, where all the talk cannot fill the absent chair. Once in a while Daphne got up to replenish their glasses, to bring bread, small cold bowls of fish, peppers, onions, olives. I could not follow it all: the andartes, EAM, ELAS, communists, Venizelists, and anti-Venizelists. . . . But there was also much I did understand – hunger, shooting, bodies in the street, how suddenly everything familiar is inexpressible. I paid such close attention that, as Kostas said, history wore me out, and around four o'clock when we moved into the garden, with the breeze and sun in my freshly trimmed hair, I fell asleep.

When I woke, it was twilight. They were leaning back in their chairs in a silent melancholy, as if the long Greek dusk had finally drawn every memory out of their hearts.

Kostas shook his head.

"It's as Theotokas says: 'Time was cut by a knife.' The tanks came down Vasilissis Sofias. Even when one German walks through a Greek street it's like an iron rod so cold it burns your hand. It wasn't even noon. We heard it on the radio. All morning the black cars made a trail through the city like a line of gunpowder."

"We closed the drapes to the sun and Kostas and I sat at the table in the dark. We heard sirens, anti-aircraft guns, yet the church bells kept ringing for early Mass."

. . . When they pushed my father, he was still sitting in his chair, I could tell afterwards, by the way he fell.

"Our neighbour Aleko came to the back door to tell Kostas and me that someone saw swastikas hanging from balconies on Amalias. They flew, he said, over the palace, over the chapel on Lykavettos. It wasn't until evening, when we saw the flags ourselves, and the flag over the Acropolis, that we wept."

. . . I could tell by the way he fell.

"At the beginning, we continued to go to the taverna, just for the company and to hear some news. There wasn't anything to eat or drink. At the beginning, the waiter still pretended, brought out the menu; it became a ritual joke. People still told jokes then, didn't they, Daphne? Sometimes we even heard the one from student days when we were so poor and someone used to call out to the waiter: 'Cook an egg, there are nine of us!'"

. . . When I was in the ground and my head was prickling, I dreamed my mother was scrubbing the lice from my hair. I imagined Mones and I skipping stones on the river. Mones once caught his finger in a door and his nail came off, but he could still make the stones jump more times.

"Daphne's brother heard that when they found Korizis, he had a gun in one hand and an icon in the other."

"After the macaronades and before the Germans, there were the British and Aussies everywhere. They took sun baths without their shirts."

"They sat around Zonar's and sang songs from *The Wizard of Oz*. They burst into song at the slightest provocation, Floca and Maxim's suddenly seemed like sets for operetta. . . . I went looking for pipe tobacco at the King George. I thought maybe there they'd still have some, but they didn't. And maybe to pick up the *Kathemerini*, the *Proia*, any newspaper I could find. A British soldier in the lobby offered me a cigarette and we had a long discussion about the differences between Greek and British and French tobacco. The next day Daphne answered the door and there he was, bringing us meat in tins."

"That's the only time one of Kostas's vices has ever been useful," called Daphne from the kitchen where she was pouring me a glass of milk.

. . . Mrs. Alperstein, Mones's mother, made wigs. She used to rub her hands with lotion to keep them smooth for her work. She gave us milk while we were studying and the glass always smelled of lotion, it made the milk taste pretty. When my father came home from work his hands were black, just like he was wearing gloves, and he used to scrub them until they were almost pink, though you could still smell the shoe leather – he was the best bootmaker – and you could still smell the polish, which came in tins and was soft as black butter.

"They made us take in a German officer. He stole from us. Every day I saw him take something – knives and forks, needle and thread. He brought home butter, potatoes, meat – for himself. He watched me cook it and I had to serve him, while Kostas and I ate only carrots, boiled without oil, without even salt. Sometimes he made me eat part of his meal in front of Kostas but wouldn't let Kostas eat. . . ."

Kostas stroked his own cheek with Daphne's hand.

"My dear, my dear. He thought it would make me crazy, but truly I was happy to see you have enough for once."

"At night, after curfew, Kostas and I lay awake and we heard the sentries marching up and down Kolonaki, as if the whole city was a jail."

"Athos, you remember how they wanted our chrome before the war. Well, when they didn't have to pay for anything, they took what they wanted from the mines: pyrites, ore, nickel, bauxite, manganese, gold. Leather, cotton, tobacco. Wheat, cattle, olives, oil. . . ."

"Yes, and the Germans stood around Syntagma Square chewing olives and spitting out the pits so they could watch the little children scramble to pick them up off the ground and suck dry whatever was left."

"They drove their trucks to the Acropolis and took tourist photos of each other in front of the Parthenon."

"Athos, they turned our Athens into a city of beggars. In '41, when it snowed so much, no one had coal or wood. People wrapped blankets around themselves and stood in Omonia Square and just waited there for help. Women with infants . . ."

"Once, after the Germans loaded up a train at Larissa, a patriot decided to liberate the cargo. The train exploded as it pulled out of the station. Oranges and lemons flew, raining into the streets. A glorious sweet smell mixed with the smell of gunpowder. Balconies glistened, lemon juice dripped in the sunlight! For days after, people found an orange in the crook of a statue, in the pocket of a shirt hanging to dry. Someone found a dozen lemons under a car – "

"Like eggs under a hen."

. . . I saw my father and Mrs. Alperstein shake hands and I wondered if they had traded smells and if all the shoes would smell like flowers and all the wigs like shoes.

"Our neighbour Aleko revived a man in the middle of Kolonaki with a bowl of milk. Aleko himself didn't even have a piece of bread to share. But soon when people collapsed in the street they didn't get up again, they simply starved to death."

"Kostas and I heard stories of whole families being killed for a case of currants or a sack of flour."

"We heard of a man who was standing early one evening in Omonia Square. Another man rushed up to him, carrying a parcel. 'Quick, quick,' he said, 'I have fresh lamb, but I must sell right away, I need to buy a train ticket to return home to my wife.' The idea of fresh lamb . . . fresh lamb! . . . was too much for the man on the corner, who thought of his own wife and their wedding supper and all the meals they took for granted before the war. The good tastes he remembered chased all other thoughts from his head and he reached into his pocket. He paid a large sum, all he had. Lamb was worth it! And the man hurried away in the direction of the train station. The man on the corner rushed off in the opposite direction, straight home. 'I have a surprise!' he shouted, and handed his wife the parcel. 'Open it in the kitchen.' Excited, they stood over the bundle of newspaper and his wife cut the string. Inside they found a dead dog."

"Athos, you are a brother to Kostas and me. You have known us many years. Who could believe we would ever have such words in our mouths?"

"When the British were still here, we managed to find things. A little margarine, a bit of coffee, sugar, sometimes a little beef! . . . But when the Germans came, they even stole cows about to calve and slaughtered both the mother and child. They ate the mother and threw away the child. . . ."

Daphne touched Kostas's arm to stop him, inclining her head in my direction.

"Kostas, it's too terrible."

"Daphne and I cheered, 'Englezakia!' as the English bombs fell in our streets, even as the smoke turned the sky black above Piraeus and sirens screamed and the house shook."

"Even I learned to recognize which planes were theirs and which were English. Stukas shriek. They're silver and dive like swallows – "

"And drop their bombs like shit."

"Kostas," chided Daphne, "not in front of Jakob."

"He's sleeping."

"No I'm not!"

"Since Daphne won't let me swear in front of you, Jakob, though you've seen so much it's only right you should know how to swear, I'll tell you instead that war can turn even an ordinary man into a poet. I'll tell you what I thought the day they abused the city with their swastikas: At sunrise the Parthenon is flesh. In moonlight it is bones."

"Jakob and I have read Palamas together."

"Then, Jakob, pedhi-mou, you know Palamas is our most beloved poet. When Palamas died, right in the middle of the war, we followed another poet, Sikelianos, in his long black cape through Athens. Thousands of us, the whole city, accompanied Palamas's body from the church to the grave. At the cemetery, Sikelianos shouted that we must 'shake the country with a cry for freedom, shake it from end to end,' and we sang the national anthem, surrounded by soldiers! Afterwards Daphne said to me – "

"No one but Palamas could so rouse and unite us. Even from his grave."

"The first weekend of the occupation, the Germans held a procession through the city. Armoured cars, banners, columns of troops a block long. But Greeks were ordered to stay inside. It was forbidden for us to watch. The few who could see anything from home peeked through their shutters while the mad parade marched through empty streets."

"On street corners, in restaurants, like sideshow acts,

black marketeers pulled raw fish out of briefcases, eggs from their pockets, apricots from their hats, potatoes from their sleeves."

. . . When it got too hard to find stones flat enough to skip, we sat on the bank. Mones had a bar of chocolate. His mother gave it to us the day we went to the cinema to see the American cowboy Butski Jonas and his white horse. We saved it because we were already planning our next expedition to the river. Inside, under the wrapper, there's always a card, with a picture of a famous place. We'd already had different palaces and the Eiffel Tower and some famous gardens. That day, we got the Alhambra and folded it and tore it in half and pledged our eternal loyalty like we always did, and Mones kept half and I kept the other half so that when we went into business together we could join them up and pin them on the wall, his half of the world and my half, everything shared right down the middle.

"The night before the Germans left Athens: Wednesday, October 11. Daphne and I heard a strange sound, not quite a breeze, very faint. I went outside. There was a tremor in the air, like a thousand wings. The street was deserted. Then I looked up. Above my head, from all the roofs and balconies people were leaning, quietly calling to each other across the city, spreading the word. The city, which had been like a jail only a moment before, was now like a bedroom full of whispering, and also in the darkness the clinking of glasses filled with whatever we could find and 'yiamas, yiamas,' to your health, rising like gusts into the night."

"Afterwards, but before the dekemvriana, the December battles, we began to hear more of what happened elsewhere. . . ."

"Daphne's sister in Hania sent a letter: 'In the middle of a field of freshly ploughed earth, nothing anywhere, you'll find someone has put up a sign: "This was Kandanos." "This was Skines." All that remains of the villages.'"

"Jakob and I also saw signs, marking where villages had once been. All across the Peloponnesus."

"They say over a thousand villages are gone."

"Jakob and I were at Kalavrita. Send the tourists to the burned-out chorios. These are our historic sites now. Let the tourists visit modern ruins."

"Here, people stood in long queues, waiting to bury their dead. The streetcleaners collected bodies. Everyone was afraid of malaria. We heard children singing the German soldiers' song: 'When the cicadas shrill, grab the yellow pill. . . .'"

"'Too many funerals crowded temple gates.'"

"Athos, you've taught Jakob well. Pedhi-mou, do you remember where the line is from?"

"Ovid?"

"Very good. Do you remember the rest? Wait, I'll look it up."

Kostas opened up a book and read aloud:

"'Meanwhile the dead were fallen all about me,
Nor were they interred by usual rites:
Too many funerals crowded temple gates . . .

. . . and none were left
To weep their loss: unwept the souls of matrons,
Of brides, young men and ancients – all vanished
To the blind wilderness of wind . . .'"

There was a long silence. Athos crossed his legs and banged the table. The dishes rattled. Kostas ran his hands through his long white hair. He leaned across the low table towards Athos.

"On the day the last German left the city, the streets were jammed, Syntagma was packed, the bells rang. Then, right in the middle of the celebrations, the communists began to shout slogans. I swear to you, Athos, the crowd went silent. Everyone sobered up in a second. The next day, Theotokas said: 'It only needs a match for Athens to catch fire like a tank of petrol.'"

"The American boys brought food and clothing, but the communists stole the crates from the warehouses in Piraeus. There's been so much wrong from both sides. Whoever has power for a minute commits a crime."

"They hunted down bourgeoisie in their beds and shot them. They took away the shoes of democrats and marched them barefoot into the hills until they died. Andartes and Englezakia had fought side by side in the mountains only a few weeks before. Now they were shooting at each other across the city. How could it be, our brave andartiko who blew up bridges and were runners for the resistance across the mountains, who disappeared in one place and reappeared in another, a hundred miles away – "

"Like a needle and thread across fabric."

"On Zakynthos a communist turned in his own brother, an old man, because once ten years ago he happened to raise his glass to the king! The communists are our sons, they know everyone's affairs just as well as they know the paths through the valleys, the mountain passes, every grove and gorge."

"Violence is like malaria."

"It's a virus."

"We caught it from the Germans."

. . . By the time Mones and I started to walk home it was misty and drizzling and our wool socks were soaked through and our feet were cold as the fish in the Nemen. Our boots were heavy with mud. Each house was connected to heaven by a rope of smoke. We would be best friends forever. We would open a bookshop together and let Mones's mother mind the store when we went to the movies. We would have plumbing in our houses and electricity in every room. My hands were cold and my back was cold because of the rain and because it was far and I was sweating too under my coat. Broken fences, sagging roads with deep wagon ruts. The tops of our socks hardened into casts. But we didn't want to get home too quickly. We stood a long time at Mones's wooden gate. We would be pious like our fathers. We would marry the Gotkin sisters and share a summer house at Lasosna. We'd row through the inlets there and teach our wives to swim. . . .

"Daphne's cousins, Thanos and Yiorgios, and hundreds of others, anyone they thought was well off before the war, were rounded up by the communists in Kolonaki Square."

. . . At Mones's gate we shook hands like men. Under his cap Mones's hair was plastered to his head. We were soaked through but would've talked longer if it wasn't dinner time. Together we'll visit Crinik and Białystok and even Warsaw! Our first sons will be born the same year! We'll never forget these promises to each other. . . .

"Daphne went out to try to buy some sugar, a treat for my birthday. Instead she found Aleko with three others hanging from the acacias at Kyriakon. . . ."

~

The first morning at Daphne and Kostas's, I was embarrassed to eat breakfast with strangers. Everyone came to the table fully clothed. However, in the days to follow, Kostas appeared less and less dressed, first without a tie, then wearing slippers, finally in his dressing gown with a belt that had tassels at the end. Athos and Kostas sat at the table each with half the newspaper, reading aloud to each other. Daphne prepared eggs with chives and thyme. She was happy to be cooking for two men and a boy, though the food shortages required inventiveness. Athos complimented Daphne's cooking at every meal. The luxury of their affection brought feeling to me, my hair tousled by a passing hand, the squeeze of Daphne's spontaneous embrace. Daphne showed me the difference it made if she placed plums in a green bowl or in a yellow bowl before she set them on the table. She took me into her painting room and made a sketch of my face with fine pencil lines. In the afternoons while Athos was attending to our move to Canada, I helped Daphne clean her paint brushes or prepare dinner, or Kostas and I practised my English in the warm garden where sometimes we both nodded off.

I listened to the ebb and flow of Athos and Kostas's political discussions. They always tried to include me, first soliciting my opinion, then debating seriously my ideas until I felt like a pundit, a peer.

When I had my nightmares, they all came to me, the three of them, and sat on my bed, Daphne gently scratching my back. They talked to each other until, in the comfort of their low voices, I fell asleep again. Then they wandered down to the kitchen. In the morning I saw the plates from their midnight party still on the table.

Once, Daphne sent me out to fetch some herbs while she was preparing dinner. I was frightened to go out alone, even just into the garden. As I stood at the back door, Kostas noticed my distress and put down the paper. "I need a stretch, Jakob, let's see what the evening air is like." And we stepped outside together.

On the eve of our departure for Canada, I sat on the bed and watched Daphne pack for me, Kostas leaping up to retrieve some extra thing to put into my suitcase, a book or another pair of his socks. Daphne patted each item carefully into place. Neither of them had been to Canada. They speculated on the climate, the people, each speculation resulting in the addition of another eccentric item – a compass, a tie clip.

I remember Daphne, on that last night, turning back at the doorway of my room after saying goodnight and coming over to give me one more fierce squeeze. I remember her cool hands on my back under my cotton pyjamas, her gentle scritch-scratch, my mother's, Bella's, soothing me to sleep.

~

Before we'd left Zakynthos, Athos said: "We must have a ceremony. For your parents, for the Jews of Crete, for all who have no one to recall their names."

We threw camomile and poppies into the cobalt sea. Athos poured fresh water into the waves, that "the dead may drink."

Athos read from Seferis: "'Here finish the works of the sea the works of love. You who will someday live here . . . if the blood chances to darken your memory, do not forget us.'"

I thought: It's longing that moves the sea.

On Zakynthos sometimes the silence shimmers with the overtone of bees. Their bodies roll in the air, powdery with golden weight. The field was heavy with daisies, honeysuckle, and broom. Athos said: "Greek lamentation burns the tongue. Greek tears are ink for the dead to write their lives."

He spread a striped cloth on the grass and we sat down to eat koliva, bread, and honey by the sea – that "the dead may not go hungry."

Athos said: "Remember. Your good deeds help the moral progress of the dead. Do good on their behalf. Their bones will bear the weight of the waves for eternity; as my countrymen's bones will bear the weight of earth.

We will not be able to exhume them according to custom; their bones will not join the bones of their families in the ossuary of their village. The generations will not be bound together; they will melt under the sea, or in the soil, desolate. . . ."

I heard in my head their cries and imagined in the waves their shiny, almost human skin, their brine-soaked hair. And, as in my nightmares, I placed my parents under the waves where it was clear and blue.

Athos lit a lamp – a jar filled with olive oil – and used a tightly wound bundle of dried quince as a wick.

Athos said: "The shepherds will not know to lament them, no prayers will be heard from distant fields amid the cries of sheep and goats. So let us pass the koliva and light the candle and sing 'Death ate my eyes' . . . If our duties – kathikonda – bring them release – anakoufisi – then the dead will send a message to us on the wings of birds."

The air was, in fact, filled with storks and swallows and wild doves. Rosemary and basil swayed like censers in the afternoon heat.

Athos said: "Jakob, try to be buried in ground that will remember you."

When we stand on the high slope above Zakynthos town, I imagine driftwood washing up on the gravelly beach below, only it's not wood but their long bones, their curved bones that have washed up with the tide. Coarse sand gleams with the polished debris. The birds don't come, there's nothing left for them. Only the skulls stay in the sea. Too heavy, they settle on the bottom; on the ocean floor is a city of white domes. They glow in the depth. Burned into the bone, last thoughts line the skulls. Silently the fish slip home through the eyes, through the mouths.

~

For years after the war, even the smallest decision was an agony. I examined my steps before I took them, even before the most trivial excursion. If I go to the store now instead of later, what will happen? I extrapolated minutely. "Jakob, I could recite half of Homer every time I wait for you. . . ."

Nothing is sudden. Not an explosion – planned, timed, wired carefully – not the burst door. Just as the earth invisibly prepares its cataclysms, so history is the gradual instant.

The week before Athos and I left for Canada, I went with Kostas for a long walk along Vasilissis Sofias, down Amalias to the Plaka. He carried a cane that he didn't use much; sometimes he wound his arm, fragile as a willow branch, through mine. He showed me the Pedagogic Academy where Daphne used to teach English. He showed me the university. We shared a gazoza in the courtyard of an old hotel.

"Did Athos tell you he was once married? No, I can see by your face he didn't. He rarely speaks of Helen even to us. Some stones are so heavy only silence helps you carry them. She died during the first war."

I felt ashamed, I felt I had betrayed Athos, that somehow I had not been worthy enough for him to have revealed this secret.

"Athos has left us many times; he's lived away from Greece for many years. But now it's different. He wants to leave. Greece will never be the same. Perhaps it will be better. But he's right to take you away. Jakob, Athos is my best friend. We've known each other forty years – you can't yet understand what that means. What I want to say to you is this: Sometimes Athos becomes very sad, you know, he can be sad for long months and there may be times when he will need you to take care of him."

My eyes went hot.

"Pedhi-mou, don't worry. Athos is like his beloved limestone. The sea will dissolve him into caves, dig holes into him, but he lasts and lasts."

On the way home we passed walls scrawled with a huge V – Vinceremo, we shall overcome – in black paint. Or M – Mussolini Merda. Kostas explained why no one wanted to erase those symbols. During the occupation, graffiti required swiftness and courage. Graffitos who were caught were executed by the Germans on sight. A single letter was exhilarating, it was spit in the eye of the oppressors. A single letter was a matter of life and death.

We passed a church and Kostas told me how, right where we stood, there had been a riot the first time the gospel was read in the demotic. "Did they think God only understood katharevousa?" "Yes, pedhi-mou, exactly!" And when the *Oresteia* was performed in the demotic for the first time, Kostas said some of the audience died in the logomachy that followed.

On Zakynthos, there was the statue of Solomos. In Athens, there was Palamas and the graffitos, whose heroism was language. I already knew the power of language to destroy, to omit, to obliterate. But poetry, the power of language to restore: this was what both Athos and Kostas were trying to teach me.

~

Athos had worked in England, France, Vienna, Yugoslavia, Poland; he went where interesting tasks took him. He had a professional reputation for both eclecticism and a very defined expertise in the conservation of waterlogged wood. But the reason we were invited to Canada was salt.

I would come to discover that Athos's interest in Scott's Antarctic travels was not entirely impersonal. In fact, Athos himself had briefly considered applying for the expedition, for he was at Cambridge at the time and, like many Mediterraneans, had a contrary passion for things polar. But Athos was newly married and never went to Scott's recruiting office in London; nor did he ever regret this, because, as it turned out, he and Helen had only five years together before Helen died. There were two geologists on the expedition, Frank Debenham and Griffith Taylor. Athos didn't know Debenham or Taylor at Cambridge. Athos met Debenham later, during the First World War. Debenham was stationed in Salonika and he heard Athos give a lecture on salt. Debenham had travelled far and seen much and known the hearts of men thrown together in dangerous places, and now he found himself sitting under a ceiling fan in a claustrophobic lecture room moved by Athos's descriptions of the desirous ionic bond. Sodium chambers like solid fog in the black earth. Miners, lovers, the sea stained with that ancient taste. The lofty salt hills of Thaikan, the baked salt cakes used as money in Kain-du.

Between the wars, Debenham had helped establish the Scott Polar Institute. He and Athos wrote to each other occasionally, and it was Debenham who told Athos that Griffith Taylor was setting up a new department of geography at the University of Toronto.

Griffith Taylor knew something of Toronto because another member of Scott's team, Silas Wright, had been born and raised there. Taylor and Wright had walked from Cambridge to the Antarctic recruiting office at St. Paul's, a waggish stunt to convince Scott of their mettle. They carried hard-boiled eggs and slabs of chocolate to keep up their strength on the twelve-hour march. Wright, used to canoeing and hiking in the wilds of Northern Ontario and British Columbia, was particularly sensitive to the suggestion that scientists might not have as much muscle as navy men, and on the voyage south he was reefing and hauling with the best of them. In fact, as soon as he returned from the hardships of Antarctica, Wright took Debenham on a camping trip in northwestern Canada.

In the midst of the very British Antarctica, Wright asserted his Canadian roots, for which he was heartily mocked. Taylor was fond of referring to Wright as "the American," a comment for which Taylor endured his due punishment. As Taylor reports in his diary: "Wright fell upon me and succeeded in tearing my pocket."

Taylor's Antarctic diary is studded with exclamation marks, as if he's continually astonished by what he's writing, as if the whole frozen experience might be an hallucination. He recounts the day trips he took with Wright, including a march to Cape Royds to find Shackleton's abandoned hut. They opened the door to a spotless cabin. A two-year-old lunch was waiting for them, the table set and laden with biscuits and jam, scones and gingerbread and condensed milk, preserved by the cold. Taylor and Wright stepped into the ghostly room, sat down and ate, as if they'd been sent an invitation by their long-absent host and two years later had arrived just in time.

It was one of Athos's regrets that he never met Wright, who had been visiting with Taylor only a week before our arrival in Toronto. The two Antarctic explorers went to the Canadian National Exhibition, where they ate snowcones, rode the midway, and attended the horse show. These were the same men who'd been the first to cross Antarctica's Dry Valley together, a mysterious zone where not a drop of moisture has fallen for over two million years. Now Wright was back in his home town, showing Taylor the fair he went to as a boy.

Taylor liked the idea of hiring Cambridge men to teach in his department, and he had heard about Athos from Debenham. Taylor and Athos arranged to meet briefly in Athens in 1938 when Taylor was touring Greece on his way to deliver his "Correlations and Culture" lecture in Cambridge. While walking through the city, they discovered that they shared the same ideas about geography and pacifism, the belief that science must be used as a peace measure, what Taylor came to call his "geopacifism." Specifically, they spoke of Nazism's "Nordic fetish" and anti-Semitism, and how geography could be used against the dangerous fabrications of politics. They impressed each other, as two men who share the same passionate convictions often do.

Taylor invited Athos to Toronto to teach and Athos accepted though, as it turned out, he wasn't able to take up the offer as early as he'd hoped, because of the war. We would only be in Toronto a few years when Taylor was diagnosed with cancer. Soon after, he retired and returned to his native Australia.

Because the Torontonian Wright went south with Taylor and Debenham; because Debenham was stationed in Salonika; because of salt – Athos and I found ourselves on a boat to Canada.

≈

Athos loved the broken hills of his country, mended by groves and sheep. He carried in his wallet a photo of the hilltop view from the house on Zakynthos.

"Love makes you see a place differently, just as you hold differently an object that belongs to someone you love. If you know one landscape well, you will look at all other landscapes differently. And if you learn to love one place, sometimes you can also learn to love another."

Before we left Zakynthos, we'd packed Athos's library and addressed the crates to the Mitsialises in Athens. Athos marked the boxes so Kostas would know which to send on to Canada and which to have delivered to the Roussos family house on the island of Idhra. Idhra is much closer to Athens, less than a day's travel from Piraeus. Athos didn't know how many years we'd be away; moving his books was a precaution against earthquakes.

Zakynthos had already endured three quakes in the past hundred years, the last just before the turn of the century. In 1953, a few years after we'd moved to Canada, again the ground hoisted up Zakynthos in spasms like a car jack, then threw the entire town to the ground. Virtually all property on the island was destroyed, including Athos's little house. Old Martin sent us a photograph Ioannis took in the zudeccha showing one lone palm tree in the wreckage, a macabre indication of where in the destroyed street he stood. Eventually Zakynthos town was rebuilt, the Venetian architecture overlooking the harbour painstakingly reconstructed. But Athos decided not to rebuild Nikos's fountain and to leave the stones of his home where they fell.

"Most of the islanders were able to save themselves," said Athos, "because they trusted the prescience of their animals. Centuries of earthquakes have taught Zakynthians to heed the warnings; a catalogue of signs has been compiled over generations. Half a day before the ground shakes, dogs and cats run into the streets howling as if mad. Nothing can be heard over the wailing. Goats kick out their stalls in panic, worms ooze out of the ground, even moles are frightened to be underground. Geese and chickens fly into the trees, pigs bite off each other's tails, cows try to tear themselves free of their halters and run. Fish leap out of the water. Rats stagger as if drunk. . . ."

In telling me this, Athos thought he was providing a reasonable explanation. But this only confirmed what

I already believed: that Zakynthians were under the protection of an unseen hand. "No," insisted Athos. "No. There was luck in the escape of the families of the zudeccha, but first Mayor Karrer had to speak out. There was luck in the islanders sailing to the mainland for safety, but first they had to heed the signs. . . . There was luck in our meeting, Jakob, but first you had to run."

Athos and I made the short trip to Idhra so Athos could visit with Mrs. Karouzos, who ran a small hotel and taverna in town. Like her mother before her, she also kept an eye on the Roussos house when it stood empty, often for years at a time. Athos explained to me that this is not unusual on the islands. Sometimes a house waits for decades for a son to return. As there are no automobiles on Idhra, Athos's crates would be carried by donkey uphill, past the old harbourside mansions of wealthy shipowners whose family fleets had broken the British blockade during the Napoleonic Wars and had traded as far as America.

The house on Idhra, like the house on Zakynthos, is suspended like a balcony above the sea. "On this terrace," said Athos, "you will always feel a breeze, no matter how hot the day. When Nikos was a boy he folded a paper airplane and sent it over the edge. It landed in the hat of a man drinking ouzo in a kafenio by the dock. On the piece of paper my brother had written a note begging to be saved from a kidnapper, and described where he was being held captive. The police came to the house and Nikos was laughing with terror at how my father would punish him, as my father chased Nikos halfway down the hill. So then everyone watching did think my brother was being chased by a criminal!"

Athos showed me photos of his parents and his brother.

We sat under the lemon trees in Mrs. Karouzos's court-yard taverna while the leaves speckled the wall with shadows, and later on the ferry back to Athens, I fell asleep with my sunburned face against Athos's shoulder.

A few days after we returned from Idhra, Daphne and Kostas saw us off at Piraeus. Kalo taxidhi, kalo taxidhi – safe voyage. Athos presented Kostas with a sealed tin of British tobacco, which Kostas said must be the last tin left in Greece, and I gave him a feeble poem over which I'd laboured, about the eve of Athens's liberation, called "The Whispering City."

On the dock, Daphne handed us a hamper of food; the hard boutimata that break your teeth unless you soak them in milk or coffee, olives and domates from her garden to eat with bread, small crumbling bunches of oregano and basil tied with string. A precious bottle of popolaro. Kostas gave Athos an edition of Sikelianos's war-time poems, *Akritika*, and he gave me his cherished copy of a pocket-sized hardcover selection of Greek poetry, planting rows of words in me that would grow for the rest of my life.

Daphne squeezed my face goodbye, and I felt my mother patting my jaw to make me a beard with her floury hands.

Daphne slipped an orange into my coat and I remem-bered Mones, who kept the precious peel in his pocket for the smell, and a half a day later opened his mouth in the schoolyard and there on his tongue lay an orange pip like a pearl.

"In xenetia – in exile," said Athos on our last night with Daphne and Kostas in their garden, "in a foreign landscape, a man discovers the old songs. He calls out for water from his own well, for apples from his own orchard, for the muscat grapes from his own vine."

"What is a man," said Athos, "who has no landscape? Nothing but mirrors and tides."

~

Athos and I stood together on deck and looked across the water at the bright city. From this distance no one would guess the turmoil that had torn apart Greece and would continue to do so for years. It was evening. In twos and threes, then like salt . . . the stars. We put on the sweaters Daphne had packed for us and stayed out in the cold wind. I could smell the wool of Athos's sleeve on my shoulder. As flames burn red then blue, so the water purified to silver blue. Then the sea began to darken, and Athens, glowing in the distance, seemed to float on the horizon like a bright ship.

It's the mystery of wood, whispered Bella.

THE WAY STATION

Like Athens, Toronto is an active port. It's a city of derelict warehouses and docks, of waterfront silos and freight yards, coal yards and a sugar refinery; of distilleries, the cloying smell of malt rising from the lake on humid summer nights.

It's a city where almost everyone has come from elsewhere – a market, a caravansary – bringing with them their different ways of dying and marrying, their kitchens and songs. A city of forsaken worlds; language a kind of farewell.

It's a city of ravines. Remnants of wilderness have been left behind. Through these great sunken gardens you can traverse the city beneath the streets, look up to the floating neighbourhoods, houses built in the treetops.

It's a city of valleys spanned by bridges. A railway runs through back yards. A city of hidden lanes, of clapboard garages with corrugated tin roofs, of wooden fences sagging where children have made shortcuts. In April, the thickly treed streets are flooded with samara, a green tide. Forgotten rivers, abandoned quarries, the remains of an Iroquois fortress. Public parks hazy with subtropical memory, a city built in the bowl of a prehistoric lake.

From the great limestone hall of Union Station, with its many tracks and tunnels, train passengers from the transatlantic docks at Montreal poured into the Toronto street. A rainy evening in early September.

There was a small crowd at the doors of the station, but from that one busy point, the city stretched deserted, like outflowing darkness beyond a small pool of lamplight. The travellers dispersed into taxis and, within minutes, even the wide plaza outside the station was empty.

Athos and I travelled north through what seemed an evacuated city, a ghostly metropolis in the rain. Past weeping stone edifices: the post office, banks, the stately Royal York Hotel, the city hall. Perhaps this is how my father felt as a boy arriving in Warsaw the first time, with his father. Trams in the desolate street, the same grey drizzle, leaves shiny as glass. Athos and I entered Toronto; towers, lights, wide avenues, big automobiles, and the bold intimacy of advertising that comes from so many living so close together: tooth powder, hair tonic, foundations, women in poses that embarrassed me.

Our taxi took us to an address on St. Clair Avenue West, a partly furnished flat that someone from the university had sublet to us. We inspected the rooms, turned on the water taps, opened cupboards. Athos spent a few minutes praising the idea of the screened window. "Electricity, running water. After Zakynthos," said Athos, "this will be like living in a hotel."

We unpacked nothing and went across the street to a restaurant that advertised itself as open "all night." I ordered my first Canadian meal: buttered toast and vegetable soup. Athos ate his first slice of pumpkin pie. Athos, who only ever smoked a pipe, bought Canadian cigarettes – Macdonald's, the one with the Scottish lass on the package – and a Toronto *Telegram*. A waitress with the name tag Aimée offered Athos coffee, which I awaited anxiously, concerned about her phrase "bottomless cup." He made a face at the thin taste. Lamps hung low over each table. From our booth at the plate-glass window, we saw that our apartment building was called Heathside Gardens. Despite the friendly clattering of dishes and the chattering waitresses in stiff white aprons, the restaurant was sad. It was the first time I'd seen people eating alone in public – a sight that disturbed me and would take me some time to get used to.

Athos was excited but tired. Early the next morning he would be meeting with Taylor at the university. We went back to Heathside Gardens. There was only one bed; I lay on the sofa. We used our coats as blankets. The street-lights filtered through the thin drapes. In the semi-dark of the city, my head full of English, I stared into the room unable to sleep, even long after the rumblings and squeals of the trams had stopped for the night.

Some time later I heard Athos trying not to wake me, walking down the hall to the kitchen on creaking floors. He looked in on me. "Sleep, Jakob, it's all right. I'll be back soon with breakfast." I could barely lift my head or open my mouth to say goodbye. Where others might have leaped up to explore their new world, I felt a stunning despair. I looked at the ceiling and counted the kounoupia, the dead mosquitoes in the light fixture, until I finally fell asleep and dreamed of the Macdonald's cigarette girl, electric shavers, and Pepsodent tooth powder.

At the university, classes were filled with men returning from the war, and the tiny faculty of the geography department was strained to its limits. Athos planned his lectures, did his own research, and managed to get out of the flat each morning after hardly sleeping. Often I watched him board the tram with papers bulging out of his briefcase and his glasses still perched on the middle of his forehead. While Athos was teaching all day at the McMaster Building on Bloor Street, I attended classes in both Greek and English at the Athena School. The tasks of shopping and cleaning I gladly took on. It pleased me to be able to take care of Athos now, to be relied upon. Athos still did most of the cooking, he liked to, it relaxed him. And each Sunday, no matter the weather, we went walking.

Athos instructed me in the subtleties of English at the kitchen table on St. Clair Avenue. The English language was food. I shoved it into my mouth, hungry for it. A gush of warmth spread through my body, but also panic, for with each mouthful the past was further silenced. At our kitchen, Athos waited patiently while I gnawed and swallowed.

The facts of the war began to reach us, through magazines and the newspapers. In our small flat my nightmares woke Athos. After a bad night, he would hold me by the shoulders: "Jakob, I long to steal your memories from you while you're sleeping, to syphon off your dreams."

A child doesn't know much about a man's face but feels what most of us believe all our lives, that he can tell a good face from a bad. The soldiers who performed their duty, handing back to mothers the severed heads of daughters – with braids and hairclips still in place – did not have evil in their faces. There was no perversion of features while they did their deeds. Where was their hatred, their disgust, if not even in their eyes, rolling invisibly back in their sockets, focused on the unanswerable fact of having gone too far? There's the possibility that if one can't see it in the face, then there's no conscience left to arouse. But that explanation is obviously false, for some laughed as they poked out eyes with sticks, as they smashed infants' skulls against the good brick of good houses. For a long time I believed one learns nothing from a man's face. When Athos held me by the shoulders, when he said, "Look at me, look at me" to convince me of his goodness, he couldn't know how he terrified me, how meaningless the words. If truth is not in the face, then where is it? In the hands! In the hands.

I tried to bury images, to cover them over with Greek and English words, with Athos's stories, with all the geologic eras. With the walks Athos and I took every Sunday into the ravines. Years later I would try a different avalanche of facts: train schedules, camp records, statistics, methods of execution. But at night, my mother, my father, Bella, Mones, simply rose, shook the earth from their clothes, and waited.

∼

Athos taught me to cook stifhados crammed with fish and vegetables, yemista – stuffed peppers, even boutimata – biscuits with molasses and cinnamon, which he ate at his desk in the middle of the night while planning his course, The History of Geographical Thought.

To celebrate our first Toronto snowfall, Athos decided we should have a banquet. He sent me out into the transformed street to buy some fish. Those first months when I went out alone, I never ventured past the few stores near the flat. That day, the street looked so extraordinary I decided to walk a bit further. I entered a new grocery, shuffled my boots on the mat and waited. A man came from the back of the store and looked down at me, his large hands dangling over the counter. His apron was smeared. In a thick accent he barked, "What do you want?" I was riveted by the sound of his shouting voice. He barked again, "What did you come here for?"

"Fresh fish," I whispered.

"No! We have suspicions." He raised his voice. "We have suspicions."

I rushed out the door.

Athos was slicing mushrooms by the sink. "What kind of fish did you get? Barbounia? Glossa? I wish Daphne were here to make her kalamarakia!" I stood in the doorway. After a moment he looked up and saw my face. "Jakob, what happened?"

I told him. Athos wiped his hands, shook his slippers off his feet, and said grimly, "Come."

I waited outside the store. I heard an uproar. Laughter. Athos came outside, grinning with relief. "It's all right, it's all right. He was saying 'chickens' not 'suspicions.'" Athos began to laugh. He was standing in the street laughing. I glared at him, heat rising into my face. "I'm sorry, Jakob, I just can't help it . . . I haven't laughed in so long. . . . Come in, come in. . . ."

I would never enter that store again.

I knew I was being ridiculous, even as I pulled away from him and walked back to the flat alone.

Language. The numb tongue attaches itself, orphan, to any sound it can: it sticks, tongue to cold metal. Then, finally, many years later, tears painfully free.

There's a heavy black outline around things separated from their names. My lame vocabularies consisted of the usual variety of staples – bread, cheese, table, coat, meat – as well as a more idiosyncratic store. From Athos I'd learned the words for rock strata, infinity, and evolution – but not for bank account or landlord. I could carry my own in a discussion of volcanoes, glaciers, or clouds in Greek or English, but didn't know what was meant by a "cocktail" or a "Kleenex."

I didn't have to wait long to hear Antarctic stories from Griffith Taylor himself. The Taylors often hosted parties in their Forest Hill mansion, and our first Christmas in Toronto the geography department was invited to celebrate. I wonder what Athos's colleagues made of us. I don't know how much of our story they knew. Almost fourteen,

I was almost as tall as Athos, and my bones and lips and dark eyebrows seemed to leap from my face. In those days, Athos gave the physical impression of a retired adventurer, of a man who might spend his evenings cataloguing his finds. Mrs. Taylor referred to us as "The Bachelors."

We were invited to garden teas, New Year's parties, end of term parties. Every occasion concluded with Griffith Taylor singing "Waltzing Mathilda." There was a romance about the Taylors – not just the house and servants, the candlelight and the sideboard heaped with delicacies. I think the Taylors were very much in love. That first Christmas, they gave me a woollen muffler. Mrs. Taylor shook our hands when we left and smiled warmly. Afterwards, Athos and I accused each other of blushing.

Athos and I hosted a few informal parties of our own. We were strays and gathered other strays around us.

Athos discovered a Greek bakery downtown and noticed that the baker, Constantine from Poros, was reading Goethe's *Faust*, in Greek, between sales of loaves of olikis and oktasporo. Constantine used to teach literature in Athens. Soon Constantine was dropping by, irregularly, two or three evenings a month, always bringing us a cake or baklava or a bag of sweet buns. Joseph, the man who came once to fix our stove and who painted portraits in his spare time, liked to visit on Saturday afternoons after his last service call. Gregor, who'd been a lawyer in Bukovina before the war and now sold furniture, sometimes asked us to go to a concert with him. Gregor was infatuated with a violinist and we always sat on the side of the hall where he could best observe her.

I learned the secrets of various trades from our visitors. Stain removal, appliance repair, portrait painting (the eyes must follow you everywhere). How to change a fuse or fix a dripping faucet, how to make a quick-rising cake. What to do on a first date (pick her up at her house, shake hands with the father, never bring her home late). Athos seemed pleased that I was learning such practicalities, while he continued to take care of my soul.

But mostly we kept to ourselves. We had little connection to the koinotita – the Greek community – aside from Constantine's family of restaurateurs whose lunch counters and dining rooms we frequented, especially the Spotlight, the Majestic, the elegant Diana Sweets, and Bassel's with its red and black leather banquettes and soft lighting. Athos worked hard, as if he knew he was running out of time. He was writing a book. As for me, I didn't make any real friends until after university. I barely met the eyes of my classmates. Instead, over the years, I came to know the city.

Donald Tupper, who taught soil science in the geography department and was known to fall asleep during his own lectures, used to organize field trips in order to point out geographical features. Athos and I often joined him and his students on these expeditions, until Tupper rolled the car into a ditch while showing us an example of a drumlin. Fortunately, I had my own private guide and companion, not only through geologic time, but through adolescence and into adulthood.

With a few words (an incantation in Greek or English) and the sweep of his hand, Athos sliced a hill in half, drilled under the sidewalk, cleared a forest. He showed me Toronto cross-sectioned; he ripped open cliffs like fresh bread, revealing the ragged geological past. Athos stopped in the middle of busy city streets and pointed out fossils in the limestone ledges of the Park Plaza Hotel or in the walls of a hydro substation. "Ah, limestone, accumulating one precious foot every twenty-five thousand years!" Instantly, the streets were flooded by a subtropical salt sea. I imagined front lawns crammed with treasure: crinoids, lamp shells, trilobites.

Like diving birds, Athos and I plunged one hundred and fifty million years into the dark deciduous silence of the ravines. Behind the billboard next to Tamblyn's Drugstore we dipped down into the humid amphitheatre of a Mesozoic swamp, where massive fronds and ferns tall as houses waved in a spore-dense haze. Beneath a parking lot, behind a school; from racket, fumes, and traffic, we dove into the city's sunken rooms of green sunlight. Then, like andartes, resurfaced half a city away – from under the bridge near Stan's Variety or from behind the Honey Dew Restaurant.

Athos showed me samples of the distinctive mottled Zumbro stone in the train station, explaining how it differed from the Tobermory or Kingston or Credit Valley stone. He pointed out Toronto's only example of lustrous black labradorite, from Nain, flashing blue in the sunlight on Eglinton Avenue.

One of our earliest excursions was a walk to Grenadier Pond, to see where Silas Wright had made his first ice experiments. Then we went to find Silas Wright's old house on Crescent Drive. I'd heard the story many times. It was Wright who first sighted Scott's tent, buried by the fatal blizzard within a few inches of its tip. Wright pointed with his ski pole into the immaculate distance and uttered the famous words: "It is the tent." It gave me great satisfaction to stand with Athos on the street one windy November morning and announce, in impeccable Canadian English: "It is the house."

It was a cold spring evening, our first spring in Toronto. It began to rain. A cracking April thunderstorm, when the sky turns dark green and the world takes on a gangrenous fluorescent glow. Athos and I ducked under the thick trusses of the Governors Road bridge. We weren't alone. A couple of young boys carrying jars filled with cloudy pond water and a teenage boy with his dog gathered for shelter. No one spoke as we stood awkwardly listening to the sewers flashflooding, the metal gutters of the bridge rushing with water, the great bone-snap of thunder. Then a screech tore the air, then another, like the cry of mammoth jays, and we saw the two boys blowing into their hands, grass pulled taut between their thumbs.

The older boy followed, the primitive reeds producing a squawking caterwaul that reverberated under the bridge. Then the sudden rain slowed, and one by one our companions fell silent and stepped out into the dripping haze as if in a trance. Not a word had been spoken.

Athos and I made up characters and stories during our Sunday walks, to practise my vocabulary. We invented a suspense serial involving two detectives, Peter Moss and Peter Bogg. In one episode, they trailed a villain who "took things for granite" (my most accomplished malapropism); he robbed museums and left, as his mark, a block of stone in the empty space. Athos created a complicated story involving a gang of British sailors who plundered dockside warehouses just so he'd have an excuse to use the title: "The Mystery of the Loch and Quay."

Puns were a kind of core sample: they penetrated into the heart of comprehension, a real test of mastery of a new tongue. Each of my terrible puns represented a considerable achievement; I recited them at dinner for Athos's praise. (What did the biologist say when he dropped his slides on the lab floor? Don't step on mitosis.)

From puns I attempted poetry, hoping that in my sonnets the secret of English would crack open under my scrutiny. "Perhaps a sonnet," suggested Athos, "is not dissimilar to the linguistic investigations of the kabbalists." I copied out well-known poems, leaving space between each line where I wrote my own version or response. I wrote about plants, rocks, birds. I wrote lines without verbs. I wrote only using slang. Until suddenly a word seemed to become itself and a quick clarity penetrated; the difference between a Greek dog and a Canadian dog, between Polish snow and Canadian snow. Between resinous Greek pines and Polish pines. Between seas, the ancient myth-spell of the Mediterranean and the sharp Atlantic.

And later, when I began to write down the events of my childhood in a language foreign to their happening, it was a revelation. English could protect me; an alphabet without memory.

As if determined by historical accuracy, the Greek neighbourhood bordered the Jewish. When I first discovered the Jewish market, I felt a jolt of grief. Casually, out of the mouths of the cheese-seller and the baker came the ardent tongue of my childhood. Consonants and vowels: fear and love intertwined.

I listened, thin and ugly with feeling. I watched old men dip their numbered arms into barrels of brine, cut the heads off fish. How unreal it must have seemed to them to be surrounded by so much food.

From wooden cages, chickens stared with a look of snobby incomprehension, as though they were the only ones who understood English and therefore couldn't make out the babble around them.

~

Athos's backward glance gave me a backward hope. Redemption through cataclysm; what had once been transformed might be transformed again. I read about Toronto's dried-up, rerouted rivers – now barely gutter streams – that once were abundant tributaries fished by torchlight. Salmon were speared and scooped from the quick vein; nets were dipped into live currents of silver. On maps, Athos outlined the regal paths of the ice ages as they surveyed the province and swept out again, gouging and strafing the land. "Their frozen robes trailed behind them, leaving a rocky wake of glacial till!" Before the city, Athos cried – showman, barker – there was a forest of conifer and hardwood, huge ancient stands inhabited by giant beavers as big as bears. At supper, we sampled native cuisine that was exotic to us, such as peanut butter, and read to each other about our new city. We read that stone spears, axes, and knives had been discovered in a farmer's field on the outskirts; Athos explained that the Laurentian People were contemporaries of the inhabitants of Biskupin. We learned of an Indian settlement under a school. We empathized with the perplexity and grumpiness of Mrs. Simcoe, the genteel eighteenth-century pioneer wife of the lieutenant-governor, transposed into the wilderness of Upper Canada. She soon came to represent, rather unfairly, a general state of disgruntledness. She inspired a private joke whenever we found ourselves at a loss, bewildered by the wordless signals that are the essence of every culture: "What would Mrs. Simcoe make of this?"

Late Sunday afternoons, we climbed from the lake bottom, covered with prehistoric ooze, to surface under a billboard on St. Clair Avenue; the tram tracks shining dully under the weak winter sun, or stropped bright under the streetlights, the evening sky purple with cold or cyanotype summer blue, the darkening shapes of the houses against the dissolving bromide of twilight. Muddy, clinging with burrs of enchanter's nightshade (stowaways on trouser legs and sleeves), we headed home for a hot dinner. These weekly explorations into the ravines were escapes to ideal landscapes; lakes and primeval forests so long gone they could never be taken away from us.

On these walks I could temporarily shrug off my strangeness because, the way Athos saw the world, every human was a newcomer.

Athos and I both kept up correspondences with Daphne and Kostas. I mailed them poems in English and reported to Daphne how well I was doing at school and how well we'd been eating, passing along pastry recipes from Constantine. Kostas's letters to Athos were filled with politics. Athos would sit at the table shaking his head. "How can he write such awful news with such a beautiful hand?" Kostas's handwriting was fluid and fine as a braided stream.

As Kostas had warned me, Athos fell into depressions, like a literal stumble into ruts in a road. He tripped, pulled himself up, carried on. Darkness dogged him. He burrowed in his room to work on his book, *Bearing False Witness*, which he knew somehow he would never finish, a debt left unpaid to his colleagues at Biskupin. He didn't come out for meals. To tempt him, I bought cakes from Constantine. When Constantine saw me instead of Athos, he knew Athos was feeling bad. "It's the illness of his work," he said. "Stale bread gives a man a stomach-ache. Tell Athos that Constantine says if he's going to keep stirring up historia, he must remember to open the lid slowly, to let the steam out of the pot."

Often I came into the kitchen at two or three in the morning and found Athos in his heavy dressing gown or, in summer, in his vest and limp boxers, dozing with his glasses on his forehead, a pen falling out of his hand. And, reverting to the habits of one who used to eat many meals alone, a book was held open on the table, an empty plate or a fork across the pages.

Bearing False Witness plagued Athos. It was his conscience; his record of how the Nazis abused archaeology to fabricate the past. In 1939, Biskupin was already a famous site, already nicknamed the "Polish Pompeii." But Biskupin was proof of an advanced culture that wasn't German; Himmler ordered its obliteration. It wasn't enough to own the future. The job of Himmler's SS-Ahnenerbe – the Bureau of Ancestral Inheritance – was to conquer history. The policy of territorial expansion – lebensraum – devoured time as well as space.

One oppressively hot summer morning, Athos and I set out on our Sunday walk, dressed as coolly as possible, almost formal in white cotton shirts. Our destination was Baby Point, which had once been the site of an Iroquois fortressed camp. Although we'd left early, the air was already thick and droning with insects.

"This week I found out that a man I went to school with in Vienna was in the Ahnenerbe."

Athos's shirt was stuck to his back. His face was pink. The trees moved in the heavy breeze, the leaves looked like wet paint splashing against the hazy sky.

"With Himmler paying his salary suddenly he found swastikas in every handful of dirt. This man, who'd been at the top of our prehistory class, actually presented the 'Willendorf Venus' to Himmler as proof that 'Hottentots' had been conquered by ancient Aryans! He falsified digs to prove that Greek civilization started in . . . neolithic Germany! Just so the Reich could feel justified in copying our temples for their glorious capital."

"Koumbaros, it's hot."

"Everything that's been destroyed: the relics, the careful documentation. These men still have their careers, even though they were hired by Himmler. These men are still teaching!"

"Koumbaros, it's so hot today. . . ."

"I'm sorry Jakob, you're right."

We stopped for lunch at the Royal Diner, which was owned by Constantine's brother, and reached Baby Point in the early afternoon. It had turned overcast, and the smell of rain filled the heat. We stood on the sidewalk and imagined the Iroquois fortress. We imagined an Iroquois attack on the affluent neighbourhood, flaming arrows soaring above patio furniture, through picture windows into living rooms, landing on coffee tables that instantly ignited. I stood on the darkening sidewalk and transformed the smells of car wax and mown lawns into curing leather and salted fish. Athos, carried away, described the murder of fur trader Étienne Brûlé. Auto da fe.

The afternoon heat was thick with burning flesh. I saw the smoke rising in whorls into the dark sky. Ambushed, memory cracking open. The bitter residue flying up into my face like ash.

"Jakob, Jakob. Let's take a taxi home."

By the time we reached the flat, the rain was falling in sheets, the smell of dust rising from the steaming pavement. I stuck my head out the car window and gulped it in. The burning smell was gone.

Koumbaros, we are lightning rods for time.

That night, I dreamed of Bella's hair. Shiny as black lacquer under the lamplight, plaited tight as a lanyard.

Sitting at the table, my parents and Bella pretended calm, they who claimed so often to have no courage at all. They remained in their seats as they'd planned they would, if it came to that. The soldiers pushed my father over in his chair. And when they saw Bella's beauty, her terrified stillness – what did they make of her hair, did they lift its mass from her shoulders, assess its value; did they touch her perfect eyebrows and skin? What did they make of Bella's hair as they cut it – did they feel humiliated as they fingered its magnificence, as they hung it on the line to dry?

≈

One of the last walks Athos and I took together was along the floodplain of the Don River, past the brick quarry and cliffs embedded with marine fossils. We intended to sit for a while in the terraced gardens of Chorley Park, the Government House, built spectacularly on the edge of the escarpment. The mansion was enormous, a Loire Valley chateau, built of the finest Credit Valley limestone.

Tourelles and pediments, tall chimneys and cornices: perched on the edge of wildness it summed up the contradictions of the New World. When Athos and I first discovered the immense estate, it no longer functioned as the lieutenant-governor's residence. There'd been complaints about the cost of upkeep by union-supported politicians. Shortly after city councillors argued over whether or not to let him replace a single blown lightbulb, the embittered lieutenant-governor abandoned Chorley Park. It was then pressed into service as a military hospital and as a shelter for Hungarian refugees. We'd visited the grounds many times. Athos said Chorley Park reminded him of an alpine sanitarium.

We were discussing religion.

"But Athos, whether one believes or not has nothing to do with being a Jew. Let me put it this way: The truth doesn't care what we think of it."

We ascended the valley. The hills were scorched with sumac and sedge, cloudy with fraying thistles and milkweed. I could see patches of sweat darkening Athos's shirt.

"Maybe we should rest."

"We're nearly at the top. Jakob, when Nikos died I asked my father if he believed in God. He said: How do we know there's a God? Because He keeps disappearing."

I heard the labour in his breath and sadness quickened in me.

"Koumbaros . . ."

"I'm fine thank you, Mrs. Simcoe."

We bent down to pass through the bushes at the edge of the hill. We emerged from the scrub of the ravine into the garden and lifted our heads to emptiness. Chorley Park, built to outlast generations, was gone, as though an eraser had rubbed out its place against the sky.

Athos, stunned, leaned heavily on his walking-stick.

"How could they have torn it down, one of the most beautiful buildings in the city? Jakob, are you sure we're in the right place?"

"We're in the right place, koumbaros. . . . How do I know? Because it's gone."

Athos was growing tired somewhere deep in his body. He worried me; I fussed over him. He waved my concern away, "I'm fine, Mrs. Simcoe!" Though he still worked late into the night, he began to take naps at odd times of the day. He wouldn't slow down. "Jakob, there's an old Greek saying: 'Light your candle before night overtakes you.'" He insisted on proving his indomitability by hauling home groceries on the tram. He would no more leave something behind, however heavy, than he would leave behind samples from a site.

We were a vine and a fence. But who was the vine? We would both have answered differently.

~

Eventually I was enrolled in the university, taking courses in literature, history, and geography, and was earning some money as a lab demonstrator in the geography department. Kostas asked a friend of his in London to send me the work of poets banned in Greece. This was my introduction to translating. And translating of one sort or another has supported me ever since. For this intuition, I will always be grateful to Kostas. "Reading a poem in translation," wrote Bialek, "is like kissing a woman through a veil"; and reading Greek poems, with a mixture of katharevousa and the demotic, is like kissing two women. Translation is a kind of transubstantiation; one poem becomes another. You can choose your philosophy of translation just as you choose how to live: the free adaptation that sacrifices detail to meaning, the strict crib that sacrifices meaning to exactitude. The poet moves from life to language, the translator moves from language to life; both, like the immigrant, try to identify the invisible, what's between the lines, the mysterious implications.

One evening I walked up Grace Street, a summer tunnel of long shadows, the breeze from the lake a cool finger slipping gently under my damp shirt, the tumult of the market left blocks behind. In the new coolness and new quiet, a thread of memory clung to a thought. Suddenly an overheard word fastened on to a melody; a song of my mother's that was always accompanied by the sound of brush bristles pulling through Bella's hair, my mother's arm drawing with the beat. The words stumbled out of my mouth, a whisper, then louder, until I was mumbling whatever I remembered. "'What good is the mazurka, my heart is not carefree; what good's the girl from Vurka, if she does not love me. . . .'" "'Black cherries are gathered, the green are left on the tree. . . .'" All the way through to the opening verses of "Come to Me, Philosopher" and "How Does the Czar Drink His Tea?"

I looked around. The houses were dark, the street safely empty. I raised my voice. "'Foolish one, don't be so dense, don't you have any common sense? Smoke is taller than a house, a cat is faster than a mouse. . . .'"

Up Grace, along Henderson, up Manning to Harbord

I whimpered; my spirit shape finally in familiar clothes and, with abandon, flinging its arms to the stars.

But the street wasn't empty as I thought. Startled, I saw that the blackness was perforated with dozens of faces. A forest of eyes, of Italian and Portuguese and Greek ears; whole families sitting silently on lawnchairs and front steps. On dark verandahs, a huge invisible audience, cooling down from their small, hot houses, the lights off to keep away the bugs.

There was nothing for it but to raise my foreign song and feel understood.

～

At night, lying in bed unable to sleep, my body pointed painfully towards its great ignorance.

I imagined kissing the girl I saw in the library, the skinny one who kept tipping over in her high heels. . . . She's lying next to me. We're holding each other but then she wants to know why I live with Athos, why I've collected all those articles about the war that are in piles on the carpet, why I stay up half the night examining every face in the photographs. Why I keep to myself, why I don't know how to dance.

When Athos went into his study after dinner, I stepped into the night. But we both entered the same convulsion of time; the events we lived through without knowing, while we were on Zakynthos. I stood on the steps of the escarpment on Davenport Road and looked out at the lit city, displayed like a circuit board. I walked past the knitwear and pencil factories, the General Electric plant, the typesetting warehouses and lumberyards, the dry cleaners and autobody shops. Past signs advertising Jerry Lewis at the Imperial and Red Skelton at Shea's. I followed the train tracks to the coal silos on Mt. Pleasant Road, or down to the rusted ships waiting by the grain silos of Victory Mills.

I took in the cold beauty of Lakeshore Cement, with its small gardens someone thought to plant at the foot of each massive silo. Or the delicate metal staircases, a lace ribbon, swirling around the girth of the oil reservoirs. At night, a few lights marked port and starboard of these gargantuan industrial forms, and I filled them with loneliness. I listened to these dark shapes as if they were black spaces in music, a musician learning the silences of a piece. I felt this was my truth. That my life could not be stored in any language but only in silence; the moment I looked into the room and took in only what was visible, not vanished. The moment I failed to see Bella had disappeared. But I did not know how to seek by way of silence. So I lived a breath apart, a touch-typist who holds his hands above the keys slightly in the wrong place, the words coming out meaningless, garbled. Bella and I inches apart, the wall between us. I thought of writing poems this way, in code, every letter askew, so that loss would wreck the language, become the language.

If one could isolate that space, that damaged chromosome in words, in an image, then perhaps one could restore order by naming. Otherwise history is only a tangle of wires. So in poems I returned to Biskupin, to the house on Zakynthos, to the forest, to the river, to the burst door, to the minutes in the wall.

English was a sonar, a microscope, through which I listened and observed, waiting to capture elusive meanings buried in facts. I wanted a line in a poem to be the hollow ney of the dervish orchestra whose plaintive wail is a call to God. But all I achieved was awkward shrieking. Not even the pure shriek of a reed in the rain.

~

I made one lasting friend through Athos's connection with the university, a graduate student of his named Maurice Salman. Maurice was even more of a stranger to the city than we were, having only just moved from Montreal when we first met. Athos invited him for dinner. Maurice was thin in those days but so was his hair, and he wore a beret pushed back off his forehead. We began to take walks together, to go to a concert or an art gallery. Sometimes he and Athos and I went to the movies where we developed conflicting passions; Athos for Deborah Kerr (especially in *King Solomon's Mines*), Maurice for Jean Arthur, and I for Barbara Stanwyck. Maurice and I were already hopelessly out of date and would remain so. We should have been dreaming about Audrey Hepburn. On the way home we stopped at a restaurant or Maurice came home with us to our bachelor kitchen where we argued over our paramours' relative merits. Kerr, said Athos, was clearly a woman with whom one could discuss Pascal's wager over breakfast, in the finest hotel or in the bush. Maurice thought Jean Arthur was a woman one could definitely go camping with or dancing all night and who would still remember where you left your keys or the children. I loved Barbara Stanwyck because she was always in a jam and was loyal to her heart and most of all because in *Ball of Fire* slang flew from her mouth like song. "Stop beating up with the gums and shove in your clutch!" "Clip the mooch!" "I'm no bungalow-apron!" She lived in a world of plenty gestanko and solid senders. She was a dish, a smooch, for whom one would need a bundle of scratch, dough, moolah, smackeroos, a two-ply poke. I was wacky about her. In these discussions none of us mentioned bare shoulders or satin over breasts; certainly no one mentioned legs at all.

But we didn't spend many evenings together because soon after we met Maurice, Athos died.

"Athos, how big is the actual heart?" I once asked him when I was still a child. He replied: "Imagine the size and heaviness of a handful of earth."

On his last night, Athos had come home from giving a lecture on the conservation of Egyptian wood. It was about half past ten. He usually reported some observation of the evening, or even recounted the main details of his talk, but since I'd typed it for him earlier that day the latter was unnecessary, and he was tired. I heated some wine for him then went to bed.

In the morning I found him at his desk. He looked as he often did, asleep in the middle of work. I embraced him with all my strength, again and again, but he would not come back. It is impossible to reach the emptiness in each cell. His death was quiet; rain on the sea.

~

I know only fragments of what Athos's death contained: no less than all the elements and their powers, ten thousand names for things, the humility of lichen. The instincts of migration: stars, magnetism, angles of light. The energy of time that alters mass. The element that reminded him most of his country, salt: olives, cheese, vine leaves, sea foam, sweat. Fifty years of intimacy with Kostas and Daphne, his memory of their bodies at twenty; his own body, as a child, at fifteen, at twenty-five and fifty, the selves that remain as we age, just as words remain on the page though darkness erases them. Two wars, which are both the rotten part of the fruit that can't be cut away and the fruit; that there's nothing a man will not do to another, nothing a man will not do for another. But who was the woman who first unbuttoned for him the two birds of her breasts in a night garden? Did he remember Helen's hands holding his or were they in his hair or were her arms outstretched when his head rested on her thighs? Did they imagine children, what words did he regret? Who was the first woman whose hair he washed, what song could have been his own voice singing of love when he first heard it?

When a man dies, his secrets bond like crystals, like frost on a window. His last breath obscures the glass.

I sat at Athos's desk. In a small flat in a strange city in a country I did not yet love.

≈

In Toronto, Athos had recreated his study on Zakynthos. It was a chaotic site from which a variety of objects could be excavated. On Athos's desk the night he died: a wooden box full of Meccano, the same set of metal wheels and hinges he had as a boy. A photomicrograph of the frail lamellae of waterlogged Biskupin oak. A photo of Kispiox totems paperclipped to an analysis of earth and weather conditions. A glass paperweight enclosing a sample of lepidodendron. A miniature birch-bark canoe. An article on the Vestfold Hills in Antarctica as a site for freeze-drying wood artifacts. Notes for an upcoming waterlogged wood conference in Ottawa. A pen and ink sketch of the fossil trees at Joggins, Nova Scotia. Kazantzakis's translations of Darwin's *Origin of Species* and Dante's *Comedy*. A cup with coffee grounds trailing the last incline of the cup to his lips.

In his desk, I found a packet of letters. . . . The intimacy that death forces on us. At first I did not want to look at them. I recognized Athos's elegant Greek script. The letters were to Helen, written when both she and Athos were studying in Vienna, the year before he went to Cambridge. I fingered the envelopes and smoothed the onion-skin. The silence of the empty flat pressed in on me with the weight of self-pity.

"When you are alone – at sea, in the polar dark – an absence can keep you alive. The one you love maintains your mind. But when she's merely across the city, this is an absence that eats you to the bone."

"My father approves of Vienna, but he still hopes to persuade me against geology. I stand firm, despite his shrewd argument that if I were an engineer I would still confront karst, while planning railways and water supplies. . . ."

While he was in Vienna, exploring intellectual and actual landscapes, honeycombed with caves and swallow-holes, tunnels and sinks, Athos also tumbled through the sense-bruised surface of things, into love.

In our flat, where no word has been spoken for weeks, I imagine Athos walking alone late at night, past the modern buildings of the Ringstrasse and pale baroque churches, streets that would soon be transformed by war. As I read his letters, written half a century before to a woman I know almost nothing of, his "H," I am shaken by my own longing. I'm embarrassed to be eavesdropping on Athos's young voice, the voice of my koumbaros when he was my age.

"Your family – your mother and your sister whom you love – want to know everything; but a real marriage must always be a secret between two people. We must guard it under our tongues like a prayer. Our secrets will be our courage when we need it."

"As for your brother's unhappiness, I'm naive enough to think that love is always good, no matter how long ago, no matter the circumstances. I'm not old enough yet to imagine the instances where this isn't true and where regret outweighs everything."

His arteries silted up like an old river. The heart is a fistful of earth. *The heart is a lake. . . .*

All I know of Athos's Helen is what I learned from the letters. There is a photograph. Her expression is so open and earnest it calls across the years. Her dark hair is piled high and woven elaborately as a corbeille. Her face is too angular to be pretty. She is beautiful.

In the same drawer as the letters and Helen's photograph, there is a thick folder containing faint blue carbons and newspaper cuttings: Athos's search for my sister, Bella.

When you've hardened yourself in certain places, crying is painful, almost as if nature is against it.

"I know the records are incomplete . . ." "Please post the following every Friday for one year . . ." "I know I have written to you before . . ." "Please check your lists . . . taking into account possible variations of spelling . . . for the period of time . . ." Athos's last inquiry was dated two months before he died.

I thought that he had given up years before. But I understood why Athos had kept this to himself. I lay on the carpet in his study. "Love is always good, no matter the circumstances . . . our secrets will be our courage when we need it." I tried to believe this but I hadn't yet learned that true hope is severed from expectation, and his words, like his search for Bella, seemed painfully innocent. But I held the file folder the way a child holds a doll.

Once in a while a tram squealed past. Through the floor I felt the heavy iron wheels rumbling on their tracks.

My father's finger, dipped in bootblack, draws a tram on a corner of newspaper, illustrating the Y-shaped wires by which Warsaw streetcars attach to the sky. "In Warsaw," my father says, "engines travel through the streets." "They move by themselves?" I ask. My father nods, "No horses!" I woke up. I turned on the light and lay down again and closed my eyes.

When I sat down to write the news to Kostas and Daphne, and to tell them I would someday bring Athos's ashes to Zakynthos, I could barely move my pen across the page. "I will bring Athos home, to land that remembers him." Koumbaros, how can a man write such news with a beautiful hand.

~

For many nights following Athos's death, I continued to sleep on the floor in his study among his boxes of random research. We had always meant to organize it together. But Athos's work on Nazi archaeology grew to take all his strength. He started documenting immediately after the war, as soon as information began to flow. Our eyes slowly became accustomed to the darkness. Athos could speak about it, he needed to speak of it, but I couldn't. He asked endless questions to order his thoughts, leaving "why" to the last. But in my thinking, I started with the last question, the "why" he hoped would be answered by all the others. Therefore I began with failure and had nowhere to go.

But in the first months of living alone, I again depended on a familiar drug; to inhabit the other world Athos and I had shared: guileless knowledge, the history of matter. During the night I dipped into the boxes, haphazardly labelled in groups of essays and notes: "the sexual adventures of conifers . . . the poetics of covalent bonding . . . a possible process for freeze-drying coffee beans." Fascinating but explicable forces; winds and ocean currents, tectonic plates. The transformations caused by trade and piracy; how minerals. and wood changed the map. Athos's essay on peat alone was long enough for a small book, as was his "A Covenant of Salt." In Vienna he'd begun collecting examples for a project on parody within cultures he called "From Relic to Replica."

He often applied the geologic to the human, analyzing social change as he would a landscape; slow persuasion and catastrophe. Explosions, seizures, floods, glaciation. He constructed his own historical topography.

During the nights among his boxes, in the months after Athos died, his thinking came to resemble in my imagination an Escher etching; walls that are windows, fish that are birds, and the brilliant leap of modern science: the hand that draws itself.

For the next three years, I compiled Athos's notes on the ss-Ahnenerbe as well as I could. Working in his study, alone now in our flat, I felt Athos's presence so strongly I could smell his pipe, I could feel his hand on my shoulder. Sometimes, late at night, an alertness would seize me and I would see him from the corner of my eye, looking in on me from the hallway. In his research, Athos descends so far that he reaches a place where redemption is possible, but it is only the redemption of tragedy.

I knew that, for me, the descent would go on and on, long after my work for Athos was finished. At that time, I was earning a part-time living as a translator for an engineering company. After the day's work was done, I slumped at Athos's desk, in despair at his many files and boxes of facts. Sometimes I went out for dinner with Maurice Salman, who now had a job at the museum. Maurice's companionship saved me; he saw I was in trouble. By then, Maurice had met and married Irena. Often Irena would cook for us while we discussed the seemingly unending task of completing Athos's book, *Bearing False Witness*. Sometimes I would look into the kitchen and see her reading a cookbook while she stood over the stove, her long yellow braid over her shoulder like a scarf, and I would have to look away from emotion. Such an ordinary sight, a woman stirring a pot.

The night I finished the work of my koumbaros, I wept with emptiness as I typed his dedication, for his colleagues at Biskupin: "Murder steals from a man his future. It steals from him his own death. But it must not steal from him his life."

≈

In our cold, dark Canadian flat, I pour fresh water into the sea, recalling not only the Greek lament "that the dead may drink" but also the covenant of the Eskimo hunter, who pours fresh water into the mouth of his quarry. Seals, living in salt water, suffer perpetual thirst. The animal has offered its life in exchange for water. If the hunter does not keep his promise, he will lose all his good fortune; no other animal will allow itself to be captured by him.

The best teacher lodges an intent not in the mind but in the heart.

I know I must honour Athos's lessons, especially one: to make love necessary. But I do not yet understand that this is also my promise to Bella. And that to honour them both, I must resolve a perpetual thirst.

PHOSPHORUS

It's a clear October day. The wind scatters bright leaves against the blue opalescence of air. But there's no sound. Bella and I have entered a dream, the animate colour surrounding us intense, every leaf twitching as if on the verge of sleep. Bella is happy: the whole birch forest gathers itself in her expression. Now we hear the river and move towards it, the swirls and eddies of Brahms's Intermezzo No. 2 that descend, descend, andante non troppo, rising only in one final gust. I turn and Bella's gone; my glance has caused her to vanish. I wrench around. I call, but the noise of the leaves is suddenly overwhelming, like a rush of falls. Surely she's gone ahead to the river. I run there and dig for clues of her in the muddy bank. It's dark; dogwood becomes her white dress. A shadow, her black hair. The river, her black hair. Moonlight, her white dress.

Like my childhood encounter with the tree, I stare a long time at Alex's silk robe hanging from the bedroom door, as if it is my sister's ghost. 1968, in our small Toronto bedroom, in the flat I used to share with Athos. In the dimness, the most liquid of Brahms's intermezzos flows on and on.

Everything is wrong: the bedroom with its white furniture, the woman asleep beside me, my panic. For when I wake I know it's not Bella who has vanished, but me. Bella, who is nowhere to be found, is looking for me. How will she ever find me here, beside this strange woman? Speaking this language, eating strange food, wearing these clothes?

Just as I leaned over her while she was reading, I badgered Bella while she practised, with the same appetite – to penetrate the mystery of the black symbols on the page. Sometimes my father would play, but he wasn't half as good as Bella, and he was ashamed of the leather polish he could never completely remove from his hands. But I loved to hear him limp through a piece and, looking back, it seems right to see work-bruised hands on a clean keyboard, as if marked by the effort of making such sounds.

I was too young to remember the composers or the names of the pieces Bella played, so if I wanted her to play something for me, I hummed the tune. I've wanted so often over the years to sing to her, so she would teach me the names of things. I knew only two pieces by title, because I asked her to play them more than anything else. A Brahms intermezzo and Beethoven's "Moonlight." When she played the Beethoven, my sister told me to imagine a deep lake surrounded by mountains, where the wind becomes trapped and the waves move in every direction under the moon. While I was skipping stones into the moonlight, perhaps Bella was constructing an elaborate fantasy about

Ludwig and his Immortal Beloved. In my memory she plays as if she understood intimately his adult passions, as if she too could imagine writing in a letter, "impossible to leave the world until I've brought forth all that is in me. . . . Providence, grant me but one day of pure joy."

The music library was a few blocks from the flat, in the middle of a park. It was what a listening library should be, wood-panelled rooms, plush chairs, trees swimming in the windows. To listen to music alone and in public, like dining alone in a restaurant, seemed a strange and embarrassing activity, yet after *Bearing False Witness* was published, it became my habit to walk there once or twice a week, after dinner. I'd decided to listen systematically through the alphabet, one composer for each letter, and then start again.

One cold night in March, I stood at the checkout desk, having just returned Fauré's nocturnes. I had the newspaper with me and was contemplating the crossword while waiting patiently for the librarian to bring me the quintets for piano and strings.

"Hip hip Fauré."

I turned around to eyes as blue as the Kianou caves. To eagerness, strength, and energy.

"I'm making a check list, is Liszt Czech?"

Her cardigan was open and, underneath, her silky blouse clung to her with static electricity.

"No," I managed. "Also," after a few seconds, ". . . nix Bach, Bax, and Bix."

"Did you get the one about the city in Czechoslovakia?" she asked, pointing to the crossword. . . . "Oslo! You know, Czech-oslo-vakia."

At that moment, the librarian came back with the quintets. Not knowing what to say I took the record and mumbled my way over to the bins of sheet music. A few minutes later I saw her put on her coat. With a jolt of courage I scrambled out the door behind her.

"I love the spring," I said stupidly, then noticed she was clutching her coat tight against the wind.

She asked me if I knew about the concerts at the conservatory.

"They're free. WEA."

I looked at her blankly.

"Workers' Education Association . . . the union . . . every Sunday afternoon at two."

I stood, helpless, watching strands of her auburn hair blow against her black wool tam. Then I looked down at my feet and at her long legs and her short fur-topped boots.

"Goodbye," she said.

"So long . . ."

"Ceylon! Abyssinia Samoa. Can't Roumania; Tibet. Moscow!"

She strode off and looking back once, gave me a jaunty salute, like a WAC in a recruiting poster.

That's how I met Alexandra.

Her father called her Sandra and she didn't mind. With him, Alex had nothing to prove. She called her father Dr. Right – which wasn't a Freudian signal but simply cockney slang for Dr. Maclean – he'll make you right as rain.

Dr. Maclean marinated his young daughter in British military pride. He told her how his fellow Londoners had carried historical treasures – including the just unearthed Sutton Hoo helmet – into the underground at Aldwych station, to protect them from the bombings. He told her stories about Major General "The Salamander" Freyberg under whom he'd served as medical officer in Crete. Freyberg had buried Rupert Brooke on Skyros and, like Byron, swam the Hellespont. Alex Gillian Dodson Maclean was regaled with tales of British intelligence agent Jasper Maskelyne who, in civilian life, came from a family of master magicians. He helped win the war with magic. Aside from concocting ordinary ruses – false road signs, exploding sheep, artificial forests disguising landing fields, and mock battalions created with shadows – Maskelyne also staged wizard japes, large-scale strategic illusions. He hid the entire Suez Canal with reflectors and searchlights. He moved Alexandria harbour a mile up the coast; each night a papier-mâché city was bombed in its stead, complete with fake rubble and canvas craters.

When she told me about these illusions, I thought of Speer's phantom architecture, his pillars of searchlights at Nuremberg, the ghost coliseum that vanished at dawn. I thought of his neo-classical columns dissolving in the sun while the chamber walls stood. I thought of Houdini, astonishing audiences by stuffing himself into boxes and trunks, then escaping, unaware that a few years later other Jews would be crawling into bins and boxes and cupboards, in order to escape.

Her mother died when Alex was fifteen. Her father hired a housekeeper. Alex and the doctor spent at least one evening a week playing Scrabble and did the London *Times* crossword together on the weekend. Alex built up an arsenal of word wit. She worked as the medical secretary in her father's clinic, which he shared with two other doctors. In spare moments she made up medical anagrams – Physician, heal yourself: Ill? Pay-shy? Our fee in cash. She thought about becoming a doctor herself, but she had too much on the go. Her passion was music; she was a professional listener. She went to the symphony, the jazz clubs, she heard recordings and could identify who was playing cornet or the piano after a few bars. Meeting Alex at the music library was like a gift of a beautiful bird on the windowsill. She was like freedom just over a border, an oasis in the sand. She was all legs and arms, gangly and elegant, all bits and pieces with one united appeal. The teenager peeped from her face or her limbs just when she was trying to be most sophisticated. This unsettled innocence was like iron filings to a magnet; she was everywhere on my heart, spiky and charged, itchy and there to stay.

I suppose I was similarly unsettled, but had no sense of how I appeared in the world. We were both skinny as lockpicks. What did she see when she looked, in love, at me? Her father had filled her with Europe, where it was always raining and romantic, where things were intense and at stake. When not in the safety of the British enclave of her schoolmates, she gravitated to the immigrant element, to union-organized events. Her father had a special respect for Greeks, ever since he'd witnessed the old women of Modhion resisting the Germans with brooms and shovels. I suppose Alex thought I was the romance he'd prepared her for.

Alex came out swinging, but was always hoping, or so she thought, for someone to wrestle her arms to her sides. She was a character in a screwball comedy searching in vain for a serious moment. She spent a lot of energy being modern to the minute and at the same time wanted a life of the mind – without all the reading. Good intentions are the last thing to vanish in a relationship. We fastened on to each other in an instant and it took five years to come apart. She would leap up and fling her arms around my neck like a child. She bought red shoes and only wore them when it rained because she liked how they looked on the wet pavement. She was a perpetual-motion machine that wanted to talk philosophy. When Alex wasn't dancing, she was standing on her head.

We sat in Bassel's or in Diana Sweets; we talked in the haze of Constantine's bakery where the smell of cigarettes obliterated even the smell of bread. She called Constantine's place "Yreka Bakery" – a palindrome. Alex adored palindromes and we habitually hauled out a few favourites on our walks downtown. "Too far Edna we wander afoot." "Are we not drawn onward, we few, drawn onward to new era?"

But Alex was most in her element sharing a mickey with her friends at the Top Hat or at the Embassy Club or the Colonial. She sat at the small, round, linen-covered tables at the Royal York and seductively dangled her leftist ideas like high heels. Once we were joined by a sad young man. His father owned a mattress factory but the son was on the side of the union. His shame had two masters. Later, walking home, Alex laughed. "Don't waste your sympathy on him! He got in trouble following a skirt through the union doors!"

Alex shocked me, just as she intended. She shrugged off expectation with language; her hardness was a form of swearing. She swaggered the delicious phrase "following a skirt" and I ached with tenderness for all the frustrated innocence in her extravagant tongue.

Alex was a sword-swallower, a fire-eater. In her mouth English was dangerous and alive, edgy and hot. Alex, Queen of the Crossword.

She went on intellectual benders, arguing all night, leaning against men in crowded bars, stuffing herself with ideals. She was stunning. But she was a political debauchée. I didn't have the confidence to argue Canadian politics with her blue-blood Marxist friends. How could I discuss their upper-class communism with them, those who shone with certainty and had never had the misfortune of witnessing theory refuted by fact? I felt maggoty with insecurities; I had European circuitry, my voltage wrong for the socket.

Alex lacked confidence in only one area. Too proud to reveal her innocence, she flirted to keep men away. I admired her armour of words, learning from her how to endure my own shyness secretly. As Maurice might say, Alex was a squeeze in a tight squeeze, a woman on the fast track who couldn't jump off her high horse for a roll in the hay. But my obvious, painful inexperience drew out her desire. She knew I was immobilized just standing close enough to smell the perfume at her hairline, the back of her neck.

When I was with Maurice and Irena, an ordinary word – jacket, earring, wrist – blinded me in the middle of a conversation. I fell dumb. If Maurice saw disaster, he also saw that Alex was lithe as an otter, a coy explosion in a fitted suit or with one trousered leg draped over the arm of a chair.

Upon first opening her eyes as my wife in our room at the Royal York, Alex yawned. "Just once I'd really like to mess up a hotel room."

Alex's sweater on a chair, her scent lingering in the wool. Tucked behind furniture were her various handbags, from which mysterious items were transferred, one to another, whenever she went out. She'd moved into the flat I'd shared with Athos and now I explored the place like a stranger. I had entered the ancient civilization of women. The polyglycols in her perfumes and makeup, in her lotions and talcs, replaced Athos's vials of linseed oil and sugar compounds, his polyvinyl acetate and microcrystalline wax, his alkylene oxides and thermosetting resins.

When Maurice and Irena invited Alex and me for dinner, Irena used her wedding silver and a lace tablecloth. Irena was a flustered and radiant hostess, and served us her poppyseed cake with an embarrassed pride. Alex wanted to enjoy these evenings but she was restless. She brought along some scotch and cigarettes and tucked her feet under her in the wingchair, but I could see she was ready to bolt. Whenever we were at Maurice and Irena's, she felt she was missing something, everything, elsewhere. If she went into the kitchen to help Irena or gave Irena a little hug when we said goodnight, my heart dilated with hope that someday Alex would really learn to love us all, as we were.

Alex could make the rest of us feel like parents and she the wilful, spirited child. She followed Irena and looked into the pots and tasted things appreciatively, then sat on the kitchen stool and smoked. While chopping vegetables, she told Irena about her father's clinic or about her latest jazz genius, then got distracted and lit another cigarette, Irena finishing the job. Marriage gave Alex moral security, her hijinks and wildness were now socially harmless. She did appreciate our conversations, our long walks; she appreciated that I cooked for us since I was doing translations now in earnest and worked at home. Alex shared the domestic work but drew the line at laundry and mending; as she would say, "Euripedes? Eumenides." I was also translating Greek poems for Kostas's friend in London. And for a while I taught night-school English to other immigrants. I still wasn't writing much poetry, but I did write some very short stories. They were always, in one sense or another, about hiding; and they only came to me when I was half asleep.

We'd been married about two years when my night-mares returned. Even so, it would be some time before Alex and I no longer considered the deep achievement of our marriage to be our nocturnal happiness.

Alex liked to go out for greasy breakfasts on rainy Sundays, followed by a matinée. Since Maurice and I had been going to the movies together for years and since the first time Maurice and Irena met Alex was when we went to see *Ben-Hur* together, it was tradition for the four of us to see whatever was playing at the Odeon near Maurice and Irena's house. We never chose the movie, instead we simply went to the same cinema every time. This was probably the one issue upon which we all agreed; whatever was playing was fine with us.

We'd just been to *Cleopatra* and I could see Maurice was developing a crush on Elizabeth Taylor. He was walk-ing ahead with Alex, who was trying to pry out of him the latest gossip at the museum, where Maurice was now in charge of meteorology. Alex turned around to Irena and me, and she pointed to a coffee shop.

"How about a 'long way home'?"

This was Alex's rhyming slang for palindrome, which in this case we all knew referred to one of the best in her arsenal: "Desserts, I stressed." Alex would never dream of saying simply, Let's stop for a rice pudding.

It was unusual for Alex to suggest extending our visits with Maurice and Irena; I deduced she was probably just hungry. She looked at me and knew what I was thinking. She rolled her eyes. Caught out.

"Jakob, your wife always wants to know what's going on at work. Doesn't she know the museum is no place to find hepcats? All I can tell her is old news. Now Alex, if you want to hear about past lives – "

"Why not? Hepcats have nine lives, don't they?"

"She's impossible," said Maurice, holding his head in mock despair.

"Well, never mind," said Alex. "Besides, I get more than enough history at home."

～

One can look deeply for meaning or one can invent it.

Of all the portolanos – harbour guides, sea charts – to survive from the fourteenth century, the most important is the Catalan Atlas. It was commissioned by the King of Aragón from the cartographer and instrument-maker Abraham Cresques Le Juif. Cresques, the Jew from Palma, founded a long-lived school of mapmaking on the island of Majorca. Religious persecution forced the Cresques workshop to relocate in Portugal. The Catalan Atlas was the definitive mappamondo of its time. It included the latest information brought back by Arabic and European travellers. But perhaps the atlas's most important contribution was what it left out. On other maps, unknown northern and southern regions were included as places of myth, of monsters, anthropophagy, and sea serpents. But the truth-seeking, fact-faithful Catalan Atlas instead left unknown parts of the earth blank. This blankness was labelled simply and frighteningly Terra

Incognita, challenging every mariner who unfurled the chart.

Maps of history have always been less honest. Terra cognita and terra incognita inhabit exactly the same coordinates of time and space. The closest we come to knowing the location of what's unknown is when it melts through the map like a watermark, a stain transparent as a drop of rain.

On the map of history, perhaps the water stain is memory.

Every day Bella practised finger-strengthening exercises; Clementi, Cramer, Czerny. Her fingers seemed to me, especially when we fought – chicken-pecking each other in the ribs – strong as ball-peen hammers. But when she played Brahms or when she wrote words on my back, she proved she could be as gentle as any normal girl.

The intermezzo begins andante non troppo con molto expressione –

Brahms conducted and composed for the Hamburg Ladies' Choir. According to Bella they rehearsed in the garden; Brahms climbed a tree and conducted from a branch. Bella adopted the choir's motto as her own: "fix oder nix!" – "up to the mark, or nothing." I imagined Brahms carving a line into the bark.

Bella memorized, repeating phrases until her fingers were so tired they gave up resisting and got it right. Unavoidably, my mother and I also learned her music by heart. But when she was finished memorizing – bar by bar, section by section – and played the piece without stopping, I was lost; no longer aware of a hundred accumulated fragments but only of one long story, after which the house would fall silent for what seemed a very long time.

History is amoral: events occurred. But memory is moral; what we consciously remember is what our conscience remembers. History is the Totenbuch, The Book of the Dead, kept by the administrators of the camps. Memory is the Memorbucher, the names of those to be mourned, read aloud in the synagogue.

History and memory share events; that is, they share time and space. Every moment is two moments. I think of the scholars of Lublin, who watched their holy and beloved books thrown out of the second-storey windows of the Talmudic Academy into the street and burned – so many books that the fire lasted twenty hours. While the academics sobbed on the sidewalk, a military band played marches and soldiers sang at the top of their lungs to drown out the cries of those old men; their sobs sounded like soldiers singing. I think of the Łódź ghetto, where infants were thrown by soldiers from hospital windows to soldiers below who "caught" them on their bayonets. When the sport became too messy, the soldiers complained loudly, shouting about the blood running down their long sleeves, staining their uniforms, while the Jews on the street screamed in horror, their throats parched with screaming. A mother felt the weight of her child in her arms, even as she saw her daughter's body on the sidewalk.

Those who breathed deep and suffocated. Those who asserted themselves by dying.

I seek out the horror which, like history itself, can't be stanched. I read everything I can. My eagerness for details is offensive.

In Birkenau, a woman carried the faces of her husband and daughter, torn from a photograph, under her tongue so their images wouldn't be taken from her. *If only everything could fit under the tongue.*

Night after night, I endlessly follow Bella's path from the front door of my parents' house. In order to give her death a place. This becomes my task. I collect facts, trying to reconstruct events in minute detail. Because Bella might have died anywhere along that route. In the street, in the train, in the barracks.

When we were married I hoped that if I let Alex in, if I let in a finger of light, it would flood the clearing. And at first, this is exactly what happened. But gradually, through no fault of Alex's, the finger of light poked down, cold as bone, illuminating nothing, not even the white point of contrast that burned away the ground it touched.

And then the world fell silent. Again I was standing under water, my boots locked in mud.

~

Does it matter if they were from Kielce or Brno or Grodno or Brody or Lvov or Turin or Berlin? Or that the silverware or one linen tablecloth or the chipped enamel pot – the one with the red stripe, handed down by a mother to her daughter – were later used by a neighbour or by someone they never knew? Or if one went first or last; or whether they were separated getting on the train or off the train; or whether they were taken from Athens or Amsterdam or Radom, from Paris or Bordeaux, Rome or Trieste, from Parczew or Białystok or Salonika. Whether they were ripped from their dining-room tables or hospital beds or from the forest? Whether wedding rings were pried off their fingers or fillings from their mouths? None of that obsessed me; but – were they silent or did they speak? Were their eyes open or closed?

I couldn't turn my anguish from the precise moment of death. I was focused on that historical split second: the tableau of the haunting trinity – perpetrator, victim, witness.

But at what moment does wood become stone, peat become coal, limestone become marble? The gradual instant.

Every moment is two moments.

Alex's hairbrush propped on the sink: Bella's brush. Alex's bobby pins: Bella's hairclips turning up in strange places, as bookmarks, or holding open music on the piano. Bella's gloves by the front door. Bella writing on my back: Alex's touch during the night. Alex whispering goodnight against my shoulder: Bella reminding me that even Beethoven never stayed up past ten o'clock.

I have nothing that belonged to my parents, barely any knowledge of their lives. Of Bella's belongings, I have the intermezzos, "The Moonlight," other pianoworks that suddenly recover me; Bella's music from a phonograph overheard in a shop, from an open window on a summer day, or from a car radio. . . .

The second legato must be a hair's breadth, only a hair's breadth slower than the first –

When Alex wakes me in the middle of a nightmare I'm rubbing the blood back into my feet after standing in the snow. She's rubbing my feet with hers and wrapping her smooth, thin arms around my side, down my thighs on the narrow wooden bunks, wooden drawers with breathing bones packed feet to head. The blanket is pulled away, I'm cold. I'll never get warm. Then Alex's firm, flat body, a stone across my back as she climbs, her leg over my side, scrambling, turning me over. In the darkness, my skin taut, her breath on my face, her small fingers on my ear, a child holding onto a coin. Now she is still and light as a shadow, her head on my chest, her legs on my legs, her narrow hips and the touch in the cold wooden bunk in the dream – revulsion – and my mouth is closed with fear. "Go back to sleep," she says, "go back to sleep."

Never trust biographies. Too many events in a man's life are invisible. Unknown to others as our dreams. And nothing releases the dreamer; not death in the dream, not waking.

~

The only friends of Athos's from the university I kept up with were the Tuppers. Several times a year I took the tram east to the end of the line where Donald Tupper picked me up, and we drove back to his house on the Scarborough Bluffs. Sometimes Alex joined me; she liked the Tuppers' sheepdog, which she and Margaret Tupper walked, out along the cliffs overlooking the clear expanse of Lake Ontario. I trailed behind with Donald, who was distracted as ever by the landscape and talked about the geography department while every so often buckling to his knees without warning to examine a stone. One autumn evening I was at least ten yards away before I realized he'd hit the ground. I turned around to find him lying on his back in the grass looking at the moon. "See how deep the maria look tonight from here, at the edge of the Great Lakes. You can almost see the silicates evaporating from the young earth to settle in the craters."

Every year the Tuppers' back yard eroded a few inches more until one summer their vacant dog house vanished over the edge of the bluffs during a storm. Margaret thought that this was taking soil science a bit too far and her husband reluctantly agreed they'd have to move inland. Alex related this to her father one night while he was visiting us. "Why would anyone build on the bluffs in the first place," asked the Doctor, "if the cliffs have been eroding for thousands of years?" "Precisely because they've been eroding for thousands of years, Daddy-o," answered my clever Alex.

∾

Every moment is two moments.

In 1942, while Jews were crammed into the earth then covered with a dusting of soil, men crawled into the startled darkness of Lascaux. Animals woke from their sleep underground. Twenty-six feet below they burst to life in lamplight: the swimming deer, floating horses, rhinos, ibex, and reindeer. Their damp nostrils trembled, their hides sweating iron oxide and manganese, in the smell of subterranean stone. While a worker in the French cave remarked, "What a delight to listen to Mozart at Lascaux in the peace of the night," the underworld orchestra of Auschwitz accompanied millions to the pit. Everywhere the earth was upturned, revealing both animals and men. Caves are the temples of the earth, the soft part of the skull that crumbles under touch. Caves are repositories of spirits; truth speaks from the ground. At Delphi, the oracle proclaimed from a grotto. In the holy ground of the mass graves, the earth blistered and spoke.

While the German language annihilated metaphor, turning humans into objects, physicists turned matter into energy. The step from language/formula to fact: denotation to detonation. Not long before the first brick smashed a window on Kristallnacht, physicist Hans Thirring wrote, of relativity: "It takes one's breath away to think what might happen to a town if the dormant energy of a single brick were to be set free . . . it would suffice to raze a city with a million inhabitants to the ground."

∼

Alex is constantly turning on lights. I sit in late-afternoon dimness, a story eating its way to the surface, when she bursts home, full of the Saturday market and crowded trams and the daily world I'm missing – and turns on all the lights. "Why do you always sit in the dark? Why don't you turn on the lights, Jake? Turn on the lights!"

The moment I'd spent half my day gnawing through misery to reach vanishes under a bulb. The shadows slip away until the next time, when Alex again barges in with her shameless vitality. She never understands; thinks, certainly, that she's doing me good, returning me to the world, snatching me from the jaws of despair, rescuing me.

And she is.

But each time a memory or a story slinks away, it takes more of me with it.

I begin to feel Alex is brainwashing me. Her Gerrard Street scene, her jazz at the Tick Tock, her coffeehouse politics at the River Nihilism, owned by an origami artist who folds birds out of dollar bills. Her Trudeaumania and her cornet mania. Her portrait painted by the artist who wears half a moustache. The length of her, the edgy sexuality of which she's now fully in control – all of it is making me forget. Athos replaced parts of me slowly, as if he were preserving wood. But Alex – Alex wants to explode me, set fire to everything. She wants me to begin again.

Love must change you, it can only change you. Though now it seems I don't want Alex's understanding. Now her lack of understanding seems proof of something.

I watch Alex get dressed to meet her friends. She is dishearteningly perfect. She clips a thick gold bracelet around a slim black sleeve. Her dress is as tight as a bud. Each item she zips, clasps, pins, lets loose the power of her beauty.

When Alex goes out with "the kids," "the cats," "the crowd," I stay home, the grim reaper. "You'll have a better time without me."

To Alex's father, to Maurice and Irena, Alex has walked out on me. But it's I who have abandoned her.

She comes in late and lies on top of me. I smell the smoke in her dress, in her hair. "I'm sorry," she says. "I won't go without you again." We both know she says this only because it isn't true. She pulls each of my fingers separately, a long stroke along each stretch of bone. She kisses my palm. A flush spreads across her skin.

I draw my hands through her silky hair. I feel the birthmark at the tip of her scalp. After a few minutes her shoes thump to the floor. I pull down the long zipper and the soft black wool separates, a wake of pale skin opening. I work out the knots in her back, from too many hours in high heels, too many precarious bar stools and hours of conversation, leaning to hear above the din. I circle her smooth hot back slowly, like kneading the air out of bread. I imagine the faint impression of her garters on her thighs. She is thin and light, the bones of a bird. Her smoke-filled hair falls over her open mouth, her mouth open against my throat. Fully clothed, her limbs outline mine under the blanket – now I'm inside Athos's coat. I feel the wetness of her breath, her small ear.

No surge of desire moves me to trace her spine with my tongue, to speak her, inch by miraculous inch.

I lie awake while she sleeps. The longer I hold her, the further Alex recedes from my touch.

There's the decrescendo in the ninth bar, and then from pianissimo to piano so quickly, but not quite as soft as the diminuendo in the sixteenth bar –

Bella sits at the kitchen table with the music in front of her. She practises fingering on the tabletop and writes on the score what she must remember. It's Sunday afternoon. My father is asleep on the sofa and Bella doesn't want to wake him. I can hear the tapping now, lying next to Alex. I can hear Bella tapping on the wall between our rooms, a code we invented so we could say goodnight from our beds.

On the way home from buying eggs for my mother, Bella told me the story of Brahms and Clara Schumann. Uncharacteristically, Bella leaped at the chance to run the errand, because it was raining and she wanted to use the elegant new umbrella my father had bought for her birthday. She allowed me to walk under it with her, but she insisted on carrying it like a parasol and neither of us stayed dry. I yelled at her to hold it straight. I pulled it from her, she grabbed it back, and then I sulked outside its precious periphery until I was soaked and she was repentant. Bella always told me stories when she wanted me to forgive her. She knew I couldn't resist listening. "When he was twenty, Brahms fell in love with Clara Schumann. But

Clara was married to Robert Schumann, whom Brahms revered. Brahms worshipped Robert Schumann! Brahms never married. Imagine, Jakob, he was true to her his whole life. He wrote songs for her. When Clara died, Brahms was so upset that on the way to her funeral he took the wrong train. He spent two days changing trains, trying to reach Frankfurt. Brahms arrived just in time to throw a handful of earth on Clara's coffin. . . ." "Bella, that's a terrible story, what kind of a story is that?"

It's said that during the forty hours he spent on the trains, Brahms's head was already filling with his last composition, the choral prelude "O Welt ich muss dich lassen" – "O World, I must leave thee."

That they were torn from mistakes they had no chance to fix; everything unfinished. All the sins of love without detail, detail without love. The regret of having spoken, of having run out of time to speak. Of hoarding oneself. Of turning one's back too often in favour of sleep.

I tried to imagine their physical needs, the indignity of human needs grown so extreme they equal your longing for wife, child, sister, parent, friend. But truthfully I couldn't even begin to imagine the trauma of their hearts, of being taken in the middle of their lives. Those with young children. Or those newly in love, wrenched from that state of grace. Or those who had lived invisibly, who were never known.

A July evening, the windows are open; I hear children shouting in the street. Their voices are suspended in the heat evaporating from pavement and lawns. The room is motionless against the rushing trees. Alex respects me enough to bother saying the words: "I can't stand this anymore." I'm too tired to lift my head from my arm on the table and I open my eyes to the blurry pattern of the cloth, too close to focus.

When she says, "I can't stand this anymore," it also means, "I've met someone else." Perhaps a musician, a painter, a doctor who works with her father. As to leaving, she wants me to watch: "This is what you want isn't it? Every last speck of me will be gone . . . my clothes, my smell, even my shadow. My friends whose names you can't remember. . . ."

It's a neurological disorder, I know what I must do but I can't move. I can't move a muscle or a cell. "You're ungrateful, Jake, that dirty word you hate so much. . . ."

When Mama and Papa first brought me here, there were thirty-two tins.

More than enough for a little boy like you, Mama said. Remember, two tins every day. Long before you run out of tins, we'll be back. Papa showed me how to open them. Long before the tins are finished, we'll be back for you. Don't open the door to anyone, not even if they call you by name. Do you understand? Papa and I have the only key and we'll come fetch you. Don't ever open the curtains. Promise to never, never open the door. Don't ever leave this room, not for a minute, until we get back. Wait for us. Promise.

Papa left me four books. One is about a circus, one is about a farmer, the other two are about dogs. When I finish one, I start the next and when I finish all four, I start again. I don't remember how many times.

At the beginning I walked around the room anytime I felt like it. Now I have one place for the morning, another for after lunch. When the sun is between the rug and the bed, then I can eat supper.

Yesterday was the last tin. I'll be very hungry soon. But now that the last tin is gone, Mama and Papa will come back. The last tin means they're coming.

I want to go out but I promised I would never leave until they came back. I promised. What if they came back and I wasn't here?

Mama, I'd even eat cooked carrots! Right now.

Last night there was a lot of noise outside. There was music. It sounded like a birthday party.

The last tin means they'll be here soon.

I'm floating. The floor is far away. What if I don't open the door, what if I leave through that little crack in the ceiling. . . .

A week has passed since Alex moved out. If she were to return, she would find me in the same place she left me. I lift my head from the table. The July kitchen is dark.

TERRA NULLIUS

I arrive in Athens at midnight. Leaving my bag at the Hotel Amalias, I walk back out into the street. Each step is like passing through a doorway. I seem to be remembering things only as I see them. The leaves whisper under the streetlamps. I climb steep Lykavettos, lurching, stopping to rest. Soon I can't feel the heat, my blood and the air are the same temperature.

I stare at the house that used to be Kostas and Daphne's and which looks recently redecorated, flowers dripping from window boxes. I long to open the front door and enter the vanished world of their kindness. To find them there, small as two children, their feet barely skimming the floor as they lean back on the sofa.

Kostas, in the last letter he sent me before he died: "Yes, we have the democratic constitution. Yes, the press is free. Yes, Theodorakis is free. Now we can again watch our tragedies in the amphitheatre and sing rebetika. But not for a day do we forget the massacre at the polytechnic. Or the long imprisonment of Ritsos – even when he accepts his honorary degree at Salonika University or reads his 'Romiosini' at Panathinaiko Stadium. . . ."

Standing outside Kostas and Daphne's house, it doesn't seem possible that they are gone, that Athos has been dead close to eight years. That Athos, Daphne, and Kostas never even met Alex.

I want to call Alex long distance, to turn around and take a plane back to Canada; as if it's essential to tell her what it was like, those few weeks with the three of them in that house when I was young. As if this is the missing information that could have saved us. I want to tell her that now I could be roused, if only she could want me back.

In my hotel room I lie awake until I'm ready to weep from exhaustion. I've been awake since Toronto; two days and two nights. The traffic never stops on Amalias. All night I hear the noise of the street as I travel out of the past.

In the morning I'm unprepared for the German language in Syntagma Square, unprepared for the tourists everywhere. I take the first flight of the day to Zakynthos. The shortness of the journey by air disorients me. But the landing strip is surrounded by fields I recognize. Wild calla and high grass sway silently in the hot wind.

I walk uphill in a trance.

The earthquake has turned our little house into a cairn. I bury Athos's ashes under the stones of our hiding place. The asphodels that we used so long ago to make bread are growing everywhere through the broken pile. It seems proper that with Athos gone, the house should also be gone. After, in the partially rebuilt town, I inquire at the kafenio and learn that Old Martin died the year before. He was ninety-three and everyone in Zakynthos attended his funeral. Since the earthquake, Ioannis and his family have lived on the mainland. A few hours later, I leave Zakynthos on *The Dolphin* and cross the channel. The orange plastic deck chairs glint like hard candy. The sky is a billowing blue tablecloth suspended by the wind. At Kyllini I board a bus back to Athens. I eat a very late dinner from a tray, on the balcony of my hotel room. When I wake in the morning, I am still fully dressed.

∾

I sailed the next day to Idhra. From the boat, I left behind a swarm of tourists. As I climbed the narrow streets, the town, with its whitewashed walls of pure sunlight, fell away.

Athos's family house – where I now sit and write this, these many years later – is a record of the Roussos generations. The various pieces of furniture give the impression of having been hauled up the hill during different decades and, rather than being carried downhill, have simply been left and added to, like aggregate rock. I've often tried to guess which item of furniture represents which Roussos ancestor.

Mrs. Karouzos seemed pleased that at last the house would be opened again. She was still a child in the twenties, when Athos's father came to Idhra for the last time. I wondered whether she found me wanting as she looked me over, whether or not she was thinking, So this is what the Roussos line has come to.

That first night, the moon in the window frozen like a coin in mid-toss, I explored Athos's library. Again I found myself in his care.

There were many volumes of poetry, more than I remembered, as well as Athos's lessons: Paracelsus, Linnaeus, Lyell, Darwin, Mendeleev. Field guides. Aeschylus, Dante, Solomos. So familiar – but not only what was inside: my hands remembered the crazed and embossed leathers, corners eroded to board, paperbacks soft from the sea air. And slipped between books, newspaper clippings fragile as mica. When I was young I searched among them for the one book that would teach me everything, just as I would look for one language, just as some would look for one woman's face. There's a Hebrew saying: Hold a book in your hand and you're a pilgrim at the gates of a new city. I even found my prayer shawl, a gift from Athos after the war, never worn, folded carefully and still stored in its cardboard box. The shawl's bottom edge the clearest blue, as if it has been dipped in the sea. The blue of a glance.

I held the lamp close to the shelves. I decided on the slim hardcovered Psalms, bound in red leather darkened by many hands. Athos had found it in a bin in the Plaka. "Perfectly right. Oranges. Figs. Psalms."

I was very tired from travelling, and the heat. I took the little book into the bedroom and lay down.

"Grief has eaten up my life, groans have eaten away years . . . those who know me are afraid when they hear my name. I have been forgotten like a dead man who is not considered, like a pot that is broken. . . ."

"My strength has dried like the baked earth . . . there are dogs around me, I am cut off by a crowd of wicked men. They have torn my hands and feet. . . . They will divide my clothes between them."

"On the day of evil he will take me into his house, he will hide me in his tent, he will lift me onto high rock. . . ."

I stretched out on the cotton bedcover. The cleansing summer wind – the meltemi – found its way under my shirt to my damp skin. Mrs. Karouzos had filled all the lamps. For the first time in almost two decades, they added their light to those of the village's below.

"I will speak a dark language with the music of a harp."

There are places that claim you and places that warn you away. On Idhra the pang of smells opened in me with the prickly sting of memory. Burros and dust, hot stones washed down with salt water. Lemon and sweet broom.

In Athos's room, in the house of his father. I heard the cries and they grew louder, filled my head. I moved closer inside myself, didn't turn away. I clutched the sides of the desk and was pulled down into the blueness. I lost myself, discovered the world could disappear. During long evenings, in the blush of the lamp, in the purity of white pages.

The child was licking dew from the grass. Zdena had no water with her, so she told the girl to suck on a finger ". . . and when you are really hungry – chew." The little girl looked at her for a moment, then put her forefinger in her mouth.

"What's your name, little one?"

"Bettina." A clean name, thought Zdena, for a girl who's now so dirty.

"How long have you been waiting here, like this, by the road?"

"Since yesterday," she whispered.

Zdena kneeled down beside her.

"Someone was supposed to come for you?"

Bettina nodded.

Zdena took the little girl's bag from her, she saw there was blood on the handle. She opened Bettina's hands, which were striped from gripping.

It was six miles back to town. Zdena carried a square of cloth filled with weeds for cooking. At home she had a bone for soup and the herbs would give flavour to the stock. Part of the time Zdena supported the girl, and sometimes the girl stood on Zdena's boots and they walked together.

While they walked, Bettina sucked the ends of her hair into wet points. She devoted her attention to the ends of her hair and did not look around her.

That evening the little girl watched Zdena make soup. She dipped her bread into the watery broth and crammed in sopping mouthfuls, her lips close to the edge of the bowl.

They lived quietly. Bettina liked to count the pattern on Zdena's dress, placing her finger in the centre of each cluster of flowers. Zdena felt Bettina's little finger through the thin cloth on different places on her body; it was like the game of connect-the-dots. Zdena took shape.

The little girl sat on her lap and listened to stories. Zdena felt her forty-year-old breasts and belly go warm against the weight of the child. The grief we carry, anybody's grief, Zdena thought, is exactly the weight of a sleeping child.

One August afternoon, the mud-locked roads now powdery with weeks of dry summer, a man stopped at Zdena's house. He *heard that she was the shoemaker's daughter (Zdena's father had no sons) and his boots needed mending.*

The man waited on the verandah in his socks while Zdena made the repairs. Each heel required five small nails. Bettina watched carefully. It was very hot. When she was finished, Zdena brought out a cup of water for each of them.

The child burrowed her face into Zdena's skirt, her small arms circled Zdena's legs. It was not clear whether she wanted to be comforted or was intent on comforting.

"She looks just like you," the man said.

I came to Idhra to press to tearing certain questions.

Questions without answers must be asked very slowly. My first winter on the island I watched the rain fill the sea. For weeks at a time, sheets of dark water draped the windows. Every day before supper I walked to the edge of the cliff and back again. I ate at my desk, like Athos, with my empty plate holding open a book.

Though the contradictions of war seem sudden and simultaneous, history stalks before it strikes. Something tolerated soon becomes something good.

I must not use so much pedal at the first ritardando –

It's Hebrew tradition that forefathers are referred to as "we," not "they." "When we were delivered from Egypt. . . ." This encourages empathy and a responsibility to the past but, more important, it collapses time. The Jew is forever leaving Egypt. A good way to teach ethics. If moral choices are eternal, individual actions take on immense significance no matter how small: not for this life only.

A parable: A respected rabbi is asked to speak to the congregation of a neighbouring village. The rabbi, rather famous for his practical wisdom, is approached for advice wherever he goes. Wishing to have a few hours to himself on the train, he disguises himself in shabby clothes and, with his withered posture, passes for a peasant. The disguise is so effective that he evokes disapproving stares and whispered insults from the well-to-do passengers around him. When the rabbi arrives at his destination, he's met by the dignitaries of the community who greet him with warmth and respect, tactfully ignoring his appearance. Those who had ridiculed him on the train realize his prominence and their error and immediately beg his forgiveness. The old man is silent. For months after, these Jews – who, after all, consider themselves good and pious men – implore the rabbi to absolve them. The rabbi remains silent. Finally, when almost an entire year has passed, they come to the old man on the Day of Awe when, it is written, each man must forgive his fellow. But the rabbi still refuses to speak. Exasperated, they finally raise their voices: How can a holy man commit such a sin – to withhold forgiveness on this day of days? The rabbi smiles seriously. "All this time you have been asking the wrong man. You must ask the man on the train to forgive you."

Of course it's every peasant whose forgiveness must be sought. But the rabbi's point is even more tyrannical: nothing erases the immoral act. Not forgiveness. Not confession.

And even if an act could be forgiven, no one could bear

the responsibility of forgiveness on behalf of the dead. No act of violence is ever resolved. When the one who can forgive can no longer speak, there is only silence.

History is the poisoned well, seeping into the groundwater. It's not the unknown past we're doomed to repeat, but the past we know. Every recorded event is a brick of potential, of precedent, thrown into the future. Eventually the idea will hit someone in the back of the head. This is the duplicity of history: an idea recorded will become an idea resurrected. Out of fertile ground, the compost of history.

Destruction doesn't create a vacuum, it simply transforms presence into absence. The splitting atom creates absence, palpable "missing" energy. In the rabbi's universe, in Einstein's universe, the man will remain forever on the train, familiar with humiliation but not humiliated, because, after all, it's a case of mistaken identity. His heart rises, he's not really the subject of this persecution; his heart falls, how can he prove, why should he prove, he's not what they think he is.

He'll sit there forever; just as the painted clock in Treblinka station will always read three o'clock. Just as on the platform the ghostly advice still floats: "To the right, go to the right" in the eerie breeze. The bond of memory and history when they share space and time. Every moment is two moments. Einstein: ". . . all our judgements in which time plays a part are always judgements of simultaneous events. If, for instance, I say the train arrived here at seven o'clock, I mean: the small hand of my watch pointing to seven and the arrival of the train are simultaneous events . . . the time of the event has no operational meaning. . . ." The event is meaningful only if the coordination of time and place is witnessed.

Witnessed by those who lived near the incinerators, within the radius of smell. By those who lived outside a camp fence, or stood outside the chamber doors. By those who stepped a few feet to the right on the station platform. By those who were born a generation after.

If I use my second finger instead, I'll be ready for the middle voice in the next bar –

Irony is scissors, a divining rod, always pointing in two directions. If the evil act can't be erased, then neither can the good. It's as accurate a measure as any of a society: what is the smallest act of kindness that is considered heroic? In those days, to be moral required no more than the slightest flicker of movement – a micrometre – of eyes looking away or blinking, while a running man crossed a field. And those who gave water or bread! They entered a realm higher than the angels' simply by remaining in the human mire.

Complicity is not sudden, though it occurs in an instant.

To be proved true, violence need only occur once. But good is proved true by repetition.

I must keep the same tempo into the pianissimo –

On Idhra I finally began to feel my English strong enough to carry experience. I became obsessed by the palpable edge of sound. The moment when language at last surrenders to what it's describing: the subtlest differentials of light or temperature or sorrow. I'm a kabbalist only in that

I believe in the power of incantation. A poem is as neural as love; the rut of rhythm that veers the mind.

This hunger for sound is almost as sharp as desire, as if one could honour every inch of flesh in words; and so, suspend time. A word is at home in desire. No station of the heart is more full of solitude than desire which keeps the world poised, poisoned with beauty, whose only permanence is loss. Of the poems I published before I returned to Idhra, Maurice had a definite opinion, which he stated in a voice of compassion for the unwise: "These aren't poems, they're ghost stories."

What he also meant but didn't say was: Before our son Yosha was born, I also thought I believed in death. But it was only being a father that convinced me.

After a year on Idhra, at the end of the summer, Maurice, Irena, and Yosha, who was still a toddler, came to visit.

Maurice and I spent many hot afternoons in the small courtyard of Mrs. Karouzos's taverna while Irena and Yosha rested.

One afternoon as we talked, Maurice rolled a lemon under his flat palm, over the blue and white tablecloth. He said: "Sa" – he always begins a remark he's particularly proud of with "c'est ca," which in his rush to make the point comes out in a slur – "you want to be like Zeuxis, master of light, who painted his grapes so realistically, the birds tried to eat them!"

I leaned back in my chair, tipping the front legs, with my head against the stone wall. The courtyard tilted. The green shutters and pure sky. Then I looked at Maurice's flushed, very round face. He and Irena were my only friends on earth. I couldn't stop laughing and soon he was laughing too. The lemon escaped Maurice's palm and wobbled down the narrow street to the harbour.

From the first, I felt at home in these hills, with broken icons hovering over every abyss, every valley, the spirit looking back upon the body. Their Lord's blue robes dimmer than the flowers, the face of their Redeemer fractured with weather. Icons in wooden boxes small as birdhouses, with peeling paint and wood fraying like rope from rain and sun. I wrote in the tranquil buzz, in the heat that shellacked the leaves, turned the houses white with sweat, red hot roofs squirming under the glare.

But I also knew I would always be a stranger in Greece, no matter how long I lived here. So I tried over the years to anchor myself in the details of the island: the sun burning away night from the surface of the sea, the olive groves in winter rain. And in the friendship of Mrs. Karouzos and her son, who looked after me from a distance.

I tried to embroider darkness, black sutures with my glinting stones sewn safe and tight, buried in the cloth: Bella's intermezzos, Athos's maps, Alex's words, Maurice and Irena. Black on black, until the only way to see the texture would be to move the whole cloth under the light.

At the close of Maurice and Irena's first visit, after climbing back up to the house and watching the boat cross the water, I didn't think I could bear to stay on Idhra alone. But that second winter, Maurice and Irena kept me company through the mail as I finished *Groundwork*, and I felt them with me as I had years before while I worked alone on Athos's book.

"Write to save yourself," Athos said, "and someday you'll write because you've been saved."

"You will feel terrible shame for this. Let your humility grow larger than your shame."

Our relation to the dead continues to change because we continue to love them. All the afternoon conversations that winter on Idhra, with Athos or with Bella, while it grew dark. As in any conversation, sometimes they answered me, sometimes they didn't.

I was in a small room. Everything was fragile. I couldn't move without breaking something. My hands melted what they held.

The pianissimo must be perfect, it must be in the listener's ears before he hears it –

Nazi policy was beyond racism, it was anti-matter, for Jews were not considered human. An old trick of language, used often in the course of history. Non-Aryans were never to be referred to as human, but as "figuren," "stücke" – "dolls," "wood," "merchandise," "rags." Humans were not being gassed, only "figuren," so ethics weren't being violated. No one could be faulted for burning debris, for burning rags and clutter in the dirty basement of society. In fact, they're a fire hazard! What choice but to burn them before they harm you. . . . So, the extermination of Jews was not a case of obeying one set of moral imperatives over another, but rather the case of the larger imperative satisfying any difficulties. Similarly, the Nazis implemented a directive against Jews owning pets; how can one animal own another? How can an insect or an object own anything? Nazi law prohibited Jews from buying soap; what use is soap to vermin?

When citizens, soldiers, and SS performed their unspeakable acts, the photos show their faces were not grimaced with horror, or even with ordinary sadism, but rather were contorted with laughter. Of all the harrowing contradictions, this holds the key to all the others. This is the most ironic loophole in Nazi reasoning. If the Nazis required that humiliation precede extermination, then they admitted exactly what they worked so hard to avoid admitting: the humanity of the victim. To humiliate is to accept that your victim feels and thinks, that he not only feels pain, but knows that he's being degraded. And because the torturer knew in an instant of recognition that his victim was not a "figuren" but a man, and knew at that same moment he must continue his task, he suddenly understood the Nazi mechanism. Just as the stone-carrier knew his only chance of survival was to fulfil his task as if he didn't know its futility, so the torturer decided to do his job as if he didn't know the lie. The photos capture again and again this chilling moment of choice: the laughter of the damned. When the soldier realized that only death has the power to turn "man" into "figuren," his difficulty was solved. And so the rage and sadism increased: his fury at the victim for suddenly turning human; his desire to destroy that humanness so intense his brutality had no limit.

There's a precise moment when we reject contradiction. This moment of choice is the lie we will live by. What is dearest to us is often dearer to us than truth.

There were the few, like Athos, who chose to do good at great personal risk; those who never confused objects and humans, who knew the difference between naming and the named. Because the rescuers couldn't lose sight, literally, of the human, again and again they give us the same explanation for their heroism: "What choice did I have?"

We look for the spirit precisely in the place of greatest degradation. It's from there that the new Adam must raise himself, must begin again.

I want to remain close to Bella. I read. I rip the black alphabet to shreds, but there's no answer there. At night, at Athos's old desk, I stare at photos of strangers.

Brahms wrote the intermezzos for Clara, and she adored them because they were for her –

I want to remain close to Bella. To do so, I blaspheme by imagining.

At night the wooden bunk wears through her skin. Icy feet push into the back of Bella's head. *Now I will begin the intermezzo. I must not begin too slowly.* There is no room. Bella's arms cover herself. *At night when everyone is awake, I will not listen to the crying. I will play the whole piece on my arms.* Her skin is coming apart at her elbows and behind her ears. *Not too much pedal, you can spoil Brahms with too much pedal, especially the intermezzos, the opening must be played clear as – water. Bar 62, crescendo, pay attention, but it's hard because that's where he's so – in love. The first time he played this for her, she listened knowing he wrote it for her.* The cuts on Bella's head are burning. She closes her eyes. *After*

*the intermezzo I will practise parts of the Hammerklavier. By
then most of the barrack will be asleep.* Against her sore scalp,
the feet are wet and send the ice into her. *The two notes at
the beginning of the adagio Beethoven added after, at the pub-
lisher's; the A and C# that change everything.* Every raw place
on her scalp bursts with cold. *Then I can play it again.
Without the two notes.*

When they opened the doors, the bodies were always
in the same position. Compressed against one wall, a
pyramid of flesh. Still hope. The climb to air, to the last
disappearing pocket of breath near the ceiling. The terrifying hope of human cells.

The bare autonomic faith of the body.

Some gave birth while dying in the chamber. Mothers
were dragged from the chamber with new life half-emerged
from their bodies. Forgive me, you who were born and
died without being given names. Forgive this blasphemy,
of choosing philosophy over the brutalism of fact.

We know they cried out. Each mouth, Bella's mouth,
strained for its miracle. They were heard from the other
side of the thick walls. It is impossible to imagine those
sounds.

At that moment of utmost degradation, in that twisted
reef, is the most obscene testament of grace. For can anyone tell with absolute certainty the difference between the
sounds of those who are in despair and the sounds of those
who want desperately to believe? The moment when our
faith in man is forced to change, anatomically – mercilessly
– into faith.

In the still house, the visitation of moonlight. It occupies the darkness, erasing everything it touches. It has taken me years to reach this fabrication. Even as I fall apart I know I will never again feel this pure belief.

Bella, my brokenness has kept you broken.

I wait for daylight before daring to move. The dew soaks my shoes. I walk to the edge of the hill and lie down in the cold grass. But the sun is already hot. I think of my mother's overturned glasses of steam that drew fevers from the skin. The sky is a glass.

～

In experiments to determine the mechanisms of migration, scientists locked warblers in cages and kept them in darkened rooms where they couldn't see the sky. The birds lived in bewildered twilight. Yet each October, they huddled, agitated, turned inside out with yearning. The magnetic pole pulled their blood, the thumbprint of night sky on their inner eye.

When you are lost to ones you love, you will face south-southwest like the caged bird. At certain hours of the day, your body will be flooded with instinct, so much of you having been entered, so much of you having entered them. Their limbs will follow when you lie down, a shadow against your own, curving to every curve like the Hebrew alphabet and the Greek, which cross the page to greet each other in the middle of historia, bent with carrying absence, cargoes from distant ports, the power of stones, the sorrow of those whose messiahs have made them leave so much behind. . . .

In the early darkness of Greek winter afternoons, in rooms cold at the windows, I raise my hands to my face and smell Alex in my palms.

I long for memory to be spirit, but fear it is only skin. I fear that knowledge becomes instinct only to disappear with the body. For it is my body that remembers them, and though I have tried to erase Alex from my senses, tried to will my parents and Bella from my sleep, this will amounts to nothing, for my body betrays me in a second. I have lived many years without them. Yet it's the same winter afternoon that draws Bella close, so close I can feel her powerful hand on my own, feel her gentle fingers on my back, so close I can smell Mrs. Alperstein's lotion, so close I feel my father's hand and Athos's hand on my head and my mother's hands pulling down my jacket to straighten me out, so close I can feel Alex's arms reaching around me from behind, and upon me her maddeningly open eyes even as she disappears into sensation, and suddenly I'm afraid, and turn around in empty rooms.

&

To remain with the dead is to abandon them.

All the years I felt Bella entreating me, filled with her loneliness, I was mistaken. I have misunderstood her signals. Like other ghosts, she whispers; not for me to join her, but so that, when I'm close enough, she can push me back into the world.

THE GRADUAL INSTANT

When they were young, Maurice Salman's sons, Yosha and Tomas, often sent strange things to me through the mail: envelopes filled with sand, drawings consisting only of loops or straight lines, pieces of plastic of unknown origin. I answered with rocks and foreign coins.

Maurice, Irena, and the boys visited me on Idhra, and I stayed with them whenever I returned to Toronto, camping in the den. Maurice's museum work required that he teach two courses at the university, including Ancient Weather: Predicting the Past. "Almost as tricky," he told his students, "as knowing what the weather will be next week." The demand for Greek–English translation grew steadily, and I was able to make a sufficient living. Over the years, aside from my own writing, I compiled two books of Athos's essays for publication and translated into Greek *Bearing False Witness*. Sometimes Donald Tupper, on behalf of the geography department, invited me to speak on Athos's work.

Maurice and Irena have always thrived on disorder. The boys' school projects – Livingstone's diary written in shaky felt marker on foolscap, the corners of the pages burned dramatically by Irena at Yosha's instruction – was swept to one side of the dining-room table at dinner time. The Gobi Desert in Plasticine and sand on the living-room floor – everyone simply walked over it. Emerging from relative solitude on the island, I was faithfully greeted by Maurice: "So. The monk runs away to join the circus."

I would hear the boys come home from school. Downstairs, Yosha would begin to practise the piano. Then I would hear the door slam and I knew Tomas was outside by himself in the yard. Yosha played with maddening care. He was afraid of making mistakes and played slow as geology rather than hit a wrong note.

In their house, in the narrow time between afternoon and evening, among familiar shadows and familiar clutter, I often found myself lying on the old burgundy sofa, my head next to Maurice's books, listening to Yosha's straining piano beautiful as light.

I love Maurice and Irena's boys, as I would have loved Bella's children, and I often yearn to tell them yet again about my ancient afternoons at the river docks, the thin autumn sun in bright stripes on the thick reeds, green fur on the rocks in the shallowest parts of the river, the biblical cities Mones and I made out of mud and sticks. The frozen shore, the faintly greenish sky, the black birds, the snow. When they were very young I crouched down to Yosha and Tomas and held their frail, bony shoulders, hoping to remember my father's touch.

I watch the boys lean against Irena, the way they still sometimes give in to her caress, resting their heads against her. Irena doesn't take this love for granted. She wasn't young when Yosha was born and never quite believed that Tomas would survive. You can see it clearly in her face.

I listened to Yosha's earnest wish to never make a mistake, his aching melody that wasn't broken but sounded as though it was; so much space between the notes.

For years after my marriage ended, Maurice and Irena pretended to envy my freedom; secretly they amused themselves with the challenge of finding me a second wife. On my visits to Toronto they connived like teenagers. Lunches, family parties, faculty dinners – every event a potential romantic minefield, with Maurice planting the bombshells. Maurice would make the introductions and then scram. I was accustomed to his refrain: "Now Jakob, I know this woman . . ." and remained unmoved.

But sometimes the world disrobes, slips its dress off a shoulder, stops time for a beat. If we look up at that moment, it's not due to any ability of ours to pierce the darkness, it's the world's brief bestowal. The catastrophe of grace.

I had been visiting Toronto part of every year for over eighteen years before she walked into Maurice and Irena's kitchen.

I don't know what to look at first. Her light-brown hair or her dark-brown eyes or her small hand disappearing into the shoulder of her dress to adjust a strap.

"Michaela is an administrator at the museum," says Maurice as he makes his exit.

Her mind is a palace. She moves through history with the fluency of a spirit, mourns the burning of the library at Alexandria as if it happened yesterday. She discusses the influence of trade routes on European architecture, while still noticing the pattern of light across a table. . . .

There's no one left in the kitchen. All around us are glasses and small towers of dirty dishes. The noise of the party in the other room. Michaela's hips lean against the kitchen counter. Voluptuous scholar.

Michaela has only recently met Irena. She's asking after her.

I find myself telling Michaela a story that's a dozen years old, the story of Tomas's birth, about my experience of his soul.

"When Tomas was born, he was very premature. He weighed less than three pounds. . . ."

I had put on a gown, scrubbed my hands and arms to the elbows, and Irena led me in to see him. I saw what I can only call a soul, for it was not yet a self, caught in that almost transparent body. I have never before been so close to such palpable evidence of the spirit, so close to the almost invisible musselman whose eyes in the photos show the faint stain of a soul. Without breath, the evidence would vanish instantly. Tomas in his clear plastic womb, barely bigger than a hand.

Michaela has been looking down at the floor. Her hair, glossy and heavy and parted on the side, covers her face. Now she looks up. Suddenly I'm embarrassed at having spoken so much.

Then she says: "I don't know what the soul is. But I

imagine that somehow our bodies surround what has always been."

Standing together on the winter sidewalk, in the white darkness. I know even less than lamplight in a window, which knows how to pour itself into the street and arouse the longing of one who waits.

Her hair and hat circle her quiet face. She's young. There are twenty-five years between us. Looking at her I feel such pure regret, such clean sadness, it's almost like joy. Her hat, the snow, remind me of Akhmatova's poem where, in two lines, the poet shakes her fists then closes her hands in prayer: "You're many years late,/how happy I am to see you."

The winter street is a salt cave. The snow has stopped falling and it's very cold. The cold is spectacular, penetrating. The street has been silenced, a theatre of whiteness, drifts like frozen waves. Crystals glisten under the streetlights.

She points out her impractical boots, "party shoes," and then I feel her small leather glove around my arm.

~

Michaela lives above a bank. Her flat is a monastic cell of a sensuous order. I've entered an old world; the specifications of a dream. Magazines – *Nature*, *Archaeology*, *The*

Conservator – and piles of books – novels, art history, children's stories – teeter on the floor next to the couch. Shoes left in the middle of the room; a shawl flung on the table. The clutter of hibernation.

Jumbled rooms breathe dimly in the shallow light. The dark autumn fabrics, the rugs and heavy furniture, a wall of small framed photographs, a child's lamp in the shape of a horse – all seem in defiance of the strict world of accounting in the bank below.

I'm a thief who has climbed in through a window only to find himself struck frozen by a feeling of homecoming. The impossibility of it; the luck.

I wait for Michaela to return with tea. I feel the malaise of the warm room, the peace of the immaculate snowfall. Michaela's crammed rooms have cast a spell. I'm already painted into the Rembrandt dimness.

She comes back, carrying a tray to the low living-room table; a silver pot, glasses edged in silver. Her shoes off, now wearing thick socks, she looks even younger. Now I see in Michaela's face the goodness of Beatrice de Luna, the Marrano angel of Ferrara, who reclaimed her faith and gave refuge to other exiles of the Inquisition. . . . In Michaela's face, the loyalty of generations, perhaps the devotion of a hundred Kievan women for a hundred faithful husbands, countless evenings in close rooms under the sheets, discussing family problems; a thousand intimacies, dreams of foreign lands, first nights of love, nights of love after long years of marriage. In Michaela's eyes, ten generations of history, in her hair the scents of fields and pines, her cold, smooth arms carrying water from springs. . . .

"Tea?" she asks, pushing newspapers onto the rug, clearing a place.

She pauses in the middle of a family story; now she's the one uncomfortable at having spoken so much. About her parents, "like embassies" – Russian and Spanish soil under them – as they sat in their Montreal living room. About her grandmother, who told Michaela stories of her life that were actually fiction, either wishing Michaela to remember her in a certain light or wishing, herself, to believe in her longest-held fantasies. Michaela's grandmother described a huge house in St. Petersburg, the details of ornate fixtures, carved woodwork, even the personalities of servants. Drapery of green and gold, velvet dresses of wine and black. But mostly she insisted on her education, telling Michaela she'd been a student, a teacher, a writer for a newspaper.

Michaela offers her ancestors to me. I'm shocked at my hunger for her memories. Love feeds on the protein of detail, sucks fact to the marrow; just as there's no generality in the body, every particular speaking at once until there's such a crying out. . . .

I am leaning forward on the sofa, she is sitting on the floor, the small table between us. It seems to be absolution simply to listen to her. But I know that if she touches me my shame will be exposed, she'll see my ugliness, my thinning hair, the teeth that aren't my own. She'll see in my body the terrible things that have marked me.

A last shudder of strangeness, a last flash of fear before longing pushes its blade into me, up to the hilt. Skinned alive. My hand reaches for hers and instantly I know I've made a mistake. I'm too old for her. Too old.

Now, impossibly – can it be without pity? – she is placing her cheek – soft sun-warmed peach – against my cold palm.

~

I begin to trace every line, her lengths and shapes, and realize suddenly that she's perfectly still, her hands clenched, and I'm appalled by my stupidity: my longing humiliates her. Too many years between us. Then I realize she's entirely concentrated, pinioned under my tongue, that she's giving me the most extravagant permission to roam the surface of her. Only after I explore her this way, so slowly, an animal outlining territory, does she burst into touch.

I'm paralyzed in the cave her hair makes. Then my hands move to feel her slim waist and suddenly I know how she would bend after a shower, twisting her hair into a wet turban, feel the shape her back would make, leaning over. I hear her small voice – long phrases of music and stillness like an oar balanced in its arc above the water, dripping silver. I hear her voice but not her words, so soft; the noise of her whole body is in my ears. Instead of the dead inhaling my breath with their closeness, I am deafened by the buzzing drone of Michaela's body, the power lines of blood, blue threads under her skin. Cables of tendons; the forests of bone in her wrists and feet. Each time she stops speaking, in each long pause, I renew the pressure of my grasp. I feel her slowly going heavy. How beautiful the blood's pull towards trust, the warm weight of the sleeper entering her orbit, pulling towards me, fragrant, heavy and still as apples in a bowl. Not the stillness of something broken, but of rest.

It's growing light when Michaela undresses, deliberate and dreamlike. Her clothes dissolve.

Even the wild molecules of objects in the room seem suddenly palpable. After years, at any moment, our bodies are ready to remember us.

She lies on top of me, the saddle of pelvis, the curve of skull, fibulas and femurs, sacrum and sternum. I feel the arches of her ribs, every breath flooding blood between the ossicula of her ears and of her feet.

But there is no tinge of death in Michaela's skin. Even as she sleeps, I see in her nakedness the invisible manifest, flooding the surface of her. I see my beloved's damp hair against her forehead, the stain of love like salt across her belly, the hipbone nudging the surface, complex with breath. I see the muscles pushing out her calves, firm as new pears. I see that she will again open her eyes and embrace me.

It's late, almost afternoon, when she says, though I may have dreamed it, though it's just something Michaela might ask: Are you hungry? No. . . . Then perhaps we should eat so that hunger won't seem, even for a moment, the stronger feeling. . . .

∼

Michaela's hands above her head; I stroke the fragile place on the back of her smooth, soft upper arms. She is sobbing. She has heard everything – her heart an ear, her skin an ear. Michaela is crying for Bella.

The light and heat of her tears enter my bones.

The joy of being recognized and the stabbing loss: recognized for the first time.

When I finally fall asleep, the first sleep of my life, I dream of Michaela – young, glistening smooth as marble, sugary wet with sunlight. I feel the sun melting over my skin. Bella sits on the edge of the bed and asks Michaela to describe the feel of the bedcover under her bare legs, "because you see, just now I am without my body. . . ." In the dream, tears stream down Michaela's face. I wake as if I've been dug out of the dream and lifted into the world, a floating exhaustion. My muscles ache from stretching into her, as I lie in sunlight across the bed.

Every cell in my body has been replaced, suffused with peace.

She sleeps, my face against her back, her breasts spilling from my hands. She sleeps deeply like a runner who's just emerged from the Samaria Gorge, who's heard only her own breathing for days. I drift and wake with my mouth on her belly, or on the small of her back, drawn home by the dream into her, her breasts soft loam, hard, sore seeds.

Each night heals gaps between us until we are joined by the scar of dreams. My desolation exhales in the breathing dark.

Our coming together is as unexpected, as accidental, as old Salonika itself, once a city of Castillian Spanish, Greek, Turkish, Bulgarian. Where before the war you could hear muezzins call from minarets across the city, while church bells rang, and the port went quiet on Friday afternoons for the Jewish Sabbath. Where streets were crowded with turbans, veils, kippahs, and the tall sikkes of the Mevlevis, the whirling dervishes. Where sixty minarets and thirty synagogues surrounded the semahane, the lodge where dervishes spun on their invisible axes, holy tornadoes, blessings drawn from heaven though the arms, brought to earth through the legs. . . .

I grasp her arms, bury my brain in the perfume at her wrists. Bracelets of scent.

To be saved by such a small body.

~

Across the city, across a hundred milky back yards, Michaela is sleeping.

I've barely put my head down when I hear Yosha and Tomas stomping along the hall and their stage-whispers outside my door. Michaela's smell is on me, in my hair. I feel the rough material of the sofa against my face. I'm heavy with lack of sleep, with Michaela, with the boys' voices. Shadows of early light line the thick curtains.

What have you done to time. . . .

I listen to the sounds of their breakfast-making, sounds that hurt. I listen to Yosha, each note learning the air. Lips of gravity press me to earth. Frozen rain clings to new snow, silver and white. On Maurice's sofa, reeds tangle along the banks, spring rain rushes in tin troughs, the room underwater with weather. Each sound – touch. Rain on Michaela's bare shoulders. So much green we'll think something's wrong with our eyes. No signal taken for granted. Again, again for the first time.

At Maurice's party where I met Michaela, there was a painter, a Pole from Danzig born ten years before the war. We talked a long time. "All my life," he said, "I've asked myself one question: How can you hate all you have come from and not hate yourself?"

He told me that the year before, he'd bought tubes of yellow paint, every shade of the brightest yellow, but he couldn't bring himself to use them. He continued to paint in the same dark ochres and browns.

The serenity of a winter bedroom; the street quiet except for a shovel scraping the sidewalk, a sound that seems to gather silence around it. The first morning I woke to Michaela – my head on the small of her back, her heels like two islands under the blanket – I knew that this was my first experience of the colour yellow.

We think that change occurs suddenly, but even I have learned better. Happiness is wild and arbitrary, but it's not sudden.

Maurice is more than delighted, he's amazed. "My friend, my friend – finally, after a million years. Irena, come here. *It's like the discovery of agriculture.*"

In Michaela's favourite restaurant, I lift my glass and cutlery spills onto the expensive tiled floor. The sound crashes high as the skylight. Looking at me, Michaela pushes her own silverware over the edge.

I fell in love amid the clattering of spoons. . . .

~

I cross over the boundary of skin into Michaela's memories, into her childhood. On the dock when she is ten, the tips of her braids wet as paint brushes. Her cool brown back under a worn flannel shirt, washed so many times it's as soft as the skin of earlobes. The smell of the cedar dock baking in the sun. Her slippery child's belly, her bird legs. How different to swim later, as a woman, the lake fingering her with cold; and how, even now in a lake, she can't swim without romance shaping her energies as if she were still a girl swimming into her future. In the evening the sky lightens with dusk, above the darkening fringe of trees. She rows, singing verses of ballads. She imagines the stars as peppermints and holds them in her mouth until they dissolve.

In our first weeks together, Michaela and I drive through many northern lakeside towns, the air laced with woodsmoke, lamps lit in small houses, or past clapboard cottages boarded up against the snow. Towns that keep their memories to themselves.

White aspens make black shadows, a photographic negative. The sky wavers between snow and rain. The light is a dull clang, old, an echo of light. Michaela at the wheel, my hand on her thigh. The joy of returning to her flat in the late Sunday-afternoon dark.

In the spring, we drive further north, past copper mines and paper mills, the abandoned towns born of and rejected by industry. I enter the landscape of her adolescence, which I receive with a bodily tenderness as Michaela relaxes and imperceptibly opens towards it: the decrepit houses of Cobalt, their doorways facing every direction except the road, which was built after. The elegant stone railway station. The gaping mouths of the mines. The faded, forlorn Albion Hotel. All this I saw she loved. I knew then I would show her the land of my past as she was showing me hers. We would enter the Aegean in a white ship, the belly of a cloud. Though she will be the foreigner, agape at an unfamiliar landscape, her body will take to it like a vow. She'll turn brown, her angles gleaming with oil. *A white dress shines against her thighs like rain.*

"My parents took to the highway at the least opportunity. Not only in summer, but in winter, in any weather. We drove north from Montreal, west to Rouyn-Noranda and further, to an esker forest, and to an island. . . . The further north you drive, the more compelling the power of the metal in the ground. . . ."

As a child, in the speeding night car, her face against the cold rear window, she imagined she could feel the pull between the stars and the mines, a metal dependency of concepts she didn't understand: magnetism, orbits. She imagined the stars straying too close to the earth and being forced to the ground. Windows open, highway air against summer skin, her bathing suit still damp under her shorts, sometimes sitting on a towel. She loved those nights. The dark shapes of her parents in the front seat.

"On the island the harbour stores smelled of wool and mothballs, chocolate and rubber. My mother and I bought cotton sunhats there. We bought old boardgames and jigsaw puzzles of bridges and sunsets; the cardboard pieces always seemed slightly soggy. . . . The pioneer museum made me afraid of ghosts of Indians and settlers and the spirits of hunted animals. I saw the clothes of men and women who hadn't been much taller than me, even when I was only ten or eleven. Jakob, their small clothes terrified me! There's a legend, that the Manitoulins once burned the island down to soil, destroying the forest and their own settlements, in order to dislodge a spirit. To save themselves, they set fire to their homes. I had nightmares of men running through the forest, a trail of torches. The island was supposed to have been purified, but I worried that the spirit was planning its revenge. I think a child knows intuitively that it's the most sacred places that are the most frightening. . . . But there was also a happiness on the island that I've never been able to recreate. Meals outside, lanterns, glasses filled with juice that had been chilled in the lake. I taught myself about root systems and mosses, I read Steinbeck's *The Red Pony* on the screened porch. We rowed. My father taught me new words that I imagined were followed by an exclamation mark representing his pointing finger: cirrus! cumulus! stratonimbus! When we were up north my father wore canvas shoes. My mother wore a scarf over her hair. . . ."

Just as Michaela is wearing, as she tells me these stories. The fabric outlining her profile, drawing out her cheekbones.

"Later, when I returned to those places, especially the beaches of the North Channel – as an adult driving north alone – I felt there was someone with me in the car. It was strange, Jakob, as if an extra self was with me. Very young or very old."

As she talks, we pass through deserted lakeside towns, sand drifting across the road from the spring beach. The poignancy of northern resort towns in off-season silence. Porches heaped with firewood, toys, old furniture; glimpses of lives. Towns that wake briefly for the short weeks of hot weather, like flowering cereus. And I can't breathe for fear of losing her. But the moment passes. From Espanola to Sudbury, the quartzite hills absorb the pink evening light like blotting paper, then pale under the moon.

Finally, Michaela takes me to one of the meccas of her childhood, a birch forest growing out of white sand.

This is where I become irrevocably unmoored. The river floods. I slip free the knot and float, suspended in the present.

We sleep among the wet birches, nothing between us and the storm except the fragile nylon skin of the tent, a glowing dome in the blackness. Wind rolls in from the distance, catches in the high antennae of branches then rolls past us into the rain, full of electricity. I cover Michaela, inside the sleeping bag, conscious of the tent as if it were a wet shirt against my back. Lightning. But we are grounded.

She rises to me unhesitatingly. What does the body make us believe? That we're never ourselves until we contain two souls. For years corporeality made me believe in death. Now, inside Michaela yet watching her, death for the first time makes me believe in the body.

As the wind gathers in the trees and then moves on, rippling through the forest, I disappear in her. Glinting seeds scatter in her dark blood. Bright leaves into the night wind; stars on the starless night. We are the only ones foolish enough to be sleeping out in the April storm. In the shaking tent Michaela tells me stories, my ear on her heart until, with the rain against the frail nylon, we sleep.

When we wake, there is pool of water by our feet. It is not on Idhra or on Zakynthos but among Michaela's birches that I feel for the first time safe above ground, earthed in a storm.

~

Accessible from only one harbour, one angle, Idhra has a crooked spine, its head turned away. We lean against the railing, my arms around Michaela's waist. The ship's flag grabs at twilight. Heat washes away under the rushing fountain of stars.

On Idhra spring stirs like a young woman after her first night of love, adrift between an old life and a new. Sixteen years a girl and two hours a woman, that's how Greece wakes from winter. One afternoon the colour of light sets, a glaze hardening on ceramic.

Olive leaves store the sun relentlessly, the strong Greek sun, until they become so dense in colour that the green turns purple, the leaves bruised by their own greed. Until they become so dark they can take in no more and, shiny, reflect the light like smoky mirrors.

High in the blue air, the light splashes like scented oil over skin. We are sticky with the musk of grapes and salt water. Michaela, clothed in summer heat, grinds coffee, sets out honey and figs.

Michaela forgets her body for hours at a time. I love to watch her while she's thinking or reading, her head leaning on her hand. On the floor or in a chair, her limbs abandoned to gravity. The more intense her concentration, the more abstract the problem she contemplates, the further her body roams. Down long roads, her legs swinging, or across open water, her hair wandering down her back. This is her body's truancy, its mischievousness. Freed from Michaela's disciplining mind, it runs away, goes outdoors. When she looks up and catches me watching her, or simply stops reading – "Jakob, Hawthorne actually pretended to be ill so he could stay home and read Carlyle's essay on heroes" – her body is there again, reappearing suddenly in the chair. And I feel deep appreciation for those heavy, sneaky limbs that have defied her mind's authority without it knowing.

She looks at me, all presence. While her body and I share our delicious secret.

Listening to Michaela read, I remember how Bella read poetry; how the yearning in her voice reached me as a child, though I didn't understand the feeling. I realize, half a century after her death, that though my sister never felt herself moving in a man's hands, she must have already loved so deeply, so secretly,.that she knew something about the other half of her soul. This is one of Michaela's blessings. Michaela, who pauses, because it has just occurred to her: "Do you realize Beethoven composed all his music without ever having looked upon the sea?"

~

Each morning I write these words for you all. For Bella and Athos, for Alex, for Maurice and Irena, for Michaela. Here on Idhra, in this summer of 1992, I try to set down the past in the cramped space of a prayer.

In the afternoons I search Michaela for fugitive scents. Basil on her fingers, garlic transferred from fingers to a stray hair; sweat from her forehead to her forearm. Following a path of tarragon as if carried by long division from one column to another, I trace her day, coconut oil on her shoulders, high grass sticking to her sea-damp feet.

We light the storm lamps, accompanied by the sound of cicadas, and she tells me plots of novels, history, childhood stories. We read to each other, eat and drink. Fresh fish bought from the village with domates baked in olive oil and thyme; eggplant and anginares grilled and soaked in lemon. *On a table graced with stillness and smells, the wild order of plums*.

Sometimes Mrs. Karouzos's son climbs up from the town to bring gifts from his mother "for old Jakob and his young bride": bread, olives, wine. Manos sits with us in the evenings, and the faint decorum he brings to our table sharpens my desire. I look at their faces across the table. Our guest's gentle privacy, his restrained affection, and Michaela, bursting with health and radiating pleasure, looking – is it possible? – like a woman well loved.

I watch Michaela bake a pie. She smiles and tells me that her mother used to roll the pastry this way. Unknowingly, her hands carry my memories. I remember my mother teaching Bella in the kitchen. Michaela says: "My mother used to cut the dough this way, which she learned from her aunt, you know, the one who married the man who had a brother in New York. . . ." On and on, casually, offhand, Michaela's mother's stories of relatives from the next town, from across the ocean, unroll like the crust. The bold dress cousin Pashka wore to her niece's wedding. The cousin who met and married a girl in America but she came from his own home town, can you believe it, he had to travel halfway around the world just to meet the neighbour's daughter. . . . I remember my mother urging Bella not to reveal the secret ingredients of her honey cake – the envy of Mrs. Alperstein – not ever, except to her own daughter, God willing. A few tablespoons of porridge so it will be smooth and moist as cream, and honey from acacias so the cake will come out golden. . . . Remembering this, I think of the ancient Japanese sword-makers who recited stories as they folded the steel – bending it thousands of times for strength and flexibility – stories timed to accompany the tempering process. So that when they fell silent, the steel was ready; the stories a precise recipe. I'm missing what Michaela's telling me, a family story about a wife who finally throws the kettle at the husband, because I'm remembering how my mother sometimes chastised Bella for her temper: "Tough birds are only good for soup," "If you're thinking bad thoughts the cake won't rise" – and here's Michaela cajoling the dough as she puts it in the oven, whispering to her pie to come out just right.

There's no absence, if there remains even the memory of absence. Memory dies unless it's given a use. Or as Athos might have said: If one no longer has land but has the memory of land, then one can make a map.

～

Now I'm not afraid when harvesting darkness. I dig with my eyes into the night bedroom, Michaela's clothes tangled with mine, books and shoes. A brass lamp from a ship's cabin, from Maurice and Irena. Objects turn to relics before my eyes.

Night after night my happiness wakes me. Sometimes, asleep, the pressure of Michaela's leg against mine translates into a dream as warmth, sunlight. Stilled by light.

~

Silence: the response to both emptiness and fullness.

The lamplight casts us in bronze. In the yellow pool waking the dark, one stares, one sleeps, both dream. The world goes on because someone's awake somewhere. If, by accident, a moment were to occur when everyone was asleep, the world would disappear. It would whirlpool into dream or nightmare, tripped by memory. It would collapse to a place where the body's simply a generator for the soul, a factory of longing.

We define a man by what he admires, what raises him.

All things aspire, even if only atomically. A body will rise quietly until caught by the surface. Then the moon pulls it to shore.

I pray that soon my wife will feel new breath inside her own. I press my head against Michaela's side and whisper a story to her flat belly.

Child I long for: if we conceive you, if you are born, if you reach the age I am now, sixty, I say this to you: Light the lamps but do not look for us. Think of us sometimes, your mother and me, while you're in your house with the fruit trees and the slightly wild garden, a small wooden table in the yard. You, my son, Bela, living in an old city, your balcony overlooking medieval street-stones. Or you, Bella, my daughter, in your house overlooking a river;

or on an island of white, blue, and green where the sea follows you everywhere. When it rains, think of us as you walk under dripping trees or through small rooms lit only by a storm.

Light the lamp, cut a long wick. One day when you've almost forgotten, I pray you'll let us return. That through an open window, even in the middle of a city, the sea air of our marriage will find you. I pray that one day in a room lit only by night snow, you will suddenly know how miraculous is your parents' love for each other.

My son, my daughter: May you never be deaf to love.

Bela, Bella: Once I was lost in a forest. I was so afraid. My blood pounded in my chest and I knew my heart's strength would soon be exhausted. I saved myself without thinking. I grasped the two syllables closest to me, and replaced my heartbeat with your name.

II

THE DROWNED CITY

The Humber River flows southeast across the city. Even a generation ago, for most of its one-hundred-kilometre course it was still a rural river, meandering through outskirts, casually linking lonely boroughs like Weston and Lambton Woods to the city downstream. For three thousand years, isolated communities, mills, and palisades were scattered along its banks.

Over time, the growth of the city could be measured by travelling upriver. As Toronto expanded, suburbs slowly spread north, filling up the wide, grassy floodplain, until even secluded communities such as Weston were embraced by the metropolis. The houses closest to the Humber cleaved to the river, nestled among cottonwood, box elder, and bur oak. Plover and blue heron wandered in back yards, among impatiens and wild grape.

Today much of the riverbank again looks as it did before the encroachment of the city. The riverine marshes, the serpentine lower reaches, are inhabited only by painted turtles and mallard ducks. The deserted plains of Weston are gentle parkland; lawn grows peacefully to the river's edge.

If you descend the short, steep bank to the water, you'll see, past the glinting surface, the river bottom glinting too. If you turn around to look at the muddy escarpment, or simply look down at your feet, you'll begin to notice the Humber's distinctive sediment, laid down in October 1954.

In the bank, four wooden knobs, evenly spaced: excavate an inch or two and the legs of a chair will emerge. A few feet downriver, a dinner plate – perhaps with the familiar and ever-popular blue willow pattern – sticks out of the bank horizontally like a shelf. You can slip a silver spoon out of the mud like a bookmark.

The books and photos have rotted by now, but the buried tables and shelves, lamps, dishes, and rugs remain. The river washes over pebbles of crockery. Fragments of a ceramic flowered border, or of the words "Staffordshire, England," are underlined by reeds.

Hidden beneath the grass, all around you, the wide, silent park is studded with cutlery.

∾

The humidity is a dense current; slow as dream time. Naomi comes from an icy shower; her skin condenses in the hot air. She lies on top of me, heavy and cold as wet sand.

You must abandon your illusions every time you speak.

It's only five o'clock but the sky is a dark front; the ions that smell always of night.

The summer we were married there was a heat wave like this, the air a blanket, cling wrap. Every inch of us slick with sweat. My shirts turning sheer and limp. We kept our small apartment in perpetual twilight, curtains drawn against it; the heat and dark were excuses to stay undressed. Like the Invisible Man, seen only by virtue of the gauze he's wrapped in, Naomi moved from room to room, her white cotton underwear glowing in the dimness.

For over a week it had been too oppressive to sleep. We drifted until morning, every few hours one re-entering the consciousness of the other, returning from the kitchen silent as a messenger through the forest. Framed by the light in the hall, Naomi's body pouring heat, carrying a glass of juice so cold its flavour was a mystery. Frozen from holding the glass, my hands on the scalding small of her back; until she whispered, "Ben," a chill rising through her. Or she rolled plums from the fridge, frosted blue ovals, along my arms to my mouth, so icy they made my teeth hurt; plum juice drying in brown tears down her neck, her skin stiffening with sweetness. Or one of us with face or feet under the faucet, the other slipping back into sleep, to the dream sound of far-off, mill-borne water.

Sometimes, even at the last, at the end of a long Sunday when we'd both been working at home, after she'd ordered fast food, which we ate without a word of importance between us, after the greasy cartons had been tossed into the sink or into the bin so we wouldn't have to look in the morning at the remains of what we'd consumed, we turned to each other in the dark, still silent, until she was a climber on a rock face, limbs precise, pinned against space, until with closed eyes she looked down between her legs from a height, and then I didn't move and meaning flooded us. Before sleep her muscles twitched, a mechanism released. Soon I felt her against me, breathing with the steady intensity of a machine.

We slept close, knowing we could not have such pleasure without such muteness.

~

There was no energy of a narrative in my family, not even the fervour of an elegy. Instead, our words drifted away, as if our home were open to the elements and we were forever whispering into a strong wind. My parents and I waded through damp silence, of not hearing and not speaking. It soaked into the furniture, into my father's dank armchair, a mildew in the walls. We communicated by slight gestures, surgeons in an operating theatre. When my parents died, I realized I'd expected sound suddenly to enter the apartment, to rush into the place so long prohibited. But no sound came into the apartment. And though I was alone, packing boxes, sorting their belongings, the silence was now eerie. Because the place itself felt almost the same as before.

I was surprised to discover not everyone sees the shadow around objects, the black outline, the bruise of fermentation on things even as light clings to them. I saw the aura of mortality like a snake that sees its prey in infrared, the pulse-heat. It was clear to me as cut fruit turning brown on the plate, a lemon peel shrivelling to scent.

I grew up thankful for every necessity, for food and drink, for my father's well-made shoes – "the most important thing." I was thankful for the whiskers that appeared on my father's face each morning because it was, he said, "a sign of health." When my parents were liberated, four years before I was born, they found that the ordinary world outside the camp had been eradicated. There was no more simple meal, no thing was less than extraordinary: a fork, a mattress, a clean shirt, a book. Not to mention such things that can make one weep: an orange, meat and vegetables, hot water. There was no ordinariness to return to, no refuge from the blinding potency of things, an apple screaming its sweet juice. Every thing belonged to, had been retrieved from, impossibility – both the inorganic and the organic – shoes and socks, their own flesh. It was all as one. And this gratitude included the inexpressible. Not more than five years old, watching my mother proud in her gardening gloves, by the roses. Even then I knew I would want for this all my life: my mother stooping to pull up weeds, sunlight, an endless day.

Even younger, I was visited by an angel in the middle of the night. She stood like a nurse at the foot of my bed and wouldn't go away. My eyes hurt from staring. She motioned to me. I went to the window to look out at the winter street, my first recognition of beauty, an ice forest, with the fineness of etched silver, in the streetlamp light. The angel was sent to wake me, so I wouldn't sleep past that vision into morning; and the sight put a temporary end to nightmares of doors axed open and the jagged mouths of dogs. I finally understood the meaning of that winter night and that moment with my mother in the garden, Jakob Beer, when I read your poems. You described your first experience of the flesh of a sleeping woman as alive, sudden as if you'd surfaced into air from under water, breathing for the first time.

When we finally met, at Irena's birthday party that late-January night, I saw that Maurice Salman hadn't exaggerated. He'd described you and Michaela perfectly – ouzo and water. Separately, clear and strong; together, you both turned cloudy. The mystery, said Salman, of two people who share "an impressive physical life." You know Salman! When he talks about you his eyes go small. He settles himself in his chair like a boulder on a beach. The sublime's his slang. What a charming combination of acuity and corn. He speaks piercingly of passion yet wears the look of a sneaky lover planning a flat tire or an empty gas tank. Straight out of the old movies he adores. He's like someone who offers an astonishing and expensive wine, then brings out a plate of peanut brittle to go with it. Perhaps I exaggerate. Salman gives the impression of offhand hyperbole but, in fact, he's astute and precise.

I'd never heard of you until, in class, Salman recommended your book of poems, *Groundwork*, and recited the opening lines. Later I saw that the book was dedicated to the memory of your parents and your sister, Bella. *My love for my family has grown for years in decay-fed soil, an unwashed root pulled suddenly from the ground. Bulbous as a beet, a huge eye under a lid of earth. Scoop out the eye, blind the earth.*

I know that the more one loves a man's words, the more one can assume he's put everything into his work that he couldn't put into his life. The relation between a man's behaviour and his words is usually that of gristle and fat on the bone of meaning. But, in your case, there seemed to be no gap between the poems and the man. How could it be otherwise, for a man who claimed to believe so completely in language? Who knew that even one letter – like the "J" stamped on a passport – could have the power of life or death.

In your later poems, it's as if history reads over our shoulder, casts its shadow on the page, but is no longer in the words themselves. It's as if you'd decided something, made a deal with your conscience. I wanted to believe language itself had freed you. But the night we met I knew it wasn't language that had released you. Only a remarkably simple truth or a remarkably simple lie could put such peace in a man. The mystery darkened in me. A birthmark in my own pallor of disorder.

And I knew I was standing on the bank watching, while you, long escaped from dusty rock, lay between the wet thighs of the river.

That night at Salman's your serenity was so profound it could only be described as sensual. Experience had wrung excess from you. Or as a geologist might say, you'd reached the pure state of residual concentration. One couldn't help but feel the force of your presence, your hand heavy as a cat on Michaela's thigh. What is love at first sight but the response of a soul crying out with sudden regret because it realizes it has never before been recognized? Of course Naomi was moved, and soon was telling you about her parents, her family. Naomi, usually so shy, spoke about the last summer with her dying father at the lake, then about my parents – for which I found myself not annoyed but curiously grateful. Tell him, I thought, tell him everything.

You listened, not like a priest who listens for sin, but like a sinner, who listens for his own redemption. What a gift you had for making one feel clear, for making one feel – clean. As if talk could actually heal. All the while with one hand touching Michaela somewhere, on her shoulder or forearm, or holding her hand. Your eyes with us, your body with her. Only once did Naomi pause, suddenly self-conscious, to say that perhaps you thought her foolish, visiting their graves so often, bringing flowers. To which you gave your unforgettable reply: "On the contrary. It seems right to keep bringing them something beautiful now and then." And I saw gratitude on Naomi's face it pains me to remember, because I'd been so annoyed with her for those visits – *my* parents! – accusing her of every pathology, of not being able to get over her own parents' deaths, of needing to live in mourning since she was eighteen. Characteristically, she didn't repeat your comment afterwards. No one's silences are more generous than Naomi's, who rarely clamps her jaw with frustration or anger (these come out in tears); her silence is usually wise. I was often thankful for this, especially in the months before I left, when Naomi spoke less and less.

By the time we were leaving Salman's that night and Naomi was pushing her arms into the sleeves of her coat, my wife's transformation was invisible yet obvious. Your conversation had wrought a change in her body. And I saw

Naomi's pleasure as Michaela admired her coat and scarf, and her flushed face when you shook her hand goodnight.

I learned something else that evening, about Maurice Salman and his wife. I saw them standing together by the window. She's so small, an impeccable package, expensive shoes, silk blouse, a face that elongates into sadness. Salman held her elbow like a teacup in his paw. He carried her sweater on his enormous suited arm, handkerchief on an elephant's back. One small gesture: she reached up, her child palm on the flatness of his huge cheek. She touched him as if he were the thinnest porcelain.

When I was at university, *Bearing False Witness* had just been reissued, thick as a small dictionary. Salman had already introduced his students to Athos's lyric geology via the salt book. Athos's impassioned descriptions – what a splendid anthropomorphist – even down to the generosity of an ionic bond. To believe there's no thing that does not yearn. Dramatic and slow earth events as well as the rise of human commerce and culture, all an evolution of longing. How could you not have been shaped by such storytelling? You were fortunate to be trained by a master. When you turned your attention to your own poems, in your *Groundwork*, and you recount the geology of the mass graves, it's as if we hear the earth speak.

I could smell the loneliness in Salman after your death, the specific loneliness that is between men, that is like no other. Salman reminisced – anecdotes about your twenties, how you walked together all night through the city, in every season, talking at first about Athos's work and then about poetry and finally about Salman's wounds though not about yours (not for many years). Stopping at the twenty-four-hour restaurant exhausted and hot, or exhausted and chilled, for pie and coffee, parting at two a.m., saying goodbye in the empty street. Salman watched you walk along St. Clair Avenue to your apartment where you lived alone after Athos died, and again years later after your first marriage ended, how disheartened you looked. . . . Salman told me about your habits, your trustworthiness, your moral seriousness. Your depressions. He told me about the perfection of Michaela, your new wife.

"Ben, when we say we're looking for a spiritual adviser, we're really looking for someone to tell us what to do with our bodies. Decisions of the flesh. We forget to learn from pleasure as well as pain," said Salman after you died. "Jakob taught me so many things. For instance: What is the true value of knowledge? That it makes our ignorance more precise. When God asked the Jews in the desert to choose no other God, he wasn't asking them to choose one God over another, but rather: choose one God or none. Jakob put great store in the incisiveness of dilemmas. You recall the opening image in his *Dilemma Poems*, one man staring at an impossibly high wall, another man staring at the same wall from the other side. . . . I remember someone at one of our parties talking about particle/wave duality. After a while Jakob said: 'Perhaps it's just that when light is up against the wall it's forced to choose.' Everyone laughed, listen to the layman talk about physics! But I knew what Jakob meant. The particle is secular man; the wave, the deist. And whether you live by a lie or live by a truth makes no difference, as long as you get past the wall.

And while some are motivated by love (those who choose), most are motivated by fear (those who choose by not choosing). Then Jakob said: 'Perhaps the electron is neither particle nor wave but something else instead, much less simple – a dissonance – like grief, whose pain is love.'"

~

We think of weather as transient, changeable, and above all, ephemeral; but everywhere nature remembers. Trees, for example, carry the memory of rainfall. In their rings we read ancient weather – storms, sunlight, and temperatures, the growing seasons of centuries. A forest shares a history, which each tree remembers even after it has been felled.

Only Maurice Salman, or Athos Roussos, would look at a student who can't decide between an interest in the history of meteorology and in literature and say: "Why not find a way to keep studying both? In some cultures a man has more than one wife. . . ." Naively, I told Salman that a formal comparison could be made between a weather map and a poem. I told him that I wanted to call my literature thesis "A Line of Weather." Afterwards, I stepped from Salman's office into the street; the October twilight was radiant with a pure pale gegenschein. I walked home, wishing for someone with whom I could share my news, wishing there was a woman waiting for me, so I could slip my cold hands under her sweater, across her warm skin, and explain what Salman had suggested instead for my thesis: the real-life objective correlative – weather and biography.

Years later when I turned my thesis into a book,

Naomi nourished my research. . . . A severe December morning in St. Petersburg, 1849. Horse-whinny hangs whitely in the air, the jangle of traces; steaming manure, wet leather, and snow. I climb from the prison coach and follow Dostoyevsky into the gelid orange light of Semyonovsky Square. He shivers in the spring coat he'd been arrested in months before, his nose turning red against waxy cheeks, pale from incarceration. Blindfolded, he and the other supposed Petrashevsky radicals are lined up to be executed in the bitter winter wind. I stare hard into his face. Even under the blindfold, his transformation is obvious. The guns are cocked. Each man experiences the bullet breaking open his chest, the hot bite, the staggering fist the size of a child's finger. Then the blindfolds are removed. Never before have I seen faces to match those, with the bare revelation that still they live, that there has been no shot. I fall with the weight of life; that is, with the weight of Dostoyevsky's life, which unfolds from that moment with the intensity of a man who begins again.

While I travelled across Russia in leg-irons, Naomi carefully placed ivory potatoes, cooked until they crumbled at the touch of a fork, into chilled vermilion borscht. While I fell to my knees with hunger in the snow at Tobol'sk, downstairs Naomi sliced thick slabs of stone-heavy bread. These edible jokes I termed the "culinary correlative." I spent afternoons in Staraya Russa, then came downstairs to a supper of sweet cabbage soup.

Reading weather is one thing: all the expected examples of thunderstorms and avalanches, blizzards and heat waves, monsoons. *The Tempest*, the blasted heath in *King Lear*. Camus's sunstroke in *The Stranger*. Tolstoy's snowstorm in "Master and Man." Your *Hotel Rain* poems. But biography. . . . The snowstorm that detained Pasternak in a dacha, where he fell in love while listening to Maria Yudino play Chopin ("Snow swept over the earth . . . the candle burned . . ."). Madame Curie refusing to come out of the rain when she heard the news of her husband's death. The Greek summer heat while the war boiled out of you like a fever. Dostoyevsky was the first example I thought of; his brutal convict march to Siberia. The prisoners stopped at Tobol'sk, where the old peasant women took pity on them. The good women stood on the banks of the Irtysh River, thirty below, and gave them bundles of tea, candles, cigars, and a copy of the New Testament with a ten-ruble note sewn into the binding. In this state of extremity, their charity permanently entered Dostoyevsky's heart. In the howling sunset and the pastel snow, the women shouted blessings for the journey to the pitiful caravan of prisoners, a slack rope drawing its line across the white landscape, the wind biting their skin through their thin clothes. And Dostoyevsky trudged on, wondering how it could be too late, so early in his life.

∼

The memories we elude catch up to us, overtake us like a shadow. A truth appears suddenly in the middle of a thought, a hair on a lens.

My father found the apple in the garbage. It was rotten

and I'd thrown it out – I was eight or nine. He fished it from the bin, sought me in my room, grabbed me tight by the shoulder, and pushed the apple to my face.

"What is this? What is it?"
"An apple – "

My mother kept food in her purse. My father ate frequently to avoid the first twists of hunger because, once they gripped him, he'd eat until he was sick. Then he ate dutifully, methodically, tears streaming down his face, animal and spirit in such raw evidence, knowing he was degrading both. If one needs proof of the soul, it's easily found. The spirit is most evident at the point of extreme bodily humiliation. There was no pleasure, for my father, associated with food. It was years before I realized this wasn't merely a psychological difficulty, but also a moral one, for who could answer my father's question: Knowing what he knew, should he stuff himself, or starve?

"An apple! Well, my smart son, is an apple food?"
"It was all rotten – "

On Sunday afternoons we'd drive into the farmland bordering the city or to their favourite park at the edge of Lake Ontario. My father always wore a cap to keep his few stray hairs from flying into his eyes. He drove with both hands gripping the wheel, never violating the speed limit. I slouched in the back seat, learning Morse code from the *The Boy Electrician*, or memorizing the Beaufort Scale

("Wind force 0: smoke rises vertically, sea like a mirror, Force 5: small trees sway, whitecaps. Force 6: umbrellas used with difficulty. Force 9: structural damage occurs."). Once in a while my mother's arm would appear over the front seat, a roll of candy dangling from her hand.

My parents would unfold their lawnchairs (even in winter) while I scrambled out alone, collecting rocks or identifying clouds or counting waves. I lay on grass or sand, reading, sometimes falling asleep in my heavy jacket under a clay sky with *The Moonstone* or *Men Against the Sea* with its waterspouts and volcanoes ("I cannot recall the hours that followed without experiencing something of the horror I felt at the time. Wind and rain, rain and wind, under a sky that held no promise of relief. In all that time, Mr. Bligh did not leave the tiller, and he seemed to have an exhilaration of mind that grew greater as our peril increased . . ."). In good weather my mother set out the lunch she'd prepared, and they sipped strong tea from a thermos while the wind searched through the cold lake and cumulus chuffed across the horizon.

Early Sunday evenings, while my mother made dinner, I listened to music with my father in the living room. Watching him listen made me listen differently. His attention dissolved each piece to its theoretical components like an X-ray, emotion the grey fog of flesh. He used orchestras – other people's arms and hands and breath – to signal me; a wordless entreaty, all meaning pressed into chords. Leaning against him, his arm around me – or, when I was very young, lying with my head on his lap – his hand on my hair absentmindedly but, for me, feral. He stroked my hair to Shostakovich, Prokofiev, Beethoven, Mahler's lieder: "Now all longing wants to dream," "I have become a stranger in the world."

Those hours, wordless and close, shaped my sense of him. Lines of last light over the floor, the patterned sofa, the silky brocade of the curtains. Once in a while, on summer Sundays, the shadow of an insect or bird over the sun-soaked carpet. I breathed him in. The story of his life as I knew it from my mother – strange episodic images – and his stories of composers, merged together with the music. Cow breath and cow dung and fresh hay on Mahler's muddy night road home, moonlight a spiderweb over the fields. Under the same moonlight, marching back to the camp, my father's tongue a thong of wool; unbearably thirsty as he walked at gunpoint, past a bucket of rain-water, its small circular mirror of stars. Praying for rain so they could swallow what fell on their faces, rain that smelled like sweat. How he ate the centre of a cabbage in a farmer's field, leaving it hollow but looking whole so no one would trace his escape from the soldiers in the grove.

I looked up from my father's lap to his concentrating face. He always listened with his eyes open. Beethoven with the storm of the Sixth in his face, pacing in the forest and fields of Heiligenstadt, the real storm at his back, at my father's back, mud weighing down his feet like overshoes, the shrill, desperate cry of a bird in the rainy trees. My father concentrating, during one long march, on a sliver in his hand, to keep his thoughts from his parents. I felt my skull under his fingers as he combed through my short hair. Beethoven frightening oxen with his windmill-waving arms, then stopping stock-still to look at the sky.

My father staring at a lunar eclipse beside the chimneys, or staring at the sun's dead light like scum on the potholes. The gun in my father's face, how they kept nudging with their boots the cup of water from his reach.

As long as the symphony lasted, the song cycle, the quartet, I had access to him. I could pretend his attention to the music was attention to me. His favourite pieces were familiar, finite journeys we took together, recognizing signposts of ritardando and sostenuto, key changes. Sometimes he played a recording by a different conductor and I experienced the acuity of his ears as he compared interpretations: "Ben, do you hear how he rushes the arpeggios." "Listen to how he draws it out . . . but if he emphasizes here, he'll ruin the crescendo later on!" And the following week we'd go back to the version we knew and loved like a face, a place. A photograph.

His absent fingers combing through my short hair. Music, inseparable from his touch.

Feeling the lines of my father's thin legs under his trousers, barely believing they were the same legs that walked those distances, stood those hours. In our Toronto apartment, images of Europe, postcards from another planet. His only brother, my uncle, whose body vanished under a squirming skin of lice. Instead of hearing about ogres, trolls, witches, I heard disjointed references to kapos, haftlings, "Ess Ess," dark woods; a pyre of dark words. Beethoven, wandering in old clothes, so shabby his neighbours nicknamed him Robinson Crusoe; the shifting wind before a storm, leaves cowering before the slap of rain, the Sixth, Opus 68; the Ninth, Opus 125. All the symphony and opus numbers I learned, to please him.

That grew in my memory, under his fingers as he stroked my hair; the hair on his arm, his number close to my face.

Even my father's humour was silent. He drew things for me, cartoons, caricatures. Appliances with human faces. His drawings offered the glimpse: how he saw.

"Is an apple food?"

"Yes."

"And you throw away food? You – my son – you throw away food?"

"It's rotten –"

"Eat it. . . . Eat it!"

"Pa, it's rotten – I won't –"

He pushed it into my teeth until I opened my jaw. Struggling, sobbing, I ate. Its brown taste, oversweetness, tears. Years later, living on my own, if I threw out leftovers or left food on my plate in a restaurant, I was haunted by pathetic cartoon scraps in my sleep.

Images brand you, burn the surrounding skin, leave their black mark. Like volcanic ash, they can make the most potent soil. Out of the seared place emerge sharp green shoots. The images my father planted in me were an exchange of vows. He passed the book or magazine to me silently. He pointed a finger. Looking, like listening, was a discipline. What was I to make of the horror of those photos, safe in my room with the cowboy curtains and my rock collection? He thrust books at me with a ferocity that frightened me, I would say now, more than the images themselves. What I was to make of them, in my safe room, was clear. You are not too young. There were hundreds of thousands younger than you.

I dreaded my piano lessons with my father and never practised when he was home. His demand for perfection had the force of a moral imperative, each correct note setting order against chaos, a goal as impossible as rebuilding a bombed city, atom by atom. As a child I did not feel this as evidence of faith or even anything as positive as a summoning of will. Instead I absorbed it as kind of futility. All my sincere efforts only succeeded in displeasing him. My fugues and tarantellas unravelled in the middle, my bourrées clumped along, so aware was I of my father's uncompromising ear. Eventually his abrupt dismissals of me in the middle of a piece, my unhappiness, and my mother's pleading at us both, convinced my father to give up instructing me. Not long after our final lesson, on one of our Sundays at the lake, my father and I were walking along the shore when he noticed a small rock shaped like a bird. When he picked it up, I saw the quick gleam of satisfaction in his face and felt in an instant that I had less power to please him than a stone.

When I was eleven, my parents rented a cottage for the last two weeks of the summer. I'd never before experienced absolute darkness. Waking at night, I thought I'd gone blind in my sleep – any child's terror. But made palpable by the dark was another old fear. I lowered my legs and thrust my arms into the dangerous air until I found the lamp. This was a test. I knew it was essential to be strong. After nights of sleeping with a flashlight in my fist, I made a decision. I forced myself out of bed, put on my sneakers, and went outside. My task was to walk through the woods with the flashlight off until I reached the road, about a quarter of a mile away. If my father could walk days, miles, then I could walk at least to the road. What would happen to me if I had to walk as far as my father had? I was in training. My flannel pyjamas were clammy with sweat. I walked with useless eyes and heard the river, modest knife of history, carving its blade deeper into the earth; rusty blood seeping through the cracked face of the forest. A fine mesh of insects on the heavy breath of the night, the slap of ferns weirdly cold against my ankles – nothing alive could be so cold on such a hot night. Slowly the trees began to emerge from the differentiated dark, as if embossed, black on black, and the dark itself was a pale skin stretched across charred ribs. Above, the far surf of leaves, a dark skirt of sky rustling against skeletal legs. Strange filaments from nowhere, the hair of ghosts, brushed my neck and cheeks and would not be rubbed away. The forest closed around me like a hag's embrace, all hair and hot breath, bristly skin and sharp fingernails. And just as I felt overwhelmed, sick with terror, suddenly I was in clear space, a faint breeze over the wide road. I turned on the flashlight and followed, running, its white tunnel back along the path.

In the morning I saw my legs were smeared with mud and tea-coloured blood from bites and branches. The rest of the day I discovered scratches in strange places, behind my ears, or along the inside of my arm, a thin line of blood as if drawn by red pen. I was certain that the ordeal had purged my fear. But I woke again that night in the same state, my bones cold as steel. Twice more I repeated the journey, forcing myself to face the darkness of the woods. But I still couldn't bear the darkness of my own room.

When I was twelve, I befriended a Chinese girl not much taller than me, though considerably older. I admired her leather cap, her dark skin, her elaborately twisted hair. Imagine a strand of hair four thousand years old! I also befriended an Irish boy and a Dane. I had discovered the perfectly preserved bog people in *National Geographic*, and derived a fascinated comfort from their preservation. These were not like the bodies in the photos my father showed me. I drew the aromatic earth over my shoulders, the peaceful spongy blanket of peat. I see now that my fascination wasn't archaeology or even forensics: it was biography. The faces that stared at me across the centuries, with creases in their cheeks like my mother's when she fell asleep on the couch, were the faces of people without names. They stared and waited, mute. It was my responsibility to imagine who they might be.

∾

Like a musical score, when you read a weather map you are reading time. I'm sure, Jakob Beer, that you would agree one could chart a life in terms of pressure zones, fronts, oceanic influences.

The hindsight of biography is as elusive and deductive as long-range forecasting. Guesswork, a hunch. Monitoring probabilities. Assessing the influence of all the information we'll never have, that has never been recorded. The importance not of what's extant, but of what's disappeared. Even the most reticent subject can be – at least in part – posthumously constructed. Henry James, who might be considered coy regarding his personal life, burned all the letters he received. If anyone's interested in me, he said, let them first crack "the invulnerable granite" of my art! But even James was rebuilt, no doubt according to his own design. I'm sure he kept track of the story that would emerge if all the letters to him were omitted. He knew what to leave out. We're stuffed with famous men's lives; soft with the habits of our own. The quest to discover another's psyche, to absorb another's motives as deeply as your own, is a lover's quest. But the search for facts, for places, names, influential events, important conversations and correspondences, political circumstances – all this amounts to nothing if you can't find the assumption your subject lives by.

~

Any details of my parents' lives before they came to Canada I learned from my mother. Afternoons, before my father came home from the music conservatory, the grandmothers and my mother's brothers, Andrei and Max, congregated in the kitchen, where all ghosts like to gather. My father was unaware of these revenant encounters under his roof. Only once do I remember mentioning any member of my father's vanished family in his presence – someone we were talking about at the dinner table was "just like Uncle Josef" – and my father's gaze jolted up from his plate to my mother; a terrifying look. The code of silence became more complex as I grew older. There were more and more things to keep from my father. The secrets between my mother and me were a conspiracy. What was our greatest insurrection? My mother was determined to impress upon me the absolute, inviolate necessity of pleasure.

My mother's painful love for the world. When I witnessed her delight in a colour or a flavour, the most simple gratifications – something sweet, something fresh, a new article of clothing, however humble, her love of warm weather – I didn't disdain her enthusiasm. Instead, I looked again, I tasted again, noticing. I learned that her gratitude was not in the least inordinate. I know now this was her gift to me. For a long time I thought she had created in me an extreme fear of loss – but no. It's not in the least extreme.

Loss is an edge; it swelled everything for my mother, and drained everything from my father. Because of this, I thought my mother was stronger. But now I see it was a clue: what my father had experienced was that much less bearable.

~

As a boy, twisters transfixed me with their bizarre violence, the random precision of their malevolence. Half an apartment building is destroyed, yet an inch away from the vanished wall, the table remains set for dinner. A chequebook is snatched from a pocket. A man opens his front door and is carried two hundred feet above the treetops, landing unharmed. A crate of eggs flies five hundred feet and is set down again, not a shell cracked. All the objects that are transported safely from one place to another in an instant, descending on ascending air currents: a jar of pickles travels twenty-five miles, a mirror, dogs and cats, the blankets ripped from a bed leaving the surprised sleepers untouched. Whole rivers lifted – leaving the riverbed dry – and then set down again. A woman carried sixty feet then deposited in a field next to a phonograph record (unscratched) of "Stormy Weather."

Then there are the whims that are not merciful: children thrown from windows, beards torn from faces, decapitations. The family quietly eating supper when the door bursts open with a roar. The tornado prowls the street, it seems to stroll leisurely, selecting its victims, capricious, the sinister black funnel slithering across the landscape, whining with the sound of a thousand trains.

Sometimes I read to my mother while she made dinner. I read to her about the effects of a Texan tornado, gathering up personal possessions until in the desert it had collected mounds of apples, onions, jewellery, eyeglasses, clothing – "the camp." Enough smashed glass to cover seventeen football fields – "Kristallnacht." I read to her about light-ning – "the sign of the Ess Ess, Ben, on their collars."

From conversations with my mother, when I was eleven or twelve, I learned that "those with a trade had a better chance of survival." I went to the library and found Armac's *The Boy Electrician* and set about acquiring a new vocabu-lary. Capacitors, diodes, voltmeters, induction coils, long-nosed pliers. I raided the "Pageant of Knowledge" series, *Electronics for Beginners*, *The Living World of Science*. Then I realized that knowing the right words might not be enough. Hesitantly I asked my father for money for my first circuit board and a soldering iron. Though he knew little about such things, I wasn't surprised that he saw the use of it and he encouraged my interest for a while. We went together to Esbe Science Supply for toggles and switches and various knobs and dials. For my birthday he bought me a microscope and slides. The rest of my equip-ment I acquired myself: my wet- and dry-bulb hygrometer, Bunsen burner, Z-tubes and funnels, pipettes, conical flasks. My mother generously cleaned out a closet to make room for my laboratory, where I spent hours alone. Even the lab coat she sewed for me from a torn sheet didn't deter me. I wasn't very good at any of it and had to follow a book at all times, having no instinct for electricity or chemistry, but I loved the smell of solder and was amazed when my first circuit lit a bulb in that dim closet.

One summer afternoon a neighbour from down the hall knocked on our door and handed me a Classics Illustrated comic book. My mother was particularly shy of Mr. Dixon, who worked in a men's clothing store and was always immaculately dressed. Mr. Dixon had bought the comic for his grandson, who, it turned out, already had that issue – #105, Jules Verne's *From the Earth to the Moon*. My mother tried to pay him, insistent, until it was clear Mr. Dixon wouldn't accept any money. Then she pressed him with thanks. Meanwhile I was on my way to the balcony, already reading: "When a man is nearly doomed to a lifetime of circling the moon, then survives the plunge of 200,000 odd miles into the Pacific, he learns not to be afraid."

After that, I wrenched money from my mother in order to collect the illustrated versions of literary master-pieces. I devoured each one from the dramatic cover to the last nagging entreaty: "Now that you've read the Classics Illustrated edition, don't miss the added enjoy-ment of reading the original." After consuming the pulp, I even chewed up the rind: edifying essays on a variety of topics filled the final pages. Brief biographies ("Nicholas Copernicus – Key Man in Study of Solar System"), the plots of famous operas, and arcana I've never forgotten. For example, at the back of *Caesar's Conquests*: "There are 6,000 men in a legion"; "Greek ships had eyes painted on their bows so the ships could see"; "Caesar always wrote of himself in the third person."

There was also a series on "Dog Heroes": Brandy, the quick-thinking setter who saved a young boy from a bull.

Foxy, Hero of the Resistance, whose master was hiding from the Hun.

The first comic I bought was a sea adventure by Nordhoff and Hall. I followed the narrator through encounters with hurricanes and mutinies ("'We've seized the ship. . . .' 'What, are you mad, Mr. Churchill?'") I chose *Men Against the Sea* because I opened it and read: "I have asked for pen and paper to write this account of all that has happened . . . to ward off the loneliness already upon me. . . ."

After weeks of importuning, when I was fourteen, my mother agreed to let me go with some school friends to the Canadian National Exhibition, an annual fair. I'd never felt such exhilaration, such unmediated, anonymous belonging as that day in the crowd. Our T-shirts were stained, our hands and the soles of our shoes were sticky – and the whole glutinous throng bubbled over energetically in the August sun. We gaped at colour television, watches that didn't require winding, and were galvanized by the wonders of circuit board technology in the Better Living Building. We toured the midway, shrieked to earth on the Flyer and the Wheel of Fire. When we needed to rest we slung over fences in the agriculture pavilions and watched the sheep-shearing and the milking machines in action. I collected glossy brochures on the latest domestic gadgets to please my mother – floor polishers, electric drink mixers, electric can openers. My shopping bag bulged with cardboard pennants and hats, pens advertising various companies and products, Beehive Corn Syrup scribblers, miniature samples of aftershave and stain remover, boxes of cereal and packets of teabags. We opened our satchels indiscriminately to anything offered to us.

When I came home I excitedly spilled everything onto the table for my mother's inspection. She looked at my bounty, then anxiously crammed it back into the bag. She couldn't believe the things I'd taken were free; she thought I must have made a mistake. She held up a handful of pens and pencils. I shouted, "They gave them away! I swear it! They're called 'free samples' because they're free! . . ." I was hysterical.

My mother made me promise not to show my father, to hide the bag in my room. Early the next morning, I walked to the corner and threw my treasure into a public trash can.

Now we had another kind of bond between us. My mother referred to the incident slyly from time to time. Though she was certain I'd taken these things improperly – admittedly by accident – she would protect me. My fault. Our secret.

From then on I began to extend my boundaries, to make detours on my way home from school. I began to learn about the city. The ravines, the coal elevators, the brickyard. Although I wouldn't have been able to put it into words then, aftermath fascinated me. The silent drama of abandonment of the empty factories and storage bins, the decaying freighters and industrial ruins.

I thought I was encouraging my mother to stop waiting for me by the window or on the balcony, to give me my freedom, not to expect me until late. I'd like to think I didn't know at the time how cruel this was. When my father and I left the apartment in the morning, my mother never felt sure we'd return at all.

I learned not to bring school friends home. I worried that our furniture was old and strange. I was ashamed by my mother's caution and need as she hovered. "What is your last name . . . what do your parents do . . . where were you born . . . ?" My mother begged my father and me for news from our world; news of teachers and classmates, my father's piano students, the personal lives of whom we knew frustratingly little. When she left the apartment for groceries, or in summer to admire the gardens in the neighbourhood (she loved gardening and watched over a window box and trellis on our balcony), my mother prepared carefully. She carried our passports and citizenship papers in her purse "in case of a robbery." She never left a dirty dish in the sink, even if she were just walking to the corner store.

To my mother, pleasure was always serious. She celebrated the aroma each time she unscrewed the lid of the instant coffee. She stopped to inhale each fragrant fold of our freshly washed linens. She could spend half an hour eating a slice of store-bought pastry as if God had baked it with

His Own Hands. Every time she purchased something new, usually a necessity (when an article of clothing had been mended too many times), she fondled it like the First Blouse or the First Pair of Stockings. She was a sensualist of proportions you, Jakob Beer, could never even estimate. You looked at me that night and placed me in your human zoo: another specimen with a beautiful wife; just another academicus dejecticus. But it was you who were embalmed! With your calmness, your expansive satiety.

The truth is you didn't acknowledge me at all that night. But I saw Naomi open like a flower.

I was about to start my second year of university and was determined to be on my own, a fact my mother had refused to accept all summer. One sun-worn August morning I carried my boxes of books down to the damp coolness of the cement parking garage and loaded up the car. My mother retreated behind the closed door of her bedroom. Only when I'd carried out the last box and was really leaving did she emerge. Grimly she prepared a parcel of food, and something was lost between us, irrevocably, the moment that plastic bag passed from her hand to mine. Over the years, the absurd package – enough for a single meal, to stop hunger for a second – was handed to me at the threshold at the end of each visit. Until it hurt less and less and the bag was simply like the roll of candy my mother passed to me from the front seat on our Sunday drives.

The first night in my own apartment, I lay in bed only

a few miles across town and let my mother's phone calls ring into the dark. I didn't call for a week, then weeks at a time, though I knew it made them ill with worry. When I finally did visit, I saw that, though my parents continued in their separate silences, my defection had given them a new intimacy, a new scar. My mother still bent towards me with confidences, but only in order to withdraw them. At first I thought she was punishing me for her need of me. But my mother wasn't angry. My efforts to free myself had created a deeper harm. She was afraid. I believe that for moments my mother actually distrusted me. She would begin a story and then fall silent. "It's nothing that would interest you." When I protested, she suggested I go into the living room and join my father. This happened even more frequently once Naomi entered our lives.

My father's behaviour remained unchanged. When I visited, I still found him either impatient, looking at his watch with desperation, or immobile, staring at a book in his room – another survivor account, another article with photographs. Afterwards, in my apartment on the upper floor of an old house near the university, I stared at the weave of my bedspread, at the bookshelf. At the dry cleaner's, flower shop, and drug store across the street. I knew my parents were awake too, our insomnia an old agreement to keep watch.

On weekends I took long self-pitying walks across the city and back again; at night, ascending into books. I spent most of my undergraduate years alone except for classes and working part time in a bookstore. I had a romance with the assistant manager. We kept on after our first embrace, just to be sure it was as joyless as it seemed. Her form was wondrously full, a firmness to everything, but especially her politics. Under her black caftan she wore shirts with slogans on them past which I never ventured: "The left hand giveth what the right taketh away." Sometimes I joined a few classmates for a meal or a movie, but I made no real effort at friendship.

For a long time I felt I had expended all my energy walking out my parents' front door.

$\sim$

My father was a man who had erased himself as much as possible within the legal limits of citizenship. So I expected a long fight when the time came for him to apply for his seniors' pension, despite the fact that the income was essential to them. I had phoned the appropriate office to find out what documents he needed and had given the information to my mother.

A few weeks later I came for dinner. My father was in his room with the door closed. My mother turned down the heat on the stove and sat at the kitchen table.

"Don't talk to your father about getting his pension anymore."

"We've been through all this – "

"He went there yesterday."

"Good. Finally."

My mother waved a hand at me as if dismissing a fool.

"You think you understand everything. . . . He went to the right place. He had all the right papers with him. He handed his birth certificate to the man at the desk. The man said, 'I know very well the place you were born.' Your father thought the man must have been from there too. But then the man lowered his voice, 'Yes, I was stationed there in 1941 and '42.' The man stared at your father, and then your father understood. The man leaned over his desk and said so quietly your father could barely hear, 'You don't have the right papers.' Your father left as fast as he could. But he didn't come home for hours."

I pushed back my chair.

"Don't, Ben. Leave him alone. If he knows I told you he won't come out of his room for dinner."

I knew he wouldn't come out for dinner anyway. My mother might even have to cancel his classes for a few days.

"You made him go. You talked him into it. You think getting things for free is so easy."

≈

Most discover absence for themselves; trees are ripped out and sorrow floods the clearing. Then we know what we loved.

But I was born into absence. History had left a space already fetid with undergrowth, worms chewing soil abandoned by roots. Rains had made the lowest parts swampy, the green melancholia of bog with its swaying carpet of pollen.

I lived there with my parents. A hiding place, rotted out by grief. Right from the start Naomi seemed to know us. She gave her heart, natural as breathing. But for me, love was like holding my breath.

Naomi stood on firm ground and stretched out her arm. I took her hand but otherwise didn't move.

Naomi didn't recognize her own beauty. Her features were strong, spare, her skin flushed as she spoke, her colour a reliable emotional indicator. She wasn't thin or extravagant, but plush as velvet. She denigrated herself, ignoring the evidence of her athletic legs and full fair hair, wishing she were taller, slimmer, more elegantly shaped; focusing on the slightest bit of flesh she hated above her waistband. As with her physical attributes, Naomi didn't acknowledge the power of her mind, ignoring all she'd read to focus on all she hadn't. Naomi could listen closely and then with painful exactitude come out with a statement that sliced to the heart of things – a swordsman cross-sectioning fruit with one sure flick of the wrist. For instance, in the car on the way home from Maurice Salman's that night. With one deft stroke, Naomi said: "Jakob Beer looks like a man who has finally found the right question."

Shortly after my teaching job at the university became permanent, I began to research my second book, on weather and war. Naomi again threatened to accompany me culinarily, with various bombes and dishes served flambé. But thankfully she decided there was nothing funny about it. The book took its title, *No Mortal Foe*, from a phrase of Trevelyan's. He was referring to the hurricane that destroyed the British naval force during the war with France. Trevelyan was correct in his identification of the real enemy: a hurricane at sea means spray crossing the deck at one hundred miles per hour, a screaming wind that prevents you from breathing, seeing, or standing.

During the First World War, in the Tyrolean Mountains, avalanches were deliberately set off to bury enemy troops. Around this time strategists also thought of creating tornadoes as a weapon, an idea never taken up, only because one couldn't be certain the tornado wouldn't turn against one's own lines.

On his way from Paris to Chartres, Edward III nearly died in a hailstorm. He vowed to the Virgin he'd make peace if he were spared from the giant stones, a promise he kept in the form of the Treaty of Bretigny. England was saved by the storm that destroyed the Spanish Armada. Hailstorms swept five hundred miles through France, ruining the harvest, creating the food shortages that contributed to the French Revolution. Russia's old ally, winter, overcame Napoleon's Grand Army. Tornadoes were created by the firebombing of Hamburg. The military term "front" was borrowed from the weatherman in the First World War. . . .

When the Germans invaded Greece, all weather broadcasts from Athens were deliberately shut down by the RAF and the Greek Forecasting Service. They had to make a hole in the Mediterranean weather map so the Germans wouldn't have the advantage of Greek forecasting for their aerial tactics.

Himmler believed that Germany had the power to alter even the weather of their occupied lands. As he rubbed Polish soil – "now German soil" – between his fingers, he speculated how Aryan settlers would plant trees and "increase dew and (form) clouds, force rain, and thus push a more economically viable climate further towards the East. . . ."

Naomi had audited one of my courses, Forms of Biography. When I first met her, she reminded me of an eccentric sister. In those days, she had a preference for loose clothes that looked as if they'd been borrowed from an older sibling. I found this extremely appealing. It made me want to get at her through her big pockets and up her ample sleeves.

Naomi's apartment was so tiny it was like living in a medicine cabinet. Out of necessity, everything was hidden behind something else, ready to topple. She kept her liquor on a bookshelf behind B for booze, behind Bachelard, Balzac, Benjamin, Berger, Bogan. Scotch was behind Sir Walter. She loved her lame jokes, the lamer the better, sent herself into paroxysms. These antics continued into our married life. On one birthday she created an elaborate treasure hunt, with the last clue leading, of course, to the cake.

Naomi was a fan of 1950s science-fiction movies, which we would often stay up late to watch. She was always on the side of the lonely monster, usually an ordinary creature that had been irradiated and subsequently grew gigantic. She called to the television screen, encouraging the oversized octopus to go ahead and crush the bridge with its expressive tentacles. Naomi claimed that the young woman scientist invariably called to the scene to destroy the atomic squid (or gorilla, spider, or bee) was her secret role model;

the nuclear physicist, the marine biologist, who made a lab coat look sexier than an evening gown.

She loved music and listened to everything, Javanese gamelan, Georgian choirs, medieval hurdy-gurdy. But her pride was her collection of lullabies, from everywhere in the world. Lullabies for the first born, for the child who wants to stay awake with his brother, for the child who's too excited or too frightened to sleep. War-time lullabies, lullabies for abandoned children.

Naomi first sang to me from the end of her couch. The window was open, a warm, windy September night. Her voice was low as whispering grass. It made me imagine the moonlight on the roof. She sang a ghetto lullaby, a sadness that seemed to me confusingly sweet. In the dark I could smell the tanning lotion on her arms and legs, and in the thin cotton of her flowered skirt. "Clasp the alphabet to your heart, though there are tears in every letter." "I sing in your little ear, let sleep come, a little handle closing a little gate."

Something in me glimmered, far down. I summoned myself: the biggest action of my life, lifting my head long enough to place it in her lap. I pressed breath kisses into her filmy skirt. Her face hung above me, half a moon, with her draping hair.

Now eight years later, Naomi still collects lullabies but listens to them by herself in the car. Old songs that I imagine make her weep in traffic. It's a long time since Naomi last sang to me. It's a long time since I've heard a riddle song or a Gypsy song or a Russian song, not a partisan song or a song from the French Foreign Legion, not a single Ay-li-ruh or Ay-liu-liu-liu to soothe fish in the sea, or a Bayushki-bayu to make birds dream on the bough.

Now all the humour has gone out of her longing.

Over the years, Naomi's non-sequiturs continued to catch me off-guard like a sunshower. In the produce section of the supermarket, I reaped the benefits of being married to a non-fiction editor. Choosing lettuce I learned that Chopin's own "Funeral March" was played for him when he died. While figuring out our taxes I was informed that "Baa baa black sheep" and "Twinkle Twinkle Little Star" share the same melody. I've learned many things while shaving or bundling the newspapers. "After World War One, a German chemist tried to extract gold from sea water to help Germany repay its war debt. He'd already extracted nitrogen from the air to make explosives. Speaking of war, did you know Amelia Earhart nursed veterans in Toronto in 1918? And speaking of nursing, Escher had to have emergency surgery when he was in Toronto to give a lecture."

For several months Naomi worked on a series on municipal affairs.

"Tell me what's happening in the city."

In bed, in her favourite grey T-shirt shapeless as an amoeba, she seduced me with details. Lawyers, architects, bureaucrats; from her descriptions I knew them all. From their tastes in books and music, to awkward incidents in public and private places – all the minutiae of prominent lives – I came to an irregular and intimate knowledge of the city. Cities are built on compromising encounters, on shared affections for certain foods, on chance meetings in indoor pools. By the third week she could tell me, with a meaningful look, of a certain politician's penchant for antique glass and I'd understand the new parking bylaws. Naomi told these stories like a courtier. Not as flabby, loose-lipped gossip, but with the cool acknowledgement that she was revealing the inner mechanisms of civic power. And sometimes, when she stopped talking, I rose to her with a pang of expectation like a taste crushed open in my mouth.

I reciprocated by feeding her bedtime stories: weather reports. When snow is ready to avalanche, the slightest disturbance will trigger the disaster: the jump of a rabbit, a sneeze, a shout. A faithful mascot waited three days by a mound of snow until someone investigated; they excavated the bewildered postman of Zurs who survived because most of freshly fallen snow is air.

In Russia, a tornado dug up a treasure and rained a thousand silver kopecks into the streets of a village.

A freight train was lifted from the tracks and placed down again, facing the other direction.

Once in a while, I admit, I made things up. Naomi could always tell. "Name your source, name your source!" she'd say, beating me with a pillow, dangling my glasses by the stem.

We used to play a game in the car. Naomi knew so many songs, she claimed she could match a lullaby or a ballad to anyone. One winter day I asked Naomi what songs she thought of when she thought of my parents. She answered almost immediately.

"For both your parents, 'Night.' Yes, 'Night.'"

I looked at her. She was flustered that I didn't understand; wary.

"Well . . . because they heard Liuba Levitska sing it in the ghetto."

I glared at her. She sighed.

"Ben, keep your eyes on the road – Liuba Levitska. Your mother said she had a beautiful coloratura, that she was a real singer. She'd sung Violetta in *La Traviata* when she was twenty-one. In Yiddish! She gave children singing lessons in the ghetto. She taught them 'Tsvey Taybelech' – 'Two Little Doves,' and soon everyone was singing it. Someone offered to hide her outside the walls, but she wouldn't leave her mother. They were both killed there. . . . Halfway through the war, she sang at a memorial concert in the ghetto for those who had already died. There was a big argument because a man complained that it was wrong to have a concert in a cemetery. But your mother said your father told him that there wasn't anything more holy than hearing Liuba Levitska's 'Night.'"

"And what song would you choose for Jakob Beer?"

Again Naomi answered too quickly, as if she'd decided long before I asked.

"Oh, 'Moorsoldaten,' definitely the 'Peat Bog Soldiers.' Not only because it's about bogs . . . but because it was the first song ever written in a concentration camp, in Borgermoor. I mentioned it to him when we met at Maurice's. Of course he'd heard of it. The Nazis didn't allow prisoners to sing anything except Nazi marching songs while they cut the peat, so it was real rebellion to invent a song of their own. It spread to all the camps. 'Everywhere we look, bog and moorland stare . . . but winter cannot reign forever.'"

We drove on for a few minutes in gloomy silence. That February day was particularly wet, and the roads were a mess. I remembered how my classmates and I used to squeeze the slush between our boots, draining the water, leaving little molehills of white ice. We worked industriously until the schoolyard was a miniature range of mountains.

"It's the only thing you can do for them," Naomi said.

"What is? For who?"

"Never mind."

"Naomi."

My wife pulled at the fingers of her wool gloves and pushed them on again. She opened the window a crack, let in a whiff of snow, then closed it.

"The only thing you can do for the dead is to sing to them. The hymn, the miroloy, the kaddish. In the ghettos, when a child died, the mother sang a lullaby. Because there was nothing else she could offer of her self, of her body. She made it up, a song of comfort, mentioning all the child's favourite toys. And these lullabies were overheard and passed along and, generations later, that little song is all that's left to tell us of that child. . . ."

Just before sleep Naomi experimented until she found the right position wrapped against me in some way. She moved about, adjusted limbs, searched for the right angles, and like a penguin under the ice, found the best breathing hole between bodies and blankets. She nuzzled, adjusted, nuzzled again, then slept with the resolve of an explorer out to conquer a dream landscape. Often she was in exactly the same position when she woke.

Sometimes looking at Naomi, the sweetness of her ways – settling into bed with her work, a little dish of licorice allsorts beside her, wearing her crazy misshapen T-shirt, such childlike contentment in her face – tightened my heart. I pushed away her papers and lay on top of the covers, on top of her. "What's wrong little bear? What's wrong . . ."

My mother taught me that the extra second it takes to say goodbye – always a kiss – even if she were simply rushing to the corner for milk or to the mailbox – was never misspent. Naomi loved this habit in me, for the plain reason one often finds a lover's habits charming: she didn't understand its origin.

What would I do without her? I began to be afraid. So I picked fights with her over anything. Over saying kaddish for my parents. And that's when she was driven to an edge: "You want to punish me for my happy childhood, well screw you, screw your stupid self-pity!"

Because she was right, Naomi was sorry for having said those words. All candour eventually makes us sorry. I loved her, my warrior who swept aside the war in fits of frustration with a single "screw you." Even Naomi, who thinks love has an answer for everything, knows that that's the real response to history. She knows as well as I that history only goes into remission, while it continues to grow in you until you're silted up and can't move. And you disappear into a piece of music, a chest of drawers, perhaps a hospital record or two, and you slip away, forsaken even by those who claimed to love you most.

~

When my parents came to Toronto, they saw that most of their fellow immigrants settled in the same downtown district: a rough square of streets from Spadina to Bathurst, Dundas to College, with waves of the more established rippling northward towards Bloor Street. My father would not make the same mistake. "They wouldn't even have the trouble of rounding us up."

Instead, my parents moved to Weston, a borough that was quite rural and separate from downtown. They took out a large mortgage on a small house by the Humber River.

Our neighbours soon understood my parents wanted privacy. My mother nodded a hello as she scurried in and out. My father parked as near as he could to the back door, which faced out onto the river, so he could avoid the neighbour's dog. Our major possessions were the piano and a car in decline. My mother's pride was her garden, which she arranged so the roses could climb the back wall of the house.

I loved the river, though my five-year-old explorations were held in close check by my mother; a barrage of clucks from the kitchen window if I even started to take off my shoes. Except for spring, the Humber was lazy, willows trailed the current. On summer nights, the bank became one long living room. The water was speckled with porch lights. People wandered along it after dinner, children lay on their lawns listening to the water and waiting for the Big Dipper to appear. I watched from my bedroom window, too young to stay out. The night river was the colour of a magnet. I heard the muffled thump of a tennis ball in an old stocking against a wall and the faint chant of the girl next door: "A sailor went to sea sea sea, to see what he could see see see . . ." Except for the occasional slapping of a mosquito, the occasional shout of a child in a game that always seemed dusky far, the summer river was a muted string. It emanated twilight; everyone grew quiet around it.

My parents hoped that, in Weston, God might overlook them.

～

One fall day, it would not stop raining. By two in the afternoon it was already dark. I'd spent the day playing inside; my favourite place in the house was the realm under the kitchen table, because from there I had a comforting view of my mother's bottom half as she went about her domestic duties. This enclosed space was most frequently transformed into a high-velocity vehicle, rocket-powered, though when my father wasn't home I also set the piano stool on its side and swivelled the wooden seat as a sailing ship's wheel. My adventures were always ingenious schemes to save my parents from enemies; spacemen who were soldiers.

That evening, just after supper – we were still at the table – a neighbour pounded at the door. He came to tell us that the river was rising and that if we knew what was good for us we'd get out soon. My father slammed the door in his face. He paced, washing his hands in the air with rage.

The banging that awakened me was the piano bobbing against the ceiling beneath my bedroom. I woke to see my parents standing by my bed. Branches smacked against the roof. It wasn't until the water had sloshed against the second-storey windows that my father agreed to abandon the house.

My mother tied me in a sheet to the chimney. The rain hit; needles into my face. I couldn't breathe for the rain, gulping water in mid-air. Strange lights pierced the wind. Icy tar, my river was unrecognizable; black, endlessly wide, a torrent of flying objects. A night planet of water.

With ropes, a ladder, and brute strength, we were hauled in. As if released from the grasp of searchlights from the shore, when our house plunged into darkness, it was swept, like every other on the street, fast downstream.

We were fortunate. Our house was not one of the ones that floated away with its inhabitants still trapped inside. From high ground I saw erratic beams of light bouncing inside upper floors as neighbours tried to climb to their roofs. One by one the flashlights went dark.

Shouts flared distantly across the river, though nothing could be seen in the pelting blackness.

Hurricane Hazel moved northeast, breaking dams, bridges, and roads, the wind tearing up power lines easily as a hand plucking a stray thread from a sleeve. In other parts of the city, people opened their front doors to waist-high water, just in time to see an invisible driver backing their floating car out of the driveway. Others suffered no more than a flooded basement and months of eating surprise food because the paper labels had been soaked off the tins in their pantries. In still other parts of the city, people slept undisturbed through the night and read about the hurricane of October 15, 1954, in the morning paper.

Our entire street disappeared. Within days, the river, again calm, carried on peacefully as if nothing had happened. Along the edges of the floodplain, dogs and cats were tangled in the trees. Alien bonfires burned away debris. Where once neighbours strolled in the evenings, they now wandered the new banks looking for remnants of personal possessions. Again, one might say my parents were fortunate, for they didn't lose the family silverware or important letters or heirlooms however humble. They had already lost those things.

The government distributed restitution payments to those whose houses had been washed away. It was only after my parents died that I discovered they hadn't touched the money. They must have been afraid that someday the authorities would ask for it back. My parents didn't want to leave me with a debt.

My father took on as many pupils as he could find. We vanished into a cubbyhole of an apartment nearer to the music conservatory. My father preferred living in an apartment building, because "all the front doors look alike." My mother was frightened whenever it rained, but she was happy to be living high up and also that there were no trees too close to the building to threaten our safety.

When I was a teenager I asked my mother why we hadn't left the house sooner.

"They banged at the door and shouted at us to leave. For your father, that was the worst."

She peered from the kitchen into the hallway to see where my father was, and then, with her hands cupped around my ear, whispered: "Who dares to believe he will be saved twice?"

~

That my mother took Naomi into her heart chafed me, a jealousy that grew intense. Like my father, I was being thrust out. The first time I was startled to attention by their familiarity, I was waiting for Naomi to finish scrubbing a pot. I had twisted the dish towel into a crown, a trick my mother had taught me. Offhand, innocently, Naomi said: "Just like your cousin Minna."

My mother held kitchen conferences with Naomi, in the guise of discussing ingredients or dress patterns, while I sat mute with my father in the living room, scanning the bookcases and shelves of phonograph records for the umpteenth time. How my mother must have pressed Naomi's hand, held on to her, conspired with her. Naomi emerging from the kitchen smiling with a recipe for honey cake. All the loving attention she lavished on my parents, the care so characteristic of Naomi – ever-considerate, generous to a fault – I began to read as insinuation, manipulation, a play of power. Later I even distrusted her visits to my parents' graves, her gifts of flowers and stones of prayer. As if Naomi were buying me a guiltless conscience the way a man buys jewellery for his mistress. Why do you do it, why? – thinking, what good does it do? She'd always say the same thing, a reply that made me ashamed, lowering her head like a felon: "Because I loved them."

How could anyone simply love my parents? How could an untrained eye see past my father's silence, his crabbed rigidity and rage, his despair; past the diminished piano teacher to the once elegant student conductor in Warsaw? How could an unskilled heart see past my bird-like mother's paisley dresses and cut-glass brooches to the passionate woman who kept a pair of elbow-length, white leather opera gloves wrapped in scented tissue in her drawer, and a postcard collection in a shoebox in her cupboard, who cooked to remember generations, who gardened on her balcony so she could have fresh flowers without my father's disapproval? By what right did Naomi earn their trust?

I began to recall the brusque affection she evoked in my father when she spoke of her own father's love for music. She was so blatant with them! For a long while I had no idea how much this hurt me. In fact, I'd even come to believe I liked this familiarity, this family feeling Naomi brought to that empty apartment. She was blunt and sweet, a crayon, when everything before her had been written in blood. She blundered in with her openness, her Canadian goodwill, with a seeming obliviousness to the fine lines of pain, the tenderly held bitterness, the mesh of collusions, the ornate restrictions. And while I now see that nothing could have pried open my father or melted him – even at the end of his life – I began to believe he had shared himself somehow with Naomi. Of course he had, but they hadn't been the sort of confidants I'd suspected. A foreigner, a stranger in our midst, Naomi entered the powderbox apartment and instead of blowing our furtiveness sky-high had simply brought flowers, sat on an ottoman, accepted our ways, never overstepping her position. Decorous, patient, an impeccable guest. What I had mistaken for confidentiality from my father was simply the relief of a man who realizes he won't have to give up his silence. It's the ease Naomi's grace encourages in everyone. She will honour privacy to the end.

~

People ask, do you dream in colour? But I wonder, is there sound in your dreams? My dreams are silent. I watch my father lean over the table to kiss my mother, she's too frail to sit up long. I think: Don't worry, I'll comb your hair, I'll carry you from the bed, I'll help you – and realize she doesn't know me.

In dreams, my father's face, with the expression he wore on Sundays listening to music, contorts; a reflection in the still surface of a lake smashed by a stone. In dreams I can't stop his disintegration.

Since his death, I've come to respect my father's caches of food around the house as evidence of his ingenuity, his self-perception. *It's not a person's depth you must discover, but their ascent. Find their path from depth to ascent.*

In the back of my mother's closet was a small suitcase, the contents of which my mother revised as I grew. This small suitcase, which I feared as a child, now represents to me the enormity of their self-control.

My mother was suddenly old. She had turned herself inside out; her skin hid behind her bones. I noticed the pull of fabric over her curved back, her thin hair over her scalp. She looked as if she might close up, clatter like a folding chair. All that was left of her were the parts that would make a terrifying sound – skeleton, eyeglasses, teeth. Yet at the same time as she was disappearing, she seemed to become more than her body. And that's when I realized how deeply Naomi's daughterly attentions were injuring me, each small jar of scented hand lotion, each bottle of perfume, each nightgown. Not to mention the distress evoked by the futility of objects that outlast us.

After my mother died, almost instantly my father slipped beyond reach. He heard things, white as whispering. When his brain was tuned to the frequency of ghosts, his mouth was a twisted wire. During one visit on an autumn Sunday about a year after my mother's death and two years before his own, I watched him from our kitchen window while Naomi made tea. He sat in our yard; the book he hadn't been reading had slipped to the grass. Someone in the neighbourhood was burning leaves. I thought about the cool, smoky air on his freshly shaven face, skin I hadn't touched for years. How strange that this memory has become beautiful to me. My father alone in the garden, lost in loneliness for his wife. He held his cardigan on his lap like a child asked to hold something without knowing why. The trace of beauty I now sense is this: perhaps, for the first time in a long life, my father was experiencing pleasure at looking back on a happier time. He sat so still the birds weren't afraid of him, plummeting from newly bare branches, sweeping a breath above the lawn around him. They knew he wasn't there. In his face the expression I now recognize from all those Sunday afternoons we sat together on the couch.

My father's last night. Holding the dial tone against my ear, waiting for Naomi to come to the hospital. I will always associate the dial tone with the mechanical horizon of death, of no heartbeat. I realized then I'd been wrong about him all my life, thinking that he wanted death, was waiting for it. How is it possible I never knew, never guessed? Truth grows gradually in us, like a musician who plays a piece again and again until suddenly he hears it for the first time.

On a March evening, about two months after my father died, I was going through my parents' closets and pockets and my father's chest of drawers. I had left the clearing out of their bedroom for last. In the humidor, which he never used for cigars, in an envelope, a single photograph. We think of photographs as the captured past. But some photographs are like DNA. In them you can read your whole future. My father is such a young man I barely recognize him. He poses in front of a piano, an infant in the bend of his arm. His other hand directs the face of a little girl towards the camera. She is perhaps three or four years old and hangs onto his leg. The woman standing beside him is my mother. If it is possible to speak without opening your mouth, without making a sound or altering the muscles in your face – that is how my parents look. On the back floats a spidery date, June 1941, and two names. Hannah. Paul. I stared at both sides of the photograph a long time before I understood that there had been a daughter; and a son born just before the action. When my mother was forced into the ghetto, twenty-four years old, her breasts were weeping with milk.

I brought the photograph home to show Naomi. She was in the kitchen. It happened in an instant. As I was taking the photograph out of the envelope, before I'd uttered a word of explanation, Naomi said, "It's so sad, it's so terrible." Then she saw the shock her words had given me and stopped scraping the plates over the garbage can.

My parents, experts in secrets, kept the most important one from me to their last breath. Yet, in a masterful stroke, my mother decided to tell Naomi. The daughter she longed for. My mother guessed that my wife wouldn't readily mention something so painful, but she knew that if she confided in Naomi, the truth would eventually be passed on. Naomi knew how much her intimacy with my parents upset me. But Naomi didn't know she was keeping a secret.

Still, I blamed her.

Privacy is the true profundity of a marriage, the place my mother's story invaded.

The past is desperate energy, live, an electric field. It chooses a single moment, a chance so domestic we don't know we've missed it, a moment that crashes into us from behind and changes all that follows.

My parents must have made a promise to each other, which my mother kept almost until the end.

Naomi explained something else I'd never known. My parents prayed that the birth of their third child would go unnoticed. They hoped that if they did not name me, the angel of death might pass by. Ben, not from Benjamin, but merely "ben" – the Hebrew word for son.

~

The snow gradually disappeared from under the trees, leaving wet shadows. Detritus hidden all winter lay strewn across lawns and floating in gutters.

In the weeks after cleaning out my parents' apartment, I began to scavenge the Humber, collecting objects that had eroded from the early-spring banks – a souvenir spoon, a doorknob, a rusted mechanical toy. I rinsed them in the river and kept them in a box in the trunk of the car. I didn't find anything I remembered.

One day the rain soaked through my coat, my sleeves and back were raw. At home I emptied my pockets of china shards, small as mosaic tiles, and washed the broken dishes in the bathroom sink. I cleaned the bottom of the river from under my nails. I sat in my wet clothes on the edge of the empty tub. After a while I changed and went into my study. I could smell supper – tomato sauce, rosemary, bay leaves, garlic wafting up from downstairs. I sat until I could no longer see the roofs of the lane and the back-yard fences, only my own lamp and bookcases reflected in the window.

I went into the bedroom and lay down. I heard Naomi climb the stairs, heard her take off her shoes. I felt her lie down beside me in her favourite position, back to back, her small stockinged feet against my calves, a gesture of intimacy that filled me with hopelessness. I imagined her staring into her view of the dark bedroom. I could have stood it, no matter how many times she said it: I thought you knew, I thought you knew. If only she hadn't put her small feet against my calves – as if nothing had changed.

I knew I must not open my mouth. The misery of bones that must be broken in order to be set straight.

~

Waking in our tiny house, on our street with the old elms and chestnut trees, I knew without raising the blinds, sometimes without even opening my eyes, whether it was raining or snowing. I knew instantly the time of morning or evening by the quality of light filming over dresser, chair, radiator, Naomi's wooden brush on the night table. Different in winter, in March, in midsummer, in October. I knew that, in half a year's time, the two sugar maples in the yard would change colour differently, one more copper than scarlet. I was sick with noticing. The pale degrees of change, the diurnal decay.

And then there are days when the atmosphere signals an anniversary of error. An unnamed moment only weather remembers. The place we'd be if all were well.

I thought about my father, who used food to forget his body. Who was alive in music, where time is an instruction.

~

You died not long after my father and I can't say which death made me reach again for your words. On Naomi's desk was your last book, *What Have You Done to Time*, and on mine was *Groundwork*.

One evening, while nervously moving our dinner around in a skillet, Naomi suggested that I help Maurice Salman, and offer to retrieve your notebooks from Idhra, now that he's no longer well enough to travel. It was Naomi's idea: a separation.

A few days later, I stood in the kitchen doorway and spoke to the back of her head.

"I've rearranged things so I don't have to teach until next January."

Naomi pressed her palms into the kitchen table and stood up. The imprint of the chair was on the back of her thighs. This made me so sad I had to close my eyes.

"But you'll be away for your birthday – the mortgage will have to be renewed soon – I already have your present. . . ."

A ship in the middle of the ocean won't perceive the

tsunami; in the trough there are eighty-five miles between crests. At that moment, fear should have stung me, I should have smelled the whiff of ether, felt the knife edge. But I didn't. Instead I squandered our life together and only said: "I'll write to you. . . ."

Naomi's body to me was so familiar a map, folded so often at the same places, tearing along the folds. I never unfurled her anymore; opened her only a small square at a time, the district I addressed in darkness.

The June night before I left for Greece, it was stiflingly hot. Naomi came dripping from the cold shower and lay on top of me. Cold as wet sand.

❧

A few years after my mother's death, during the brief time he lived with Naomi and me, my father seemed to give up sleep entirely. At night we heard him wandering around the house. Finally, I convinced him to see a doctor, who, to my relief, prescribed sleeping pills. But, suddenly able to answer the dilemma of hunger that had plagued him so long, he took them all.

VERTICAL TIME

I came to Idhra with the meltemi, the cool Russian wind evaporating off the Balkans, which swells Greek sails and snaps shirts in the summer afternoon. I arrived with the intrepid shearwater, which flies south thousands of miles from the Arctic Circle, white as ice chips off glaciers and bergs. They skim the purled sea, their sharp wings tear open the blue envelope of sky. The meltemi is a horsetail of a wind, preventing the humidity from settling. It scrubs the air until you can see the grain of a wooden door under its paint; until you can see the pores in lemon skin and the crease of ice in a glass on a table in a harbour-side café; until you can see the dampness of a dog's snout as it sleeps in the shadow of a wall – twenty minutes before you land. No matter your age, the meltemi tightens your skin, it soothes the desperate traveller's brow, the traveller who has not yet travelled long enough to have left his future behind. If you open your mouth on deck, the meltemi will scour and rinse your skull smooth as a white bowl, every thought will be new, and you will be filled with an appetite for clarity, the pull of precise muscles, precise desires. You will feed pinches of your past like bread to the seabirds, watch the pieces bloat and sink, or be scooped up by sharp beaks and swallowed mid-air.

From every angle but one, Idhra is bare blue rock, barnacled with lichen, a whale in a shallow pool. The ship curves one last time and the island suddenly lifts its head, opens its eyes. A bouquet of wildflowers pulled from a magician's sleeve. For hundreds of years, whether on a fifteen-ton sakturia or a fifty-ton lateen-rigged latinadika, sailors of this route through the Saronic Gulf – from the ports of Constantinople to Alexandria, Venice, Trieste, and Marseille – as they round the curve into the steep amphitheatre of Idhra harbour have heard newcomers gasp. They haul and pull, ignoring the gleaming gold lamé of nets strewn on the dock, ignoring the lava-red roofs liquid with light, the saturated blue or yellow doors of a hundred white houses gleaming as if with wet paint. And you feel foolish for the strain in your throat, for the eagerness of your eyes.

∾

Salman warned me that the boat would arrive too late in the afternoon to walk to your house the first day. He wrote ahead on my behalf, to Mrs. Karouzos, whose quiet hotel is converted from an admiral's mansion and is run by her son, Manos. Mrs. Karouzos's is about halfway to your house; from there, according to Salman, the rest of the way can easily be achieved in the morning. The rooms look out onto a central courtyard, which is an outdoor dining room. It's probably just as Salman remembers it. A dozen small tables. Lanterns hanging from the stone walls. I washed my face and lay down. From the bed, the window was a square of porous colour, a blue painting.

Voices from the courtyard below woke me, the window was now black and sprayed with stars. I listened to the clinking of silverware and dishes.

I added water to my glass and watched the ouzo turn to fog.

When I arrived on Idhra I was convinced I'd succeed for Salman, who is haunted by the idea of your notebooks languishing somewhere in your house. You would be pained to see your old friend, who longs for one last conversation. He hoped that he'd be recovered enough to search for himself, to visit Greece once more. Mrs. Karouzos shipped him your papers, but your journals weren't there. So Salman thinks they must look like books, hardcover, because he'd told her not to bother sending any books. I promised him I would excavate gently.

I would spend weeks inside your house, an archaeologist examining one square inch at a time. I looked in drawers and cupboards. Your desk and cabinets were empty. Then I began to go through your library: immense in scope and size, climbing almost every wall of the house. Books on the aurora borealis, on meteorites, on fogbows. On topiary. On semaphore signals. On Ghana high life, pygmy music, the sea shanties of Genoan longshoremen. On rivers, the philosophy of rain, on Avebury, the white horse of Uffington. On cave art, botanical art, on the plague. War memoirs from several countries. The most vigorous collection of poetry I've ever seen, in Greek, Hebrew, English, Spanish.

I would be distracted by marginalia, slips of paper tucked between pages, scraps of bills used as markers. I handled carefully books that were falling apart, that had been read and reread; like *A Guide to Classical Architecture*, a ruin itself that practically crumbled in my hands.

I would lose an hour in a book on ceremonial head-dress, another two in the life of a dock worker in Athens who became a labour organizer. Once I pulled Michaela's record book of expenses off the shelf, and another listing things to be sought out on various excursions to Athens or on trips back to Canada. One thick hardbound book turned out to be Michaela's masters thesis on ethics in museology, which focused on the tragedy of Minik, the Greenland Inuit who was turned into a living exhibit at the American Natural History Museum. Minik discovered that his own father's skeleton was part of a display. Michaela's writing style was not academic, and the sorrow of Minik's story and the afternoon heat suddenly filled me with uselessness.

In the end, when it was clear I wouldn't find your notebooks easily, I began to imagine you'd hidden them outside among the rocks, like the paper brigade which saved precious books during the war by burying them in the grounds around Vilna's Strashoun Library. Like all the letters of witness buried under the floorboards of houses in Warsaw, Łódź, Cracow. I even considered digging in your garden and in the sparse patches of stony soil surrounding the house. I imagined breaking apart the walls.

But my mistake would be to look for something hidden.

~

From your front door, I gazed down to the distant harbour – from this height, only a tiny abstract of colours, as if an overturned cart had spilled its goods into the bay.

A boat, drydocked and badly in need of paint, sat near the edge of the cliff overlooking the sea. It seemed ready to sail into the air at any moment. It must have taken a dozen strong men and mules to haul it to the hilltop.

It was a perfect morning. The breeze kept the heat away. I stood for a while on the stoop before I went inside.

Wands of light from the edges of the shutters crisscrossed the room. Alarm rushed across my skin. Waiting in the dimness, naked to the waist except for her hair, a woman gleamed. I stared into the room until I realized she was wood, a ship's figurehead, so large she was disorienting, as if the whole ship was behind her and had crashed into the house.

I went back outside and unhooked the shutters from two windows, then stepped through the wide door for the first time. The light was speckled with dust. Some of the furniture was shrouded with sheets and looked like snow drifts, eerie in the intense heat.

A rough wooden parapet encircled the main room, like the deck of a ship. From this walkway you could look down into the living room. The upper walls were lined with sagging, overburdened bookcases. Later I saw that beyond this balcony was your small study, tucked into a corner of the roof. It too was filled with books. A floorlamp made from a branch, with a paper shade, a hammock, a wing-chair piled with more books, a porthole of a window looking out high above the garden and the waves. Several paintings of atmospheric phenomena, including a lovely old impression of a paraselena. On the desk, various stones, an oil compass, a pocketwatch with a sea monster engraved on the case, and a shallow dish filled with an exotic collection of buttons. Buttons shaped like animals, like fruit; gold sailor buttons embossed with anchors, buttons of silver, glass, shell, wood, bone.

The house was bigger than it seemed from outside, twisting back into the hill, rooms full of treasure. Old ornamented barometers. Wind charts, tide charts, bells. Several globes, including a blank one made of slate, presumably so a student could learn the positions of the continents and countries by drawing them. Several smaller figureheads, flying from the walls, one of them an angel of salt-eaten wood, with her hand over her breast, the sea wind in her tangled hair.

The house was a breccia of affections. Everything was wind-worn or sea-worn, old and odd, mostly only of personal value.

A dozen ships in bottles, a map of the moon. An old sea chest with black iron ribs arching across the lid. A glass case across one wall with a jumbled collection of fossils. Sills with fantastic shells, stones, bottles of blue glass, of red glass. Postcards. Driftwood. Candlesticks made of ceramic, wood, brass, glass. Oil lamps of every size and shape. Door-knockers of different sizes, each shaped like a hand.

Mrs. Karouzos, too old to care for the house herself, had sent her daughter to cover the furniture. Even the clothes in the cupboards were draped with sheets. It's a strange relationship we have with objects that belonged to the dead; in the knit of atoms, their touch is left behind. Every room emanated absence yet was drenched with your presence. When I uncovered the couch, I found a blanket still dripping from one end of it, and the indentations of your bodies – invisible weight – still in the cushions. Pottery from Skyros with plumes and swirls the colours of watermelon and waves. A wide wooden table with a chair pushed from it, as if you or Michaela had only just stood up.

In the kitchen, a well-used cookbook of Greek-Jewish cooking, open to the page on pastry dough, and an equally used and obviously mislaid copy of Pliny's *Natural History*. I imagine you came into the kitchen to read a passage to Michaela and absentmindedly left it there. Or perhaps she called to you to take down something for her from a high shelf, or to ask your advice about a sauce, and you embraced her and dinner was temporarily forgotten, the book left behind.

When I saw your jumble of sandals by the door, I saw my parents' shoes, which after their deaths retained with fidelity not only the shape of their feet, but the way they walked, the residue of motion in the worn leather. Just as their clothes still carried them, a story in a rip, a patch, their long sleeves. Decades stored there, in a closet or two. A house, more than a diary, is the intimate glimpse. A house is a life interrupted. I thought of the families frozen into stone by the eruption of Vesuvius, with their last meal still in their bellies.

Here was evidence of a life so achingly simple: days spent in thought and in companionship. Reading alone; reading aloud. Days of planting vegetables, of swimming, and of sleeping in the heat of the afternoons, hours to work out an idea, to think, until it was time to fill the lamps.

I sat on your terrace and looked at the sea. I sat at your table and looked at the sky.

I felt the power of your place speaking to my body. Imperceptively, my envy dimmed. My legs grew stronger from the daily climb to your house, from the pure food I carried each day – fruit, cheese, bread, olives – to eat in the shade of your garden. One morning my bad dreams of the night before paused halfway up the hill and hesitantly turned around to float back down, as if they'd reached an invisible border. I began to understand how here, alone, in the red and yellow of poppies and broom, you had felt safe enough to begin *Groundwork*. How you descended into horror slowly, as divers descend, with will and method. How, as you dropped deeper, the silence pounded.

Every day I discovered another talisman of beauty, clues of the life you and Michaela shared: stubs of candles, hard pools of wax in shelters of rock in the garden where you must have sat together at night, no doubt your *cleft of stone opened by flame*. Your images were everywhere.

I discovered your various stations on the terrace by patiently following the sun's circadian trail across the flagstones. Scraping chairs following the shade. The place where oil had dripped each time the lamps were replenished.

Above the bed, a broadsheet of "What Have You Done to Time," the Greek translation written in ink under the English, a shadow; the Hebrew translation written above, an emanation. You wrote of meals in night air, meals where one comes to the table perfectly hungry, starving after a swim, a climb, or love; ravenousness that will be sated and will return. The *circular language* of Michaela's arms.

In the evenings, sitting on your terrace, wrapped in the overgrown drapery of lavender and rosemary, I thought about the meaning of your "Night Garden," and didn't place the emphasis on the first word of the title. The one moment you bring your life entire to another. *Shaking like a compass needle.* A moment of pure decision.

The house did possess the silence that is the wake of a monumental event. Evident in the furniture, in the wild garden with its sleep-inducing fragrances that have absorbed a thousand daydreams. In the cushions by the windows. In a forgotten cup on the terrace, now filled with rain.

Your poems from those few years with Michaela, poems of a man who feels, for the first time, a future. Your words and your life no longer separate, after *decades of hiding in your skin.*

You sat on this terrace at this table, and wrote as if every man lives this way.

∾

Is there a woman who will slowly undress

Far below, salt pulls the heavy scent of lilacs into the sea, the fragrance drowns, sweet purple, in piercing blue. The sweetness drowns without a sound. Ecstatic.

The leaves, a million hands greener than energy, soundless past the closed window. The hot room, the smell of wooden sills and floors baking in the sun. Looking out at the dry hills, so bright, the eye manufactures shadows.

Is there a woman who will slowly undress
my spirit

If I could draw, I'd hold a square of paper up to this view from your window and let the landscape burn into it, seep into it like a grasp leaving its stain, like photosensitive paper turning dark with desire for a place one will never apprehend. The hills dissolve as I look; but the loss I feel is that of one who has already passed the point of apprehension. Like writing to a man who no longer wishes to be found.

Is there a woman who will slowly undress
my spirit, bring my body

Until the lemon bending the branch, the weight of the shadow separating one leaf from another, presses that place in you. Until the hills burn your eyes, until you give in. Until *the seam of density that separates leaf from air/is not a gap, but a seal.*

Is there a woman who will slowly undress
my spirit, bring my body to belief

Until the beautiful buzzing of flies wakes me.

For weeks I drifted in the heat, in the smell of rooms long closed, slowing down more and more in my search for your notebooks. From the open door, the wafting fumes of scorched grass.

One afternoon my eyes sprang open. I felt with a rush of adrenalin that you and Michaela might appear in a doorway. A shadow had passed through the house, as brief as a thought, though nothing had changed from one moment to the next.

The idea seized me: you're still alive. You're hiding, to be left alone in your happiness.

An energy of intention I'd never experienced before crackled through me.

PHOSPHORUS

B efore the eighteenth century, lightning was thought to be an emanation from the earth or the friction of clouds rubbing together. It was a popular pastime to try to discover its true nature because no one fully realized the danger. Lightning can't be domesticated. It is a collision of hot and cold.

A hundred million volts accumulate between earth and cloud, until a white-hot dart shoots down, followed by another, and another – the zigzag of ions that form a channel for lightning to surge up from the ground – in a fraction of a second. The surrounding air molecules glow.

In the electrified area beneath the thundercloud, between strikes, rocks have been heard to hum shrilly, and metal – a watch, a ring – to sizzle like oil in a frying pan.

Lightning has evaporated glass. It has struck a field of potatoes and cooked them underground, the harvester turning them up perfectly baked. It has roasted geese in mid-flight, which have rained down, ready to eat.

The sudden intense heat can expand fabric. People have found themselves naked, their clothes scattered around them, their boots torn from their feet.

Lightning can so magnetize objects they are able to lift

three times their own weight. It has stopped an electric clock then started it again, the clockhands moving backwards at twice their normal speed.

It has struck a building then struck the fire alarm, bringing firemen to put out the blaze it started.

Lightning has restored a man's sight and also his hair.

Ball lightning enters through a window, a door, a chimney. Silently it circles the room, browses the bookshelf and, as if unable to decide where to sit, disappears through the same air passage by which it entered.

A thousand accumulated moments come to fruition in a few seconds. Your cells are reassembled. Struck, your metal melted. Your burnt shape is branded into the chair, vacancy where once you inhabited society. Worst of all, she appears to you as everything you've ever lost. As the one you've missed most.

Petra chose a table at the edge of the Karouzos's courtyard. She sat alone. One could tell immediately from her clothes and manner that she was American.

Her hair was a sleek curve of water. Her large mouth and blue eyes. The sun was in her skin, from long days spent entirely outside. *A white dress shines against her thighs like rain.*

She tossed her head back. My desire a rough edge of metal that suddenly appears smooth in a glare of light.

Sometimes, when lightning passes through objects and then through human tissue, it imprints the object onto a hand, an arm, a belly – leaving a permanent shadow, a skin photograph. Whole landscapes have appeared on the sides of animals. Across the courtyard, I imagined Petra had the divine tattoo: in the middle of her back, a Lichtenberg flower. I imagined she'd been imprinted as a child, that the rubber tires of her bicycle had saved her. In the small of her brown silky back, past an invisible down of hair, the faint breath of electricity remained. A flower so faint you feel it could be washed away or, like a frost flower, vanish with your gasp. "From your lips to the ear of God." But your adoration will not have the slightest effect. The flower is ghostly and permanent; maddening stigmata.

~

I adorn Petra's wrists and ears. The rushing sound of lemon leaves, and her bracelets slipping together down her arms as she lifts her heavy hair from her neck: the sounds of green and gold. After meals, bottles and glasses, crusts and dishes, intimate as clothes scattered around a bed.

Her casualness stabs me: "When we leave the island," "Back home," "My friends . . ."

Her hair drips from her swim. On her wet body, a bathing suit of grass.

Blindness drips into my eyes. Afternoon into evening, the window blue, then deeper blue. Like conversation drifting up from the courtyard, single words rise into consciousness: Petra, earth. Salt.

She sleeps with an abandon that is almost shocking, her black hair splashed on the sheets.

In the morning, when Petra's hair disappears under her cotton dress, I feel the coolness over my own shoulders.

I learn Petra's smells, her hair still damp in its thickness, close to her scalp, at the back of her neck. I know the line of sweat under her breasts, the smell of her hands and wrists against my face. I can identify her in darkness, *the tastes that aren't erased by the sea*. I know her body, every smoothness, every line between light and dark, every shape. Each line of bone stretching the surface, each crease traced before birth – the line behind the knee, behind the elbow, the lines in the palm, on the neck. I memorize the curve of her eyebrows, the contours of her feet. I know her teeth, her tongue. My tongue knows her ears, her eyelids. I know her sounds.

≈

Late September. At night the wind lifted the corners of the tablecloths in the courtyard. Except for Stavros the architect, on the island to restore a portion of the harbour, Mrs. Karouzos's was empty. I'd been on Idhra almost four months, known Petra for almost three. Every day before she swam – *her slim legs, long as the tails of quarter notes/firm as a fish in the shallows* – Petra slipped off the bracelets I'd bought her, the rings of Saturn. Afterwards she put them back on, two lines of honey glowing on her tanned arms. She lay on the rocky ledges and let the waves stroke her legs. Maybe she wanted to be an actor, a teacher, a journalist, she hadn't decided. She was twenty-two, she didn't want to go home.

She told me about her school friends; about the first part of her travels, in Italy and Spain. About the Australian computer salesman who proposed to her in Brindisi on the dance floor. "Right there in the middle of the Café Luna."

I confess I didn't listen too closely. As she talked I slipped stones under the bands of her underwear or her bathing suit until they were salty and dark. I retrieved them, put them in my mouth. Lost parts.

We followed your footsteps, Jakob, over the island. In our weeks together, like a tour guide, I recounted all the facts Salman had so faithfully preserved and passed on to me, on a hand-drawn map of Idhra: Here's where Jakob began "The Compass." Here's where he and Michaela swam. Here's where they read the newspapers every Saturday.

I told her how sometimes you and Michaela used to take the boat to Athens to buy books and odd condiments at a shop that sold British products – HP Sauce and curry powder, Cadbury's Drinking Chocolate and Bird's Custard – then spent the night at a little hotel in the Plaka, returning to the island the next day.

I told her how you wrote "In Each Strange City" – *in each strange city I learn again/your distant and beloved face* – when you were staying alone in a London hotel and above the bed hung the same Monet waterlilies as on the postcard at home on Michaela's night table.

I wanted Petra to wear clothes I bought for her. I loved to watch her taste food from my plate or drink from my glass. I wanted to tell her everything I knew about literature and storms, to whisper into her hair until she fell asleep, my words inventing her dreams.

In the mornings, my body was dull and sensitized with pleasure. *I shook myself free of a million lives, an unborn for every ghost*, over Petra's firm belly and brown thighs and slept carelessly, while souls seeped into the extravagance of sheets and flesh. Having emptied myself completely, I slept as though too full to move.

∽

At last, I took her to your house. Petra sensed that your place had become a shrine and walked through the rooms as if in a museum. She exclaimed at the view. She undressed in the afternoon sun, warm even in mid-October, and stood fully naked on the terrace. I held my breath. I saw Naomi, the day before I left, in the green rain light of the back yard, the wet sheets in her arms. At the back door, Naomi peeled off her shorts, soaked to the skin; her drenched shirt on the kitchen counter, trickling into the sink. I saw my wife's beauty and didn't embrace her.

Petra led me inside, and I followed her upstairs. She opened the door to your study, then to the room beside it, then found your bedroom. She opened the curtains and the simple room turned resplendent; everything startlingly white except for the turquoise cushions on the bed, as if the tide of sunlight had rushed in and left behind fragments of sea.

Then Petra started to pull down the heavy bedcover.

We found Michaela's note where she'd left it. Planned as the surprise ending to a perfect day. Among the cushions, waiting for your discovery, the night you and Michaela never returned from Athens. Two lines of blue ink.

If she's a girl: Bella
If he's a boy: Bela

I stripped away the rest of the bedcover and Petra and I lay on the floor.

Petra, perfect, not a blemish or a scar. I pounded myself into her until I hurt us both. Tears streamed down her face. I clenched my jaw and poured myself onto her belly, into the air. I stained the bedcover and lay back, sweating, and drew her hair over my face.

There was a lullaby my mother sang to me: "Shtiler, shtiler – Quiet, quiet. Many roads lead there, but no roads lead back. . . ."

My father was offered his first conducting job in the town where he was born. Shortly before the war, my parents moved there from Warsaw. Nearby was a peaceful old forest. My parents used to go there for weekend picnics. In 1941, the Nazis removed the name of the forest from the map. Then, over three years, they killed in that little grove. Afterwards, the remaining Jews and Soviet prisoners were forced to reopen the seeping pits and cremate the eighty thousand dead. *They dug the bodies out of the ground. They put their bare hands not only into death, not only into the syrups and bacteria of the body, but into emotions, beliefs, confessions. One man's memories then another's, thousands whose lives it was their duty to imagine. . . .*

The workers were chained together. Secretly, for three months they also dug a tunnel over thirty metres long.

On April 15, 1944, the prisoners carried out an escape. Thirteen made it through the tunnel alive. Eleven, including my father, reached a partisan group hiding deeper in the forest. My father and the others had dug the tunnel with spoons.

Naomi says a child doesn't have to inherit fear. But who can separate fear from the body? My parents' past is mine molecularly. Naomi thinks she can stop the soldier who spat in my father's mouth from spitting into mine, through my father's blood. I want to believe she can rinse the fear from my mouth. But I imagine Naomi has a child and I can't stop the writing on its forehead from growing as the child grows. It's not the sight of the number that scares me, even as it bursts across the skin. It's that somehow my watching causes it to happen.

I'll never know whether the two names on the back of my father's photograph, if they had ever been spoken, would have filled the silence of my parents' apartment.

Lying with Petra, I returned to the kitchen to find my mother weeping at the table surrounded by ingredients for supper. To find, at the same table, Naomi holding my mother's hand.

I returned to the kitchen where Naomi recognized the photo my father had kept hidden so many years; where Naomi and I sat in silence, the scraps of our dinner swelling with dishwater.

The night you and I met, Jakob, I heard you tell my wife that there's a moment when love makes us believe in death for the first time. You recognize the one whose loss, even contemplated, you'll carry forever, like a sleeping child. All grief, anyone's grief, you said, is the weight of a sleeping child.

I woke to find Petra in front of the bookcase; volumes scattered on the table, left open on the chair and couch as she rummaged through your possessions. Her perfect nakedness, while she desecrated what had been for years so lovingly preserved.

I sprang, held her wrists.

"Are you crazy?" she screamed. "I'm not doing anything. I'm just looking around – "

She grabbed for her clothes, pushed her feet into her sandals and was gone.

The heat was astounding. Drops of sweat fell onto the precious leather bindings in my hands. I stood at the door and watched Petra's black mane swinging above her hips and heard her swearing as she slipped past the rocks, down the path.

I looked back at the gaps on the shelves.

It was difficult to leave things as she'd left them; not to put things back as they'd been. I hesitated at the door for some time.

~

The boat arrives in late afternoon then circles back to Athens. Petra had returned to Mrs. Karouzos's with plenty of time to pack.

I was the only guest that night. Manos fastened down the tablecloth and I ate alone in the gusty courtyard.

Manos lowered his eyes, raised his shoulders, and I knew he was thinking: When it comes to a woman who's not your wife, what can a man say?

I remembered someone I knew in university who'd confided in me once, with almost adolescent curiosity – had I experienced this as well? – that after lovemaking, his mind always flooded with childhood memories. For years he mistook this deep feeling of well-being, the restoration of boyhood simplicity, for love of the women. Then he realized it was purely physiological. The body, he said, fools us perfectly. At the time, I'd envied him the women. Now I envied him the solace of his nostalgia.

All the nights, stunned with complexity lying next to Petra, she was waiting to leave.

By nine o'clock, there was a Force 5 wind. It was cold enough for a sweater and socks.

Even a moderate storm batters the beach with six hundred waves an hour. Every day, a half a ton of air presses down on your head. When you're asleep, five tons press you into the bed.

～

All the next day your house turned darker with the coming storm. I lit the lamps. Finally, it began to rain. I watched the soil turn soft and full: Petra's hair.

It was raining so hard I thought the walls might leak at the seams. The seaward windows rattled constantly. In patches throughout the house the lamps wore through the dimness.

The established absence had been replaced by fresh

loss. But all mysticism had vanished. The house seemed empty.

I wished that the bad weather would lure back your spirit and Michaela's, that you would take shelter in the shadows beyond the lamps.

I wished I could lure you back with one of Naomi's songs: "When you reach deep water do not drown from sorrow. When you reach a great fire do not burn from sorrow. . . . Little dove, little dove . . . " Naomi told me that when Liuba Levitska tried to smuggle a parcel of food for her mother into the ghetto, she was locked in solitary. Word soon spread that she was comforting the other prisoners. "Liuba is singing in the tower." And each in his distress heard "Two Little Doves" from behind the walls.

I hadn't realized the extent of Petra's rampage. In the space of perhaps an hour, she had pillaged every room.

She had done the most damage in your study. The items on your desk rearranged, your desk drawers left hanging, books glanced at then cast aside, piled haphazardly, open on a chair. Your room appeared ransacked by a scholar who'd been granted a single minute to find the reference upon which his life depended.

Slowly I restored the house, pausing to appreciate each book as I smoothed its bent pages, sitting down to read a few paragraphs, to admire illustrations of ships and prehistoric plants.

It was when I was replacing the books in the room next to your study that I found them. Not in a stack abandoned by Petra, but merely revealed by the space on the shelf beside them. There were two books, both bashed at the corners, probably from having been often stuffed into a pocket or a picnic hamper. One looked slightly water-swollen, as if you'd left it out on the terrace over-night, perhaps after reading aloud to Michaela by the light of the storm lanterns. Inside the first, your name and the date, June 1992. In the second, November 1992; four months before your death.

Your writing was neat and small, like a scientist's. But your words were not.

By late afternoon the rain had slowed; it meandered down the black windows. I could still hear the wind. I sat at your desk for a long time before I opened the first notebook. Then I read randomly.

Time is a blind guide. . . .

To remain with the dead is to abandon them. . . .

One becomes undone by a photograph, by love that closes its mouth before calling a name. . . .

In the cave her hair makes. . . .

~

It was well into the evening by the time I leaned your jour-nals, with Michaela's note tucked inside, by the front door next to my jacket and shoes.

I started to drape the sheets over the furniture.

Science is full of stories of discoveries made when one error corrects another. After revealing two secrets in your house, Petra had uncovered one more. Lying on the floor beside the couch, Naomi's scarf.

You can't fall halfway. For the first second over the edge it feels as though you're ascending. But you will be destroyed by stillness.

In Hawaii, silence is an earthquake warning. It's a ghastly silence because you only notice the sound of the waves when they stop.

I pick up the scarf and examine it under the light. I smell it. The scent is not familiar. I try to recall when I last saw Naomi wearing it.

I remember the night you stole Naomi's heart. How tenderly you answered her. "It seems right to keep bringing them something beautiful now and then."

I know it isn't hers; I know she has one just like it. The scarf is a tiny square of silence.

Naomi, who I've known for eight years – I can't tell you what her wrists look like, or the knot of bone of her ankle, or how her hair grows at the back of her neck, but I can tell her mood almost before she enters the room. I can tell you what she likes to eat, how she holds a glass, what she would make of a certain painting or a headline. I know what she makes of her memories. I know what she remembers. I know her memories.

Naomi would go downstairs to start coffee then join me in the shower, our smells still on her, my soaped skin snuffing them out as I embraced her. I know that in our last months she longed for those winter mornings we woke early and drove, stopping somewhere outside the city for breakfast, all the small diners in the small towns – the Driftwood, the Castle, the Bluebird – wandering down roads, past fallow ground, the sketch of hills. Sometimes we stayed somewhere for the night, all the foreign beds we woke in, and I wasted love, I wasted it.

～

I looked back into the house for the last time. The sheets glowed faintly. The bright pillows and rugs, the figureheads, the sills crowded with pieces of the world collected on various journeys, your sultan's tent, sea captain's cabin, laird's study – swallowed up.

From your stoop I could see the lights of Idhra town, like a scatter of coins. The wind was astringent.

I went back inside, climbed the stairs to the bedroom, and returned Michaela's note.

I'm not sure whether I did this for your sake or in order to spare Maurice Salman, your old friend who so deeply misses you.

～

The dark wind had pushed the mass of clouds out to sea, and the night sky above the island was startlingly clear. In the beam of my flashlight the rain-flattened fields glistened.

I circled the house, fastening the shutters.

THE WAY STATION

A cumulonimbus theatre towered over Athens's Syntagma Square. The mist smeared under the wipers, the cab window squealing.

Rain in a foreign city is different from rain in a place you know. I can't explain this, while snow is the same everywhere. Naomi says this is also true of dusk, that it's different wherever you are, and once told me of the time she was walking in Berlin alone, lost on New Year's Day, trying to find her way back to her hotel. She found herself at the end of a blind street, at the Wall, cement on three sides, in the near dark. She says she started to cry because it was twilight and New Year's Day and she was alone. But I think it was Berlin that made her cry.

I felt a surge of companionship with the eaters around me as they took comfort from the bulwark of hot food and drink. It was the third day of wet weather. People chewed thick slabs of bread with a crust that worked their jaws, dipped buns and biscuits into massive mugs of steaming milky coffee.

Tavern, oasis, country inn on the king's highway. Way stations. Dostoyevsky and the charitable women in Tobol'sk. Akhmatova reading poetry to the wounded soldiers in Tashkent. Odysseus cared for by the Phaiakians on Scheria.

Animal and field smells rose from wet wool and oiled jackets, even at the most popular café in downtown Athens. The restaurant was a cavern of noise; the espresso machine, frothing milk, loud conversation. A flash turned my head and I saw the two cuffs of gold snuffed out by her hair as Petra lifted its black mass from her neck. Then they reappeared, the rings of Saturn. She stood up. A man, his hand on the middle of her back, steered her between the tables into the crowded street.

I reached the door of the restaurant just in time to see them pass, like the bracelets lost in her dark hair, through the wall of light at the edge of the square. I watched as they disappeared into the unlit lanes of the Plaka.

It had stopped raining. People were already beginning to wander back out into the streets. Even the moon was emerging. Only the noise of cafés penetrated the darkness, and soon even the loud voices of drinkers dimmed into silence as I followed the dark lanes further into the Plaka, like an ant lost in the black type of a newspaper.

I found myself twisting up the mountain, the narrow market alleys gradually giving way to broken pavement, grass growing between the stones, empty lots between houses. Soon Athens in the valley was barely visible, flickering like moonlight on water, below the giant prow of the escarpment.

Jagged sidewalks, industrial fence, old wire and broken bottles, pinpoints of moonlight. Box gardens, clothing leaning over balconies, kitchen chairs left outside, the flooded remains of a meal forgotten on a small table. The houses were more settled in the rock, more decayed and vital, the higher I climbed. The debris of use, not abandonment.

The road emptied into an urban field littered with broken furniture, cardboard boxes, soggy newspaper. The garbage gave way to wildflowers. I waded through the soaked grass and looked out for a long while at the city below. The air was cool and new.

Then I realized I was sharing the darkness. I knew by their voices that the lovers weren't young. I didn't move. The man made his small shout, and a few moments later, they laughed.

It was not the proximity of their intimacy that unlocked me, it was that little laugh. I thought of Petra, turning to me in the dark, her eyes serious as an animal's. I heard their faint voices and imagined them rearranging each other's clothes.

On the boat from Idhra I'd overheard one young man explaining to another that in countries of big families husbands and wives often have to sneak from their small houses into the fields to escape the ears of the children. "No first born is conceived in the grass, but all the rest! Besides, a woman likes to look up at the sky."

I heard the skim of their clothes as they crossed the field.

The light turned flimsy. By the time I found my way back to my hotel, the sky seeped with day.

When we married, Naomi said: Sometimes we need both hands to climb out of a place. Sometimes there are steep places, where one has to walk ahead of the other. If I can't find you, I'll look deeper in myself. If I can't keep up, if you're far ahead, look back. Look back.

In my hotel room the night before I leave Greece, I know the elation of ordinary sorrow. At last my unhappiness is my own.

∾

For hours, leaning against the cold window, above the thick unmoving Atlantic, I foresee my return.

It's five-thirty, Naomi's just getting home. I imagine her at the front door struggling with her keys. A book, perhaps Hugill's *Shanties from the Seven Seas*, in one hand. In the other, a bag of groceries. Tangerines, their fragrant skins, their sweet vitamins. Bread creased by the oven's heat, soft dough forced open from the inside. Naomi's face pink with cold and mist, the backs of her stockings spattered with slush.

In the night cab from the airport I look out from the back seat of my parents' car, remembering winter Sundays as a boy. We pass through the haunted emptiness bordering the lit city, pass flat farmland under the congealing

November sky. The first starlight is a skin of frost over the fields. My boy's feet are cold in my boots. Small city lawns, streets narrow with snow. The sound of a walk being shovelled somewhere in the neighbourhood, an idling car.

The cab passes the yellow glow of windows above purple lawns; perhaps Naomi isn't home, the lights on in every house but ours. . . .

– In Greece I saw someone with a scarf just like yours. I remembered you wearing it. Do you still have it?

– Hundreds of women must have that scarf. It's from Eaton's. What's so important about a scarf anyway?

– Nothing, nothing.

Now, from twenty thousand feet, the ragged edge of the city appears, the wobbly boundary of a cell wall.

In bed I'll tell Naomi about waterspouts that inhale luminous creatures, seaplants, in their path and become glowing, twisting tubes, swaying across the midnight ocean. I'll tell her about the half-million tons of water lifted from Lake Wascana and the tornado that rolled up a wire fence, posts and all, like a ball of wool. But not about the couple who hid in their room until the tornado passed, opening their bedroom door to find the rest of the house had disappeared. . . .

Naomi sits in the dark kitchen. I stand in the doorway watching her. She says nothing. It's November but the screens are still on, damp leaves stuck to the mesh. The screens blur to grey glass and I'm frightened by the way she looks down at her hands on the table.

My wife shifts in her chair, her hair slashing her face in half. And when her face disappears like that, the sound will be in my mouth: Naomi.

I will stop myself from confessing I was on Idhra with a woman, that her hair fell from the edge of the bed to the floor. . . .

Naomi, I remember a story you told me. When you were a little girl you had a favourite bowl, with a design painted on the bottom. You wanted to eat everything, to find the empty bowl full of flowers.

The plane descends in a wide arc.

Once, I saw my father sitting in the snow-blue kitchen. I was six years old. I came downstairs in the middle of the night. There had been a storm while I slept. The kitchen glowed with new drifts piled against the windows; blue as the inside of a crevasse. My father was sitting at the table, eating. I was transfixed by his face. This was the first time I had seen food make my father cry.

But now, from thousands of feet in the air, I see something else. My mother stands behind my father and his head leans against her. As he eats, she strokes his hair. Like a miraculous circuit, each draws strength from the other.

I see that I must give what I most need.

ACKNOWLEDGEMENTS

"When the ship was endangered, he remembered them. . . ."
— *Nikos Pendzikis*

Many books assisted me in my research of the war — original testimony as well as the work of historians; in particular Terrence Des Pres's *The Survivor* renewed my resolve in the course of writing. My resolve was also strengthened by the work of John Berger. I would also like to acknowledge *The Politics of the Past*, edited by Gathercole and Lowenthal, and Apsley Cherry-Garrard's *The Worst Journey in the World*. The brief quotations from Theotokas are from Mark Mazower's *The Experience of Occupation, 1941-44*; quotations from Wilson, Bowers, and Taylor are from Griffith Taylor's *With Scott, The Silver Lining* and Edward Wilson's *Diary of the Terra Nova Expedition*. The translations of Yiddish song lyrics in Part I are from J. Silverman's *The Yiddish Song Book*; in Part II, from Shoshana Kalisch's *Yes, We Sang*, which also provided long-sought answers to specific questions. Quotations from *The Psalms* are from the translation by Peter Levi. The quotation from George Seferis is from the translation by Rex Warner.

A most special thank you to Jeffrey Walker for his invaluable encouragement.

Thank you to Ellen Seligman for her editorial acuity, her commitment and support. And to Heather Sangster for her insightful copyediting.

Thanks also to Sam Solecki, Vivian Palin, Bob and Grace Bainbridge, George Galt, David Sereda. Also to Beth Anne, Janis, Linda, Herschel, Dor, Luigi, and Nan — the granite-thief is for you. Thanks to the Michaelses, particularly Arlen and Jan. And an especial thanks to David Laurence.

Finally, my thanks to Nicholas Stavroulakis of the Jewish Museum of Greece and to Avraam Mordos and his family for their kindness in Athens.